Peace

David's Gift

a novel by

Kay Moser

Seton St. Clare Books

Copyright © 2001 by Kay R. Moser
All Rights Reserved. First Edition.

Seton St.Clare Books, a division of Seton St.Clare Communications
P.O. Box 8543, Waco, Texas 76714-8543

Printed in the United States of America
by AMA Printing/Finishing, Inc.

Cover art by Don Magid
Cover design by Patti Neckar and Frances Green of TLC Digital Imaging
and Chuck Petree of AMA Printing/Finishing, Inc.

Library of Congress Cataloging-in-Publication Data

Moser, Kay.
  David's Gift / by Kay Moser.—1st ed.
    p.   cm.
  ISBN 1-890236-16-0
   1. Women—Southern States—Fiction. 2. Contemporary—Fiction
I. Title.
  2000   Library of Congress Control Number: 00-092673

In honor of my parents,

Ruth Small Moser and Leslie Moser,

who have given me the greatest gift of my life—
knowledge of God's love for me and for all humankind.

ONE

David Randolph's eyelids jerked erratically as he lay sleeping next to his wife, Caroline, in their Dallas home. Tightening his lips and tossing his head from side to side, he moaned the sounds of a frightened child as he dreamed. Caught in his nightmarish past, he was no longer 45 years old; he was only 10, and it was not a refreshingly cool, autumn night in Dallas. It was a sweltering July day, and his father was teaching him to play tennis. The sun blazed down on the tennis court where he stood, anxiously awaiting his father's next serve. Before his frightened eyes, the sun whitened the concrete into a steaming, rolling sheet which melted into the net. He gripped the large, wooden racket like a life-saving weapon as his small body tensed to defend itself. Suddenly a white ball whizzed straight at him, and he jumped aside to avoid it. Immediately he hated himself.

"Don't run from the challenge!" his father's disembodied voice boomed across the blinding whiteness of the court as David squinted through the glare, struggling to see the giant who could make such a commanding sound. "You're my son—not a sniveling coward! Take control—always take control."

"You're too hard on him, Morgan," David's mother, Audra, insisted from the sidelines. "He's only—"

"Nonsense! He has to learn!"

"Morgan, he's a child—"

"He's the future of Randolph Industries. Go in the house, Audra!"

"But, Morgan—"

"Go!" David heard his father shout. Seconds later he stood, petrified, as he watched his father's looming presence appear out of the shimmering concrete and stalk toward him. His mother, openly crying, disappeared from the periphery of David's vision. Faster and faster his pulse raced as he watched his father effortlessly vault over the net. Then David heard a distant, muffled sob from his mother, and a flush of empowering fury shot through him. He came to life.

"You made mother cry again!" David shouted at his approaching father as he angrily banged his racket on the concrete.

"Women cry all the time. Get used to it."

"I hate it when you make her cry!"

His father stopped a few feet from the net and challenged him across the hot concrete. "So what are you going to do about it?" he sneered.

David jerked a tennis ball from the pocket of his shorts, threw the ball into the air, and raising the racket as far over his head as he could reach, he drove it directly at his father's chest.

"Good!" his father shouted as he sidestepped and easily volleyed the ball back to David. "Now you're acting like a Randolph. Give it to me! Slam it back," he called over his shoulder as he vaulted back over the net to the opposite court. Driven by his anger, David scrambled to return the ball. He stretched his right arm as far as it would reach, and when he felt the racket make contact with the ball, he threw his entire body into his swing to drive the ball back across the net.

When the sleeping, 45-year-old David flung his right arm over the edge of the bed, he awakened suddenly. His heart pounding inside his sweaty body, he struggled to understand he had been dreaming again. He forced himself to breathe more slowly. Finally he was calmer, so he wiped his brow with the sheet and cautiously looked over his shoulder at his sleeping wife. Thank God, he thought, at least she won't know about *this* nightmare. She's already beginning to suspect something is going on. As he slipped back into the fog of sleep, he warned himself again, as he had for years, she must never know about any of it, especially not about—

Once again David lost consciousness, and the past, like a seductive, but destructive, mythical Greek Siren, took control of his mind. He found himself walking down an endless, white-tiled hall with a silent, sullen nurse who carried a massive set of oversized keys. As they passed locked door after locked door, the keys jangled, and the shiny white tiles ricocheted the noise back on his strained nerves. A voice inside his head began its usual litany, *"Failure, failure, hide her away. Never tell, never tell. Failure, failure, hide her away!"*

"She's in here," the nurse interrupted the hypnotic singsong in his head as she halted at a door. Suspiciously she eyed David. "Are you sure you want to do this?"

"Of course!" he answered far too confidently as the voice in his head returned and grew more insistent. *"Failure, failure hide her away. Hide, hide!"* Mesmerized by the voice, he fell silent and helplessly stared at the blinding white door as she inserted a shiny key.

"You're sure?" she asked again before turning the key.

A louder interior voice snatched David's attention. *"Take control! Be a Randolph! Take control!"*

"Don't be ridiculous!" he snapped at the nurse. "Open the door!"

The nurse turned the key, and David flinched as his nerve-wracked ears heard the bolt shoot back with the sound of a sledgehammer against steel. Slowly, slowly the solid, white metal door began to swing inward, revealing the room. David's pulse hammered wildly as he fought for control of himself.

"Well?" the nurse sneered at him. "Afraid to go in?"

Unable to maintain his previous bravado, he struggled to force his leaden legs to move through the open door. Inside he stopped and fearfully gazed around him. White bounced off the walls and floor; the very air seemed milky. Slowly he turned full circle, looking for her, hoping against hope that he would not find her there. And he didn't. She wasn't there; it had all been a mistake, an outrageous, vicious mistake. He trembled with joy. "She's not here!" he shouted jubilantly at the nurse, but she raised her white-sleeved arm and pointed to a seated figure who was facing a window. His joy turned to suffocating fear.

"Go and see," the nurse insisted as she began to laugh.

"I can't!" David cried.

"But you must," the nurse taunted. "You know you must, and I haven't got all day."

"I can't," David's cry became a whimper. "I can't, I can't."

"She's over there," the nurse laughed gleefully, stretched out her white-sleeved arm again and pointed at the figure, "and there's nothing you can do about it. Go and see!"

"No!" David screamed angrily. "She can't be! I won't allow it! Not Danielle! Not Danielle!"

"David! David!" Caroline shook her husband as she tried to awaken him. "Wake up! You're having a nightmare."

"No! Not Danielle!" David screamed again as Caroline stood up from her side of the bed and rushed to the opposite side to shake him harder.

"Wake up, David! You're having another nightmare. Everything is okay. You're dreaming." Slowly David became conscious of Caroline's face and heard her soothing voice. "You're okay. It's all right. Everything's all right."

"Caroline?" he whispered as immense relief flooded over him. "Caroline, it's you. You're not—I mean, I'm not—"

"It was just a dream, and everything is fine," she stroked his head as she spoke.

"Yes, a dream," he finally agreed, "just a dream."

"What on earth were you dreaming about? You were tossing and trying to shout and finally you screamed, 'No! Not Danielle!'"

David tensed as his mind raced, frantically searching for an explanation she would accept without further question.

"What were you dreaming about?" she asked again.

"I don't know," he lied. "I don't know."

"I think I do," she said, and David's heart lurched when he heard her words. "I know what you were dreaming about, and we need to talk about it."

He said nothing.

"You're worried about me and the birth of our baby. That's obviously what all these nightmares you've been having are about." She paused for him to respond, but he remained silent. "Look, David," she continued, "I know you don't want to admit it, but you're afraid, and it's okay for you to be afraid. Don't you see?"

"Not really," he managed to say.

"It's simple. When you have these nightmares, you always scream out something about Danielle. You're just remembering the way you felt when she died trying to give birth. You loved her. She was your wife, so when she and the baby died, naturally you were very shaken. You're just replaying all that horror in your dreams because we're going to have our baby soon."

Wide awake now, David gratefully snatched at the explanation Caroline offered. "Right. I'm sure you're right, honey. It's just an old tape."

"But you don't need to worry about me. I'm not Danielle; I'm strong, and everything is going to be just fine."

"You're right, of course," he agreed more eagerly, "everything is fine. It's just the past creeping into my dreams."

"That's the major problem, David," she paused, obviously unsure whether to go on, "but I think there's more to it than that."

David's pulse began to race again, but he kept his voice steady as he asked, "Like what?"

"You're exhausted. You've been traveling too much lately. You just don't ever catch up on your sleep. I don't care what you say; no one can sleep well on a jet to Tokyo. No wonder you're having all these nightmares."

He intentionally shifted the focus of the conversation, "You shouldn't be standing there in your nightgown; you'll catch cold."

"David, we need to discuss this travel thing."

"We will, but not tonight. We both need some sleep." He patted the mattress next to him. "Come get back into bed; we have to take care of you and the baby; come get warm."

"I won't take one step until you promise to talk about cutting back on your travel schedule."

"Okay, okay, just get back in bed."

As she walked around to her side of the bed, he threw back the covers for her, and after she slid into place, he covered her with the silky sheet and warm blankets. Then he pulled her close to him. "You're shivering," he murmured as he wrapped his arms around her.

"I'm fine, David; don't start worrying about me. It's you we need to talk about."

"Not tonight; I can hardly keep my eyes open."

"David!"

"In the morning, I promise."

She sighed as she cuddled closer to him, and he held her tightly until he heard the even breathing that signaled she was asleep.

Thank God she doesn't even suspect, he thought, and she must never find out. But how can I keep the truth from her if I keep having these nightmares? I must! But how? They're getting worse and more frequent. She's smart—too smart. It's just a matter of time before she starts wondering if there is something else. She's going to start asking questions. Then what will I do? I better fake another emergency business trip—just get away until I can regain control of myself. I'll say I've been called to London. She'll be furious, but anything is better than having her find out. Besides, if she gets really angry with me over business trips, she'll convince herself that these nightmares I'm having come from wearing myself out traveling. Then she won't keep looking for other explanations.

* * *

"You are what?" Caroline demanded as she dropped a silver fork on her breakfast plate. "What did you say?"

David avoided looking at the rising anger in her eyes; instead he intentionally took his time picking up a coffee cup and taking a long drink. When he settled the cup back on its saucer, he finally answered her with stubborn resoluteness in his voice, "I said I'm going to London tonight."

"But you just came back from Tokyo, David! You have only been home for forty-eight hours. You're so exhausted you're having horrible nightmares again."

"I know, Caroline." David picked up his fork and calmly continued eating his breakfast. He appeared to be maddeningly indifferent to the fact that he had once again tripped the major land mine in their marriage.

"Is that all you have to say?" she demanded.

"What else is there to say?" David asked quietly between bites. "I'm going to London tonight on business. There's nothing unusual about that. I go to London often."

"Yes, you do!" Caroline shot her words at him in the sharp, staccato sounds of an automatic weapon. "You go to London and Tokyo and Hong Kong and Mexico City and every other far-flung place on the face of this earth."

"I'm running an international business—an *international* business, Caroline. As the owner and CEO of that business, I must travel abroad."

"Don't you dare state the obvious to me in that condescending tone. I am pregnant, not mentally deficient. We've been married seven years, and you've always traveled a lot, but things are supposed to be different now—"

"As far as the business is concerned, nothing has changed," David's icy interruption warned Caroline that she had better change tactics; anger would get her nowhere. Burying her fury deep inside herself, she sought to reason with him.

"But, David, we agreed that we would change our priorities—both of us. We agreed that we would seek to establish a family life, especially now that the baby is coming. I decided to become involved in the community, and you agreed that the business would not be your only interest."

"The business is not my only interest." David started to rise from the polished, walnut table. "I have many interests."

"Well, one of them should be the fact that your wife is seven months pregnant!" Caroline's control over her tone snapped.

"I haven't forgotten that." He scraped his chair back across the wooden floor.

"David," Caroline struggled to stand up in spite of her well-rounded form. "Don't you dare walk out on me. I insist you sit down and talk to me. I'm worried about you; I'm worried about us."

"I'm fine, Caroline; we're fine. There is nothing more to say. I'm going to London tonight on business, and that's final."

"When did this London trip suddenly come up?"

"Yesterday afternoon," he lied.

"Why didn't you tell me? You've known since yesterday afternoon that you were leaving tonight, and you didn't say anything?"

"I didn't want to fight with you. Every time I have to make a business trip you over-react and get hysterical."

"I do not get hysterical!" Caroline finally managed to stand up. "How dare you say that! I'm only thinking of you—of us. You need some rest, and we need time together."

"There you go again, Caroline. I haven't got time for your irrational nonsense this morning." David turned his back on her and began to walk out of the breakfast room.

"David," Caroline called after him. "At some point you have to quit running away from this relationship. No wonder you have those awful nightmares. You never face emotional things and release them."

He paused at the door, turned to look back at her, and intentionally goaded her into greater fury. "Caroline, if you start throwing the same trite, meaningless psycho-babble at me again, I'll stay in London."

"It is not trite, meaningless psycho-babble!"

"You sound like a parrot these days, always repeating the words of that psychologist you go see."

"It was your idea that I go see a psychologist, and I wanted you to come with me, you may recall."

"I recall it all, Caroline," David said sarcastically, "You have been consistently upset since you decided to become pregnant. You have gone through some kind of absurd personality change that I can only hope will go away once the baby comes. Until then, I can do nothing but just wait it out, and I might as well get on with my business." With those words, he stalked out of the breakfast room.

"David," Caroline raised her voice as she followed him into the main hall. "Is that what all this running away is about? Are you still angry because I'm pregnant?"

"I'm not running away, and I'm not angry. I have accepted the fact that you broke your word to me and tricked me into a pregnancy, but you can hardly expect me to be delighted about it. Let's just drop it; I'm going to pack."

"But David—"

"Caroline! I'm going to the office; then I'm flying to London. I have a business to run, a business, I might add, that supports you in a very elegant fashion. Nothing has changed, Caroline."

"But David," she gentled her voice and walked toward him in a conciliatory manner. "Don't you see? That's the problem. Nothing has changed. When we were in Charleston last spring, we agreed to make some changes."

"I agreed to accept the fact that you secretly quit taking your birth control pills and became pregnant. I agreed not to get a divorce over the matter. I agreed to support and try to love this child when it comes into the world. I did not agree to change my whole lifestyle."

"I'm not asking you to. Just don't be so distant. Share your life with me, like you promised you would in Charleston. David, you're avoiding a meaningful relationship with me."

"That's ridiculous!"

"It's not ridiculous. You used to relate to me; you wanted us to be together. Take travel, for instance. You used to ask me to come with you, but since we came back from Charleston, we have had a revolving door relationship. You are here for a day and gone for a week."

"Business is business, Caroline. It changes from day to day. You ought to know that by now. World markets don't stay static just because you're pregnant." With those harsh words, he walked away from her, and Caroline stood and listened as his heels clicked across the polished, wooden floors and up the staircase.

"He hasn't changed a bit, she thought bitterly. What did all those fine words he spouted in Charleston mean? I thought he understood that discovering the truth about my family history had changed my priorities and that I wanted him to share that change. I thought he was embracing family life—real family life—based on openness and intimacy. Why doesn't he want that? I must have done something wrong; I must not be communicating with him. If only I could make him see how wonderful our lives could be."

She, too, left the hall and labored slowly up the stairs. When she entered their bedroom, she found her husband packing a suitcase. She went and sat on the edge of their bed. "David, please, listen to me," she intentionally kept her voice even. "Just listen to me."

"Caroline, I have had all of the angry hysterics that I want to hear."

"I'm not angry, and I'm not hysterical. I simply want to reason with you. I want to define the basis of our lives."

"That sounds like more of that psychological gibberish to me." David turned his back on her, walked across the room, and opened a dresser drawer.

"Forget the vocabulary and where it may have come from," Caroline pleaded. David said nothing as he pulled out neatly pressed and folded items of clothing and walked back to the suitcase. Caroline sighed, then sat up straighter with more resolve. "David, when we were in Charleston last spring—"

"Oh, not that again," David muttered.

"Please, just listen, really listen this time. David, you are brushing aside the most important part of what happened last spring. I discovered that everything I had been taught was wrong—"

"I know, Caroline," David interrupted her impatiently, "I've heard this before."

"You may have heard it, but apparently you haven't listened. When I discovered the incredible deceit in my family's history and realized I was going down the same destructive path, I decided to change my values, to find a better way. I have found a better way—"

"Your Great-Aunt Kathleen's philosophy," David interrupted again. "Look, I like your Great-Aunt Kathleen. She's quite a lady, but I don't think we need to adopt her values and change our whole lifestyle."

"We do need to adopt her values because she's right," Caroline insisted.

"Caroline, in less than an hour I have to be in my office for a whole day of business meetings; then I need to get on a plane to fly to London. Can't we talk about this later when I get home?"

"No, David, we can't. All these months since last spring, there has never been a 'later.' There are always business meetings; there are always trips. In fact, they seem to have tripled in number since we came back from Charleston."

David pushed the suitcase aside and sat down on the bed beside her. "Caroline, we simply don't agree on this. You came back from Charleston with some starry-eyed idea that you wanted to change yourself totally and to make the world a better place and that I was going to do the same. Well, I have made it possible for you to be whoever you want to be, however idiotic your choices seem to me. I have accepted the fact that you have given up most of our social life, even the part that furthers my business interests. Most significantly, I have accepted the fact that, much against my will, I'm going to be a father."

"Are you going to be a father, David?"

"Of course! You're sitting there with a well-rounded stomach, and the doctor assures us you're pregnant."

"But are you going to be a father—really be a father? You haven't been a husband in five months. Are you going to be a father when the baby comes?"

"I'm going to be myself, Caroline. If you choose to change yourself, I'll support you, but don't try to change me."

"I see." Caroline sat silently and fought back the tears stinging her eyes. When she had regained control, she continued, "David, since you're going to be yourself, I assume that that means you will continue being emotionally distant as well as being physically absent." She paused, waiting for him to respond, but he said nothing. "I would like to ask you a favor. It means a great deal to me."

"I give you everything you ask for, Caroline. I've never denied you anything."

"I want this to be your last business trip until the baby is born. Frankly, I'm afraid, as I think most first-time mothers are. And this is an experience—the birth of our baby—that I want to share with you."

"The baby is not due for two more months."

"I know. But I also know that this trip of yours, which you say will last about a week, may very well turn into two weeks, and you may go from London to some other city before you come back to Dallas. Promise me that for the last six weeks of this pregnancy, you'll stay in town."

"I can't promise that, Caroline."

"You can!"

"I can't quit doing business for six weeks just because you're pregnant!"

"David, I can't stand the thought that I will go into labor and you will be in Hong Kong or some other place on the other side of the world."

David rose and started packing again. "That isn't likely to happen."

"The doctor says it could happen. First babies often come early, or complications arise."

"Well, if you do go into labor and I'm somewhere else, I will, of course, take the first plane home. It's not like you're alone here, Caroline; you have your mother and father and all the medical support you could possibly need. And we chose not to do that Lamaze stuff, so I won't really be a part of this birth anyway."

"*We* didn't choose not to do Lamaze. You refused to participate."

"Let's don't get into that again; I'm not the delivery room type. I think I have stretched myself as far as I can be expected to.

Do try to remember that when we married, you promised me that I would never have to go through childbirth with you. In case you have forgotten, I lost my first wife and child in childbirth, and you promised that you would never put me in that position again."

"Of course, I haven't forgotten David. I was wrong to deceive you, and I've begged you to forgive me. I feel even worse now that I see you suffering through these dreadful nightmares, but surely you want to be a part of this pregnancy in some way."

"Frankly, I just want it over."

"Well, so do I. At least the part between now and the birth, but I'm stuck with this. I'm carrying this child, but it's your child too."

"But it was your choice to become pregnant!" His sharp, biting words were hurled at her like spears.

Stunned by his willingness to hurt her, she was speechless for a moment. Then she asked sadly. "It always comes back to that, doesn't it, David?"

"Well, you're the one who's always talking about the incredible impact of deceit in your family, and you're the one who chose to be deceitful. Yes, it does come back to that. Now I have to go." He slammed the suitcase shut and started out the door.

"David, please don't go! Please stay and talk about this."

"There's no more to say, Caroline. I'll be in my office all day. I'll take the seven o'clock flight to London tonight, and I'll see you in a week or two."

"David, why are you doing this? What is going on? What is really going on?"

"No more, Caroline!" He jerked up the suitcase and left.

Caroline sat on their bed and listened to David's footsteps growing softer and softer as he moved further away from her. Finally she heard the front door open and close firmly. He was gone. She looked around the beautifully decorated room, glanced out the window, and noted that it was a bright, sunny, fall day. The first cold front of autumn had finally forced its way as far south as Dallas and pushed the steamy Gulf air down into the hill country. The result was a very special day in Texas—the first fall day with cloudless, blue skies, crisp air and cheerful, yellow sun. The day Texans eagerly await every summer had finally arrived, the first day of the long Indian summer that could very well last until Thanksgiving. All across Dallas the residents were reminded once again of a major reason they loved Texas. The leaves on the trees moved ever so slightly in the northern breeze, and Caroline watched them a long time, mesmerized by their gentle movements as they danced against the bright-blue sky. They were so vivid, so vital, so engaged with the breeze—so engaged with life.

She sighed heavily, stood up and walked toward the window. When she arrived, she placed her right hand on a pane of glass as if she were reaching for the dancing leaves. She placed her left hand on her extended stomach where she felt the movement of her child. Things are changing so fast in some areas of my life, she thought, and yet, they are standing stock-still in other areas. How confusing it is. David is gone again. The same repetitive coming for a short time, then suddenly going away. The same shallow involvement with life. Why does he keep acting this way? Why can't I get close to him? What is it that holds him at a distance from me and from deep involvement with life? I, of all people, should be able to understand. Just last year I was exactly like David. For both of us life was no deeper than the social engagements on our calendar, and we liked it that way. We had no real relationships. All we had were chatty telephone calls, cocktail-party conversations over dinner or the exhilarating, yet exhausting, raised-voiced non-conversations at balls or other large gatherings.

But life has changed for me. It changed when I realized I was pregnant. I almost ran away from it; I almost aborted my child. Oh, God, forgive me! And thank You that I did not destroy my child. Thank You that I did not bow to my basest, pleasure-seeking instincts and deny the life that was in me. Thank You that I decided, finally, in Charleston that I would risk everything to have my child. Since then, life has been so much more meaningful for me because this precious, dependent being living inside me has become my focus. And it has pulled me out of myself and made me cast my attention, my heart on it. Amazingly my love for my baby has even made me love other children and want to care for them.

Surely the change in me is some form of maturing. Why can't David see that I'm becoming a better person? At least I'm trying to. But he doesn't seem to want me unless I go back to being no more than an ornament at his side. We are out of sync, and it's my fault. I'm the one who has changed, but I refuse to go backward because the Caroline of a year ago was almost nobody, a woman so shallow she was sheer, almost invisible. These months of carrying my baby and working with Mother in the homeless shelter have made me more of a real person, a participant in life. Why doesn't David want to change too? What happened to all of our fine plans for a greater intimacy between us, a deepening of our relationship that would spill over into the world somehow and help others? And why does he keep having those awful nightmares?

Well, I'm not going to figure out anything standing here at the window. And since David is going to be gone for the next few days, I might as well go down to the shelter and try to be of some use there. Caroline turned away from the window and started toward the closet to choose her clothing for the day. She dressed as quickly as she could, put on a minimum of makeup and brushed her long, auburn hair back into a ponytail at the nape of her neck.

"There," she said, looking at herself in the mirror. "That ought to do. Oh, wait a minute. The weather has changed. I'll need a sweater or something." She left the bedroom and went out into the hall to a cedar-lined closet. After opening it, she peered down the row of carefully organized winter clothing. "I wonder if any of this will fit me now," she murmured. Then she noticed an over-sized, long cardigan sweater. "That will do." She reached for the garment and slid it off of its hanger. As she slipped into it, she glanced around the closet until her eyes lighted on a white, cardboard box on one of the higher shelves. "James Bradford's vest!" she exclaimed. "I haven't thought of it in months." Drawn to the container, she reached for it and carried it back into the bedroom. Placing it carefully on the bed, she sat down beside it and slowly opened the box and folded back the many layers of acid-free paper. Finally she uncovered the intricately embroidered, silk vest of her great-great-grandfather, James Bradford, of Charleston, South Carolina.

It's still beautiful, she thought, and it used to look so impressive hanging on the drawing room wall. I'm ashamed to admit it now, but this vest used to be the center of my identity. I was so proud to be the direct descendant of James Bradford and so determined to continue the legacy of his life—the legacy of elevated social position and the enjoyment of the elegant life that wealth supposedly brings. How odd it is to find this vest hidden away in a cedar closet. I guess I've changed more than I thought.

Caroline carefully removed the vest from its protective cocoon and held it up to the light, to enjoy once more the intricate embroidery. How many hours some woman must have poured into this project, she thought. And I wonder how many days my great great-grandfather actually wore it. These creases in the silk, these stains here and there make him so real to me. How powerful a personality he had! He shaped the character of his granddaughter, Judith, who became my grandmother. And through her, he shaped my life. I didn't know how much he had impacted me until that storm hit the house last spring, and for the first time in over a century, this vest was no longer behind glass. I finally held it in my hands, and quite unexpectedly it changed my life. How odd to think that a single item of clothing, like this vest, could change the direction of my life, but it did.

Caroline slipped her finger into a pocket of the vest, as she silently remembered. Actually it was the piece of paper I found in the vest that started everything. Such strange words were written on that paper: "He knows nothing. Meet me at midnight." Naturally I was curious and asked Grandmother about them, but she just became furious and refused to answer. Instead she began to act totally irrationally, burning all the Bradford family papers, destroying all the family history she had exalted so long. There was no stopping her; she was frantic. It was obvious she had been hiding some horrible secret from me. And trying to cover up that secret cost her her life. How I wish I could have stopped her! I still can't believe she's dead.

What a horrible week that was, and when it was over, I needed some answers, and I knew I could only find them in one place, in Charleston. So I went there to find out what Grandmother had been hiding, and there I met Great Aunt Kathleen. And she told me the truth. I discovered that there was nothing admirable about James Bradford or my grandmother or the way of life she had taught me. It was all selfish to the core, and so was I. What a sickening discovery! But something good did come out of that journey. I met Great Aunt Kathleen and saw how happy her life has been. She gave me a better model for my own life. I knew then that I wanted the child I was carrying, and I wanted to tell David the truth about its conception.

This vest used to be almost a holy object to me. It stood for all the things I treasured and the high social position I valued. Now it only serves to remind me of the self-centeredness I'm capable of. Great Aunt Kathleen always says, "Life is about relationships, about day-to-day relationships." She's right, so right. And for me that means a deep relationship with David and my baby. I want us to be a real family, and I don't plan to let any part of the past—not even those horrible nightmares of his—get in the way.

TWO

"Caroline!" her mother, Marian, exclaimed as she saw her walk through the door of the shelter for homeless women and children. "What on earth are you doing down here? I thought you were spending a few days at home with David."

"He's going to London, Mother."

"Oh, but I thought—" She stopped herself as she realized that they could be overheard.

"I'm yours for the day." Caroline changed the subject abruptly. "What needs to be done down here?"

"Well, let's talk about that," Marian followed Caroline's lead and began to talk about the shelter as she steered Caroline down the hall. "If you have time now, it would be great to draft the preliminary plans for the preschool room so we can start looking for donors."

"I have time," Caroline answered despondently, "plenty of time."

"Are you sure you're up to working?"

"I need to do something, Mother. I don't need to sit home and think about what's happened. What room do you have in mind for the preschoolers?"

"This one." She took Caroline by the arm and ushered her through a door, but as soon as she had closed the door behind her, she demanded, "What's happened?"

"I wish I knew. He just suddenly announced that he's flying to London tonight."

"After he promised to stay home a few days?"

"Right. And after he had another one of his nightmares."

"Nightmares?"

"Yes, I haven't mentioned them because I thought they would stop, but they're becoming more frequent."

"Do you know what the nightmares are about?"

"Not really. He won't talk about them, but he always says 'Danielle' right before he wakes up. The way he says it, well, I can tell he's yelling it in his dream. Do you know what I mean?"

"Yes, like a muffled scream or something."

"Exactly. What does all this mean, Mother?"

"What do you mean by 'all'? What else is there?"

"He obviously wants to stay as far away from me as he can." When tears suddenly appeared in Caroline's eyes, she turned away from her mother and struggled to regain her composure, "There's no space in David's life for me or our child," she finally added.

"Now, Caroline, that can't be true," Marian put her arm around her daughter's shoulders. "Why do you say such a thing, dear?"

"Because he keeps leaving!" Caroline cried. "Because he keeps putting business before everything personal—before our relationship, before our baby. When he is at home, he won't talk about anything personal. He won't even touch me, Mother. He just gets away from me as quickly as he can."

"It's not you, Caroline. I'm sure it's the past haunting him. He must be afraid of losing you the way he lost Danielle."

"I know; I know he's afraid, but he lost his first wife over twenty years ago. Shouldn't he have made his peace with it?"

"Yes, he should have, but that doesn't mean that he has."

"Will he—ever?"

"Of course he will, dear, but it may not be until your baby is safely delivered and you are okay. I know you need his support now, but you may just have to do without it. Many women go through childbirth without their mates' enthusiastic support. Even if tragedy hadn't touched David's life 20 years ago, his reaction to the baby might have been just the same. Many men don't really want their children until they see them; they're not eager to give up their exclusive relationship with their wives. We have to remember that David, like other men before him, can't visualize his child the way you can. You have an advantage; you can feel your child inside of you. It's just very different with mothers and fathers, especially at this stage, before the child is born."

"But he can see me! I'm still here. I need him to love me, Mother. He's my husband, for heaven's sake."

"I think he's afraid to love you, Caroline. In spite of David's jet-setting around running a huge corporation, he's actually a very frightened person. He seems to allow little, if any, intimacy in his life."

"Tell me about it! I've tried to talk to him about that, but he won't even discuss it. Mother, why did he agree to go on with our marriage after he found out I was pregnant? He had the perfect excuse to leave. After all, I tricked him into this pregnancy. When he came looking for me in Charleston last March and found out I was pregnant, why did he agree to continue our life together?"

"I'm sure he agreed with the best of intentions, Caroline. Words are so easy, but backing them up with actions is much harder. You, yourself, have discovered that. When you were in Charleston last spring, you made some promises to yourself that were hard for you to keep once you returned to Dallas and got caught up in your everyday world again."

"I know. I decided I would quit living the empty life of a socialite and become involved with homeless women and children down here in the shelter. And I've done that, Mother."

"I know you have, dear. But was it easy?"

"No, it was one of the hardest things I've ever done."

"Right. But it was very easy to make the decision to do it in Charleston, while you were sitting on the piazza of your Great-Aunt Kathleen's beautiful ante-bellum home, or while you were walking arm in arm with David through the azalea gardens. Under those circumstances it was easy to decide to change anything, but when you actually flew back to Dallas and decided to get your hands dirty down here, you had quite a battle with yourself. Remember?"

Caroline blushed. "I do remember. I remember some pretty bad scenes down here when I got impatient or angry and just stomped out. For a while I thought I was a horrible person because I couldn't make the transition immediately. I would just look at all these dirty, ragged children and these women who were so coarsened by life, and I just, I just—"

"You just wanted to run off to a fashionable spa and let them pamper you or fly to one of your favorite resorts in the south of France."

"Yes, that's exactly what I wanted to do, but I didn't do it. I came back down here, and I kept trying. David hasn't even tried to keep his promises to work out of his Dallas office more and to be involved in this pregnancy."

"It was a bigger change for David, Caroline. He's a very important man in the world's eyes, in his own eyes. And he's spent 30 years in a frenetic lifestyle hopping on his corporate jet and flying off wherever the global economic situation called him."

"I guess you're right; it has been a bigger change for him, but still, we have to spend time together if we're ever going to have a meaningful relationship. And frankly, Mother, David has become more distant than he ever was."

"I hear what you're saying, Caroline," Marian sighed and stared out the windows of the dilapidated room. "You know, in a strange way you had a great advantage over David. You see, we forget that David was in London during that critical week last March, that week that changed your life."

"You mean the week when Grandmother died?"

"Yes. David didn't experience what you experienced. Every change that you've been able to bring about in yourself—in your values or in your actions—all of those changes are based on what you experienced that week plus what you discovered in Charleston about the family. But David had none of those experiences. You endured a wrenching event, the death of your grandmother, that produced a unique revelation in your life. In a single week's time, you went from being a spoiled brat—I'm sorry, dear, but it's true—to being a grown woman. You went from being a pampered ornament to a flesh-and-blood woman who suddenly had not only to watch the death of her beloved grandmother, but also face the way she had deceived you. You had to face the fact that your grandmother's way of life, which you had adopted, was wrong. That week was one shock after another for you. And as if those things weren't difficult enough, you also had to face the consequences of your pregnancy."

"You might as well say it the way it was, Mother. I lied to David. I told him I was taking the pill when I wasn't. I deceived him into the pregnancy when I knew he would hate the idea."

"Okay, say it anyway you want to. You were pregnant. You were facing the decision of whether or not to get an abortion in order to keep your princess lifestyle going. Then suddenly the grandmother who had encouraged you into that fairy-tale lifestyle died. Almost immediately you discovered that that lifestyle—those values of hers—were based on a lie. You were a brave woman, Caroline. You could have buried your head in the sand and gone right on living the shallow life you were living, but you didn't. When you found papers that led you to believe there was a lie in your grandmother's version of the past, you went to Charleston, and you ferreted out the truth. You found out that all that your grandmother stood for, the legacy of the famous James Bradford, was based on deceit and selfishness. You had to face the fact that you were continuing that legacy of deceit in another generation by lying to your husband."

"I know all of that, Mother. Believe me, I haven't forgotten one moment of it."

"No, of course you haven't, but what you have to remember is that David never experienced any of that. He was in London, so sick with pneumonia that he couldn't even get home for your grandmother's funeral. As soon as he could get out of his sickbed, he flew to Charleston, found you, and was suddenly hit with all this information—not experience—information."

"I hadn't thought of that. It must have been overwhelming for him."

"Of course it was."

"There was no easy way to make him understand. I simply had to sit him down on the piazza at Great Aunt Kathleen's and tell him all the events that I had just lived through, as well as all the revelations about the family, and how they had impacted me."

"And he listened, and he heard, but he did not experience it. There's a big difference between hearing about something and living through it," Marian observed.

"So you're saying that I cannot expect the degree of change in him that I have experienced because he doesn't have the basis for change."

"Right. Even if he had been in Dallas and had gone through that week with you, it would not have been his grandmother who had betrayed him, who had lied to him. Even if he had followed the trail back with you as you looked into your ancestry, it would not have been his great-great-grandfather who started this path of suffering that split the family and confused so many lives. And as much as I'm sure David likes your Great Aunt Kathleen, she could never have impacted him like she impacted you."

"You're right. He thought Great Aunt Kathleen was interesting, but he never really saw her depth, the wisdom of her life values."

"You had more reason to accept Aunt Kathleen's values because you were carrying a baby and you want the best for it. Through the whole situation, Caroline, there has been more at stake for you. First, you had to decide whether to abort your baby. Then you had to decide whether you wanted your baby to grow up with the values you were embracing. The importance of what you had at stake gave you the courage to start making changes in yourself and in your lifestyle."

"But I don't know how to help David start, Mother, and I can't live in this kind of isolation."

"I hate to say it, dear, but you may have to accept the fact that there is nothing you can do to change David or his views on life. You may have to let God take care of that."

"I can't imagine that even God could change David."

"I know, I know," her mother laughed and gave her a hug. "That's a common feeling that wives often have about their husbands, but believe me, God can think of something."

"And if He doesn't?"

"Well, then you will have to make some choices. Surely you have noticed that your own father has not changed his life since I changed mine."

"That's true. Daddy has gone on the way he always did. Even after you left society and started giving your life to the people down here, Daddy didn't change. How can you stand that?"

"I just had to make my peace with it, Caroline. Your father is not a clone of me. If God wants to change him, He will. But I don't know that your situation is exactly comparable with mine. By the time I saw a better way to live, you, my youngest child, were in your early teens. We must pray very hard that David does have his eyes opened and that he does make some changes because your precious child is coming into the world, and your child needs both parents and needs them living in some kind of harmony."

"You and Daddy could have gotten a divorce."

"We could have," Marian agreed, "but we love each other, and we love our children, so in the end, we just agreed that I would do my thing and that he would not make it difficult for me to do so."

"You seem to be telling me two opposing things. On the one hand, to let go of David—let him go his own way—and on the other, you're warning me that I will soon give birth to a child who needs a united family."

"Your child most likely won't be born into the united family that we want for it. I just can't see David changing that quickly. But at the very least your child needs to have a mother who is sure of her direction. And you seem to be sort of wobbly at the moment about how you feel about things. I'm sorry that David left. I had hoped you two would have some quiet time together now before the baby comes."

"I know. I had hoped we could get away together for a few days. I need to get away before the baby comes."

"Then why don't you go somewhere, Caroline, if the doctor says you can?"

"Where shall I go?" They looked at each other for an instant, then both laughed. "I can't believe I asked that question. There's only one place I want to go."

"To Charleston!" they said in unison.

"To visit Great Aunt Kathleen," Caroline added.

"Oh, she would dearly love to see you, and you won't be able to travel much longer. Call the doctor. See what he says. If he doesn't want you to travel alone, I'll gladly go with you."

"Oh, it would be wonderful to see Great Aunt Kathleen. And it would be heaven on earth to be in Bradford House, to stand on the piazza and look out at Charleston Harbor."

"Goodness! You're making me hope the doctor says you need an escort so I can go. At any rate, get on the phone, Caroline, and call the doctor. Take your trip while you can."

*   *   *

The evening Dallas-to-London flight was two hours into its journey, and the passengers had been fed a light supper. For the most part, the first-class passengers had put away their work, reclined the seat backs and snuggled close to pillows to capture some rest during the long hours of flight ahead. David's overhead light remained on as he struggled to continue working. He made little headway with the papers he was reviewing because his mind was constantly drawn back to Caroline and the fight they had had that morning before he had left the house. Being a man particularly capable of compartmentalizing his mind, he had managed not to think of the disagreement through his workday, but now that he was suspended over the Atlantic with nothing but darkness outside the window and a seemingly interminable business report in front of him, his mind broke loose.

Maybe I should tell Caroline the truth, David considered, but

I have suppressed that part of my past for so long that I don't know if I can face it now. He stared out the window at the darkness. "No one must ever know what happened here," a commanding male voice from the past wafted through David's mind. He squeezed his eyes shut to force it away, but it would not be silenced. "You do understand, don't you, David? No one must ever know what happened here." David had a sudden, overwhelming urge to jump out of his skin, to jump out of the plane and run, but instead he slammed the business report back into his briefcase, snapped the case closed, pushed the tray table forward, latched it, and thrust the briefcase under the seat in front of him. A stewardess was immediately at his side.

"Would you like a pillow, Mr. Randolph?" she asked quietly as she held one out to him.

"Yes, yes, fine," he answered brusquely.

As she turned to leave, he reclined the seat, placed the pillow behind his head and crossed his arms across his chest as if he were composing himself to sleep. In actuality, he had crossed his arms across his chest to hold on to himself, to keep himself together somehow. Relax, he told himself, just relax. Listen to the plane engines, the steady drumming sound, and relax. He directed all his powers of concentration to the sound of the engines, and his muscles slowly began to go limp. He was slipping into a very welcome sleep, a reprieve from the pain he kept so deeply buried inside of himself.

An image appeared in David's mind's eye, and he saw himself once again moving an iron cover across the top of a deep, deep well. It was an image he had used often to promise himself that the past demons of his life were contained, that they could not come to the surface again and haunt him. Nor could they pull him into the well and drown him. The plane engines droned on, and David slipped slowly into sleep. At some indefinable, immeasurable moment, the constant mechanical sound changed to a soft voice, his own voice murmuring, "Danielle, Danielle, Danielle," and he became blissfully happy. He dreamed.

He was in his early twenties—a Texan—tall and strong. His polished good looks and sophisticated manner were the calculated results that only old money can buy. The best schools, world-wide travel, a well-nurtured, keen interest in the best of everything—all these had produced the poised, proud, young Texan who watched a young woman named Danielle run along the banks of the river ahead of him. She was laughing, carefree, totally without constraint as she frolicked through the grass like a young colt. The bright sun glistened off her short, bouncing, brunette curls as she tossed her head; her eyes glittered as she laughed. It was obvious that the world belonged to her, and he was fascinated by her. She was fire and spirit. She thawed the cold reserve that was so much a part of his nature, and he felt lightened by her presence. He knew he could never be like Danielle, free-spirited and blithe, but to be near her meant he could borrow some of her fire and feel twice as alive as he had ever felt in his life. Compelling desire surged through him; he had to claim her for his own, so he ran after her, calling her name.

"Danielle! Danielle! Wait!"

She glanced back over her shoulder at him, laughed and tormented him by continuing to run away. Her contagious, powerful laughter enslaved his senses, encouraging him to run faster. Certain he could catch her, he was also certain that she wanted to be caught. His heart pounded with the excitement of the chase as his young muscles sprang eagerly to action. She darted this way and that to escape him, the skirt of her white dress flapping in the breeze as she ran. Zigzagging back and forth through the trees, she challenged him to catch her, to overpower her. Finally, she turned and ran toward the bank of the river. He followed eagerly, so intent on catching her that he hardly noticed when his feet left the soft soil and landed on the wooden planking of a long pier that stretched out into the river. When he realized that she would soon reach the end of the pier, a thrill of triumph filled his mind. I've got her now! She can't run into the river. Danielle did reach the end of the pier and turned to face him, laughing between gasps as she struggled to breathe. He stopped a few feet from her and drew huge gulps of air into his lungs. Quickly strengthened by the oxygen and pressed by his desire, he said triumphantly, "I've got you now," and reached out to grab her waist.

In one quick, fluid movement, she placed her hands on his upper arms as if she would succumb to his embrace, and at the same time, she threw her weight against him, and he plunged over the edge of the pier into the cold river. His body sank deep into the water as his mind struggled to deal with the shock of this unexpected turn of events. A surge of angry frustration rose in him as he turned himself in the water and swam upward, but when he broke the surface, ready to scold her, his anger melted as her beauty blazed down at him. For a moment he was mesmerized by her sparkling brown eyes and full, laughing lips. He grinned and demanded, "How am I going to return to the picnic now? I'm a muddy mess."

"Oh, who wants to go back there?" she asked gaily. "They're all a bunch of stuffed shirts."

"But it's your party! They're your guests. You have to go back."

She paused for a moment, obviously thinking about what he had said, then exclaimed, "Not necessarily!" and suddenly dove into the water beside him.

David was so surprised that his mind recorded the event like a slow-motion, movie camera. One moment she was poised on the edge of the pier, her clean, crisp, white dress flapping in the breeze, her face surrounded by a halo of gleaming brown curls; then suddenly, she was flying through the air, her arms over her head, descending to the water and slowly disappearing beneath the surface. The last thing he saw was her white, high-heeled sandals. He was aghast at her action, but strangely pleased.

Then a stronger emotion overtook him, and he was afraid for her. He dove back under the water, his eyes open, searching for her in the murky world of the river. Almost instantly he saw her white dress, and after a few kicks, he reached her side. Her skirt was billowing around her slender legs, her curls were floating around her face, and her eyes were open; but what startled him most was that she was smiling at him. He realized that she was not drowning;

she was waiting for him. She held out her arms; he wrapped his around her tiny waist and began to kick to propel them both up to the surface. As soon as they reached the air, he demanded, "Are you crazy?"

"Yes," she cried as she threw her arms around his neck, "and don't you love it?"

Yes, he loved it. Inebriated by her flamboyant actions, he pulled her to him and pressed his lips against hers, but they began to sink under the water again. Frustrated but determined, he made the common sense decision that he would never gain his kiss until he got her back on the shore, so he put his arm around her and began to swim the short distance to the muddy shoreline.

By the time he got her back up on the bank, they were both covered with mud and green slime from the river, but she was laughing. Eagerly he kissed her, and when she did not resist, he pressed his lips more passionately to hers. Far too soon for him, she drew her lips back and gasped for air. He wanted her desperately but was afraid he would push her too fast, and she would refuse him. Gently he smoothed her wet curls away from her cheeks, and to calm himself, he thought of the guests they had left behind at her party. "What will the others say?" he asked.

"All kinds of deliciously wicked things," she responded happily. "And every time they tell the story, it will get worse and worse, so we might as well enjoy ourselves." She reached up and pulled the straps of her dress off her shoulders and as the wet, white cloth slipped down her arms, David's control slipped too. He lifted her into his arms and carried her to a more secluded spot where he lowered her to the ground. She unbuttoned his shirt, and he shrugged it off. The tall, damp river grass was cold against his naked skin, but her lips were soft and warm, and her arms held him so close—

"Mr. Randolph. Mr. Randolph." He heard an unfamiliar woman's voice. "Mr. Randolph," the voice became more insistent, and he felt someone shaking his shoulder. Slowly he emerged from the depths of his sleep, reluctant to leave behind his world of sunshine and youth. Opening his eyes, he looked toward the source of the voice. A woman was leaning over him, saying. "I need you to prepare for landing." He stared at her blankly, so she repeated, "I need you to prepare for landing, Mr. Randolph. We'll be landing soon in London."

"Oh," was all he could say, but he shook his head vigorously, trying to force himself back into the present.

"If you'll put your seat back up straight and tighten your seat belt—"

"Yes, yes, of course," he agreed groggily. Then as she turned to walk away, he reached back and took the pillow from behind his head, fumbled for the button on the armrest, and raised the back of the seat to an upright position.

The stewardess reappeared at his side and handed him a cold, wet cloth. "Perhaps this will help," she suggested.

He took it gratefully and rubbed it across his face. It was wet like the river, but it smelled of disinfectant, and the sharpness of that smell totally catapulted his mind back to the present. "Thank you," he said briskly as he handed it back to her. He was awake now, but he could still feel Danielle's skin under his hand. Why? he demanded silently. Why did it have to happen? Why did it have to end that way?

When David entered his London townhouse, he was greeted by his housekeeper, Mrs. Watson's cheerful, "Good morning, sir." He nodded stiffly to her, and his exhausted manner set off an immediate surge of maternal concern from her. "Sir, you look completely done in. But never you mind, I've got some breakfast all ready for you. Just go freshen up, sir, and I'll have a hot pot of coffee ready when you come back down."

"No caffeine," David ordered as he slowly started toward the stairs.

"Sir," Mrs. Watson paused and peered at him as she chose her words carefully, "Sir, if you don't mind my saying so, you don't look up to the office just yet. Perhaps you should—"

"No office this morning," David cut her off. "I've got to get some rest. I'll go in this afternoon."

"I've already laid out the table, sir, but I'm going to bring a tray of breakfast upstairs for you. That way you can get to bed faster and—"

"That's fine, Mrs. Watson. Just give me fifteen minutes." David headed more determinedly for the stairs, so she wouldn't prolong the conversation.

After he had showered and eaten the breakfast Mrs. Watson had brought him, David collapsed into a comfortable chair in the master bedroom of his London townhouse and let his head hang for a moment. He was so exhausted he wasn't certain he could make it over to the bed to sleep, but after a few moments of sitting in the chair, his lower back began to ache. "Eight hours sitting in a plane," David mumbled. He leaned forward to stretch his back. "I've got to stay out of planes for a while." Still too tired to stand, he leaned backward against the chair and stretched his legs out in front of him as far as they would go. At the same time, he turned his head sharply to the left in an attempt to loosen the crick in his neck. His gaze fell on an ornately framed picture on the draped table next to the chair. It was a picture of Caroline in her wedding dress. Momentarily forgetting the aches and pains of his body, he picked up the frame and studied the picture of his wife.

"Caroline," he whispered. "My beautiful, regal Caroline. I do love you. I do." His throat tightened, and tears came into his eyes. "If only I could tell you everything. If only I could tell you about the past, but I can't. I won't! I want our life to be separate from that horror. I want only good things for us—the way it was on the day we married." The lines of weariness on his face softened and faded as he lovingly examined the portrait of the fine-boned, petite woman with her mass of auburn hair, her creamy skin and her blue-gray eyes. She was wearing her grandmother's wedding gown, an old-fashioned, ivory silk dress. Yards and yards of its sheer fabric had been delicately embroidered in ivory silk thread. Her long, auburn hair was piled on top of her head in soft curls, and a mantilla style veil fell to her shoulders and trailed down her back to the floor where it was carried by the train of the dress.

"Oh, Caroline," David murmured. "Why did things have to change? I wanted us to stay just the way we were in the beginning. Why couldn't you leave it alone? It was perfect, unblemished, safe, and now—" Hurriedly, he put the picture back on the table. "I've got to get some rest," he scolded himself and stood up suddenly.

As quickly as he could, he undressed and slipped into a pair of pajamas. He turned off the lamp by the chair, walked to the bed and pulled back the bedspread. He grabbed the corner of the white, crisp sheet and roughly snapped the top sheet back out of his way. To his exhausted eyes, the bright white sheet glared in the bedside lamplight, so he turned the lamp off, slipped between the sheets and jerked the white sheet back over him. "I wish she was here," he murmured, "looking just like she does in that picture." It took no more than a minute for him to fall into a deep sleep, and soon he was dreaming of Caroline coming down the aisle in the church.

He could see her at the back of the vast church, a blur of filmy, ivory fabric. Slowly she walked forward, far too slowly for him as he waited eagerly for the moment when he could clearly see her face. He squinted his eyes and expectantly held his breath. Any second she would pass under the first chandelier, and the mellow light would reveal the woman he had waited for so long. She approached the circle of light the chandelier cast on the marble floor, but as she walked through the light, her ivory dress turned to a sharp white tone, and the softness of the filmy fabric became the hard surface of gleaming satin. The antique, family veil was gone. The long, luxuriant, auburn hair had turned to short, brown curls, and he was looking into the face of Danielle.

She smiled at him nervously and clasped her father's arm more tightly. A sense of foreboding overwhelmed him, and he muttered in his sleep, "No, not Danielle. I want Caroline—not Danielle," but Danielle continued to walk down the aisle grasping her father's arm. When she reached the front of the church, his feeling of fear disappeared, and he was consumed by longing for her dazzling beauty. How ridiculous to be afraid, he thought. What's wrong with me? I am about to marry the most beautiful woman in the world. Then he remembered the cause of his anxiety: she's late, very late. I thought she wasn't coming. I paced and paced in the room next to the sanctuary. I wanted to run, to go look for her, to find her and chain her to my side, but what does all that matter now? She is here at the altar, ready to marry me, and I love her so!

The minister asked, "Who gives this woman to be married?"

Her father said, "I do," and began to step back. Confidently David stepped toward her to take her hand, but her smile suddenly disappeared, her lips began to quiver with fear. She looked into David's eyes for one panicky moment, then whirled around and cried out, "No, Daddy! No, I can't do it!"

What is it? What's wrong with her? David's mind whirled with anxiety. The enormous church was full of people. There was a dead silence until Danielle spoke again in a high-pitched, hysterical voice, "Oh, Daddy, I can't help it. I can't do it!"

This isn't happening, David thought. It can't be. I won't let it happen; I won't lose her. She loves me. She has to love me! She has to marry me! The blazing white of Danielle's dress blurred as David fought his fears, determined to push back the faintness attempting to knock him off his feet.

Danielle suddenly faced him. "I love you, David," she insisted, "really I do, but I just can't—" She began sobbing. David's mind went blank, and he stood as rigid as a statue. Her father took her by the arms and quickly escorted her out a side exit of the sanctuary. David stared after her; he was so shocked, he could not move.

Finally the minister spoke. "Let us give these two young people a few moments," he suggested diplomatically as he patted David on the shoulder.

The minister's touch snapped David back into control of himself. "She loves me," he muttered, "she just said so." He turned and raced after Danielle. When he found her, she was standing in a small office sobbing on her father's shoulder.

"Danielle!" he raced to her side, took her from her father's arms and held her at arm's length so he could see her face. "Talk to me," he demanded. "What's wrong? You said you love me."

"I do. I do." She turned to face him as water continued to stream from her eyes. "I do love you, David."

"Then what's wrong?" He demanded again, but before she could answer, he continued, "I don't care what it is; we can handle it if we're together. I love you, Danielle, more than anything in the world. I want you to be my wife."

"It's just a case of nerves," her father spoke up. "I'm afraid she's been having a hard time of it all day, but it's just a case of nerves, son. It'll pass as soon as the ceremony's over."

"That's not true, that's not true!" Danielle started crying hysterically and beating on David's chest with her right fist. "It's not true. If only someone would tell the truth. Oh, Daddy, we have to tell the truth!"

"No!" David shouted in his sleep. "Not the truth. No one must ever know. No one must ever—"

"Mr. Randolph! Mr. Randolph!"

David tried desperately to drag his sleep-drenched mind to total consciousness when he heard the incessant voice.

"Mr. Randolph! Wake up!" the voice continued, and someone began to shake him.

Finally he understood. It was Mrs. Watson's voice. He sat up in bed, breathing heavily, and shook his head to clear it.

"You were yelling, sir; I didn't want to invade your privacy, but I had to be sure you are all right." Mrs. Watson apologized.

"Fine, fine," David stammered. "Thank you."

"A bad dream, sir?" she asked.

"Yes, yes that's all it was. Thank you, Mrs. Watson. You may go."

"Yes, sir," she hesitated a moment, then turned to leave.

Drenched with sweat, David collapsed back onto his pillow.

"Oh, God, why can't I make it go away?" he demanded of the ceiling. "Why can't I just make it go away? It was twenty-five years ago." He got up, went into the bathroom, and took a bottle from the medicine chest. After swallowing a sleeping pill, he returned to the bed and settled back down.

"I've got to let this go," he warned himself. "It's going to ruin my life; it's going to hurt Caroline. It *is* ruining my life because it's ruining my marriage to Caroline right now. I've got to let this go.

I'm a grown man, and a man takes control. I'm a Randolph, and a Randolph controls! I *will* let this go." He repeated his resolve over and over again as he sank into a deep sleep.

THREE

When Caroline saw the seat belt light in the plane go off, she loosened her seat belt and reclined the seat into a more comfortable position. If only I could put my feet up, she silently wished, but at least we are finally off the ground and free of the delay at the Atlanta airport. How I wish they had a flight straight from Dallas to Charleston. Oh well, at least this flight will be short, and then I'll finally be in Charleston. Just the thought of arriving at Bradford House makes me smile. I can't wait to stand on the upper piazza and look out at the harbor and down on the gardens. It will be like stepping into another world, and right now I could use another world, especially a serene one.

And Bradford House is serene. At least it is these days, but Aunt Kathleen's stories about the family history that took place in the house certainly prove it wasn't always peaceful. And whose fault was that? James Bradford's. My great-great grandfather's. When he came back from the Civil War and found his fiancee, Diana, married, he started the chain of events that wracked the Bradford family for two more generations and even reached into my life. Since he couldn't have the woman he wanted, Diana, he married her cousin, Mary, but that fact didn't keep him from having an adulterous affair with Diana. So he ended up fathering two children, a son by his mistress, Diana and a daughter by his wife, Mary.

Poor Mary. Apparently she knew all along about his affair and chose to remain quiet about it. How awful for her—to know her husband loved another woman and, at the same time, to be carrying a baby she knew he didn't want. I can certainly guess how she must have felt; all I have to do is look at how I feel about David's reaction to my pregnancy, and he's not even having an affair— Caroline stopped her thoughts as her mouth flew open and she exclaimed, "Oh no! No, that's not possible!"

"Are you okay, young lady?" The alarmed man seated next to her asked. When Caroline continued staring straight ahead instead of answering him, he demanded more firmly. "Do you need help?"

"I don't know," Caroline murmured as tears gathered in her eyes. "I don't know."

"I'll call a stewardess."

"That's not necessary," Caroline managed to drag her thoughts away from the specter of David's possibly having an affair long enough to answer.

"You're sure?"

"Yes, absolutely," she turned and smiled feebly at him. "I was just thinking about something—uh—something unpleasant. I'm fine, really I am." She turned to look out the window as she hurriedly wiped her tears away. Dear God, she thought, please don't let it be true. I never thought of such a thing until now, but David is treating me just like James Bradford treated his wife, Mary. He's ignoring me, staying away from me. What am I going to do? What if there is another woman?

"Do you need some help?" a stewardess broke into Caroline's thoughts, and she realized the man had ignored her and called for help in spite of her objections.

"No, thank you," Caroline murmured, eager to dismiss the woman so she could return to her thoughts.

"You're sure?"

"Yes, yes, I'm just fine. I think I'll just take a little nap." Caroline closed her eyes to encourage the woman to move on down the aisle. Immediately her question came back to her. What am I going to do? What if David has found someone else? I have to have a strategy in case it's true. What did Mary do? She just endured it; she just endured what James Bradford dished out. What else could she do in the late 1860's? And what was the result of Mary's passive acceptance of her husband's infidelity? He fathered a son, Robert, by Diana, and he fathered a daughter, Carrie, by her. What a horrible mess!

Caroline sighed audibly and squirmed in her seat as she continued remembering the family story her great aunt had told her. The situation got worse, she thought, much worse when those two children grew up and eloped with each other. Then there was another baby conceived—but definitely unwelcome—in the world, Carrie's baby. But Carrie didn't knuckle under to James Bradford the way her mother had. Carrie annulled the marriage to her half-brother, Robert. Then she refused to marry the man her father lined up for her; she refused to deceive him into thinking her baby was his. Instead she married an older man she knew loved her, and in the end she overcame all the scandal and had a happy life.

But how did she turn it all around? How did she take control of her life? There she was, pregnant with a child only she wanted. She couldn't go on living with the love of her life, Robert. *I have* to know how she managed her own feelings, how she managed to make something good out of such a catastrophic beginning.

Caroline opened her eyes again and stared out the window. Huge, fluffy clouds floated by, but she hardly noticed them as she worried about David and how she was going to handle whatever was going on. It's a good thing I'm going to Charleston, she thought. I need to be at Bradford House now; I need information and advice, and Great Aunt Kathleen is the only one who can give it to me. I need the feeling I get there. At Bradford House I feel like anything is possible, like I can solve absolutely any problem. And I've certainly got some problems to solve.

"Please drop me off at the garden gate," Caroline said to her cousin's driver, who had picked her up at the airport and was escorting her to Bradford House.

"Are you sure, Miz Randolph?"

"Yes. I want to go in by the garden gate. You can turn into the driveway and take the bags into the house. And if you don't mind, take them on upstairs."

"Yes, ma'am." He stopped the Lincoln at the curb in front of the elegant, wrought iron gate that Caroline loved so dearly. He hastened out of the car, opened the door for her and helped her slowly emerge from the Lincoln.

"Thank you," she smiled at him when she had finally gotten her bulky form upright and steadied. "Wait. I want to give you a little something as a token of my appreciation for your special care."

"Oh, no, Miz Randolph. You mustn't do that. Your Cousin John, he already taken care of everything."

"Are you sure?"

"I's positive. Don't you worry about me now, but you take your time. You's had a long trip."

"I will."

"And I'll get these bags up wherever Miz Kathleen tell me to put them."

"Thank you." She stood still while the man re-entered the driver's seat of the Lincoln and carefully maneuvered it around the corner toward the driveway. Then she turned and placed her hand on the beautiful, old gate.

I have a sense of two time-frames running at the same time, she thought. It seems like only yesterday that I stood here for the first time and opened this gate with no idea what I would discover about my family or my own life. It seems like only yesterday, and yet, so much has changed in my life, it seems like years ago. She ran her fingers along some of the intricate curves of the wrought iron and wondered. How many Bradfords have entered this gate over the years? In spite of all the rains and winds that must have come in the last two centuries, it still seems like all their fingerprints are on this gate, and that by touching it again I can reconnect to them.

Dear God, I hope the wisdom I need is really here waiting for me. Overcome by a confusing combination of anxiety as well as a sense of finally coming safely home again, she just stood there, unable to enter.

"Caroline! Caroline!" She heard the genteel voice of her Great Aunt Kathleen calling her, prompting her to take courage and open the gate into the garden to find the source of that welcoming voice. "Caroline," her aunt called again; Caroline raised her eyes to the second-story piazza of the old house.

"Aunt Kathleen!" she called back and waved. For a moment they stood, Caroline in the garden and her Great Aunt Kathleen standing high above her on the second story piazza of the mansion, but when their eyes met, even at that great distance, an amazing kindredship between them flamed up. Great Aunt Kathleen suddenly clasped her hands together in obvious delight.

"I'll be right down!" she called.

"Take your time," Caroline warned, remembering the steep, circular staircase, that amazing architectural achievement that was the focal point of the marvelous, old house. For a moment Caroline was worried that her elderly aunt might fall in her haste to reach the garden, but then she heard the voice of Betsy, the housekeeper, in the distance.

"Now, Miz Kathleen, you slow yourself down. I's going down that staircase with you." Betsy's voice dwindled away, and Caroline relaxed, knowing that her great aunt was still in the care of the ever-vigilant Betsy.

Caroline started her own slow journey down the winding path of the garden that led to the lower piazza. The azaleas still billowed over the walk, but the beautiful rosy-reds and pinks and whites of last spring had now turned to the green and bronze tones of the fall. In general, the garden was not the riot of color that it had been the previous spring, but when Caroline saw her great aunt's roses, she couldn't resist smiling. "Great Aunt Kathleen. How does she do it? I believe she probably keeps her beloved roses blooming all year long." Caroline paused next to a pink rosebush and gently touched one blossom. It was velvety soft, and she thought of her baby's skin with a thrill of expectation. For a few seconds she stood there running her fingertips over the surface of the delicate petals and remembering the first time she had entered this garden last spring. Great Aunt Kathleen had suddenly appeared from these roses, thrust a bowl of water into her hands and proceeded to give her a lesson on the proper way to cut a rose. Caroline shook her head and lightly laughed at the memory.

"Caroline!" Great Aunt Kathleen now called to her from the lower piazza, and Caroline moved more quickly along the winding path to join her Great Aunt Kathleen and to throw her arms around the diminutive woman.

"We're together again!" Great Aunt Kathleen proclaimed.

"But one of us is more obviously present now," Caroline responded as she moved back from Aunt Kathleen for a moment and put her hand on her abdomen.

"Yes, yes," Great Aunt Kathleen agreed gleefully. "The baby. Oh, Caroline! I can't wait to see it." She once again clasped her hands in excitement. "Oh, Betsy," she called to the housekeeper who stood a few paces away, "isn't it wonderful? We could hardly imagine that there was really a baby coming when Caroline was last here, but now look at her."

"I sees her," Betsy smiled as she stepped forward.

"How are you, Betsy?" Caroline gave the old woman a hug. "Thank you for continuing to take care of this incorrigible great aunt of mine."

"I thought we agreed to drop that 'great' stuff a long time ago," Great Aunt Kathleen objected "'Aunt Kathleen' will do just fine."

"Yes, Aunt Kathleen."

"Besides, if there is anyone looking a little great around here, it is not I."

Caroline shook her head woefully. "Pregnancy definitely doesn't do much for one's vanity."

"Beauty don't just come only from the shape of a woman," Betsy insisted.

"Betsy is right as usual," Aunt Kathleen agreed. "You should see your face; you are absolutely glowing. Motherhood becomes you; it's obvious already."

"Part of that glow comes from seeing you two and this wonderful garden and the house again. I'm so glad to be back in Charleston!"

"And we's glad to have you here," Betsy said.

"We certainly are, my dear. Come on inside and let's get you settled in and have some tea. How was your trip?"

"It wasn't bad at all, although it did seem incredibly slow, probably because I was so eager to get here."

"What you need now is some rest."

"I haven't been doing anything but sitting. What I want to do is wander around the garden and then look at every room of this house."

"I'm ready; let's go! Just name the direction, the garden or the house? Which shall we see first?"

"The house, Miz Kathleen," Betsy dictated. "Neither one of you's got the sense you's born with. You two needs a good sensible person taking care of you. Miz Caroline got to come in the house and freshen up a bit before you two goes traipsing around the garden. If I don't keep my eyes on you, you two will be out sauntering round on the Battery in the next five minutes."

"What a delightful idea, Betsy, the Battery! There's no better way to get re-acquainted with Charleston than to walk on top of the sea wall and enjoy the harbor. Caroline, shall we take a walk on the Battery?"

"Don't you dare!" Betsy declared. "Miz Caroline got to take care of herself. She can't be walking on no sea wall."

"But exercise is the best thing for Caroline in her condition, Betsy," Aunt Kathleen argued.

"Not right this minute, it ain't. She just got off a plane. She need to get herself settled and have a proper tea."

"I hate to admit it, but she's right, Caroline. Let's get you freshened up and settled in your room. Then Betsy can force whatever food and drink she wants to on you." Aunt Kathleen gave Betsy a playful look.

"I ain't gonna force nothing on nobody," Betsy declared indignantly, "but it's late afternoon, and I's got some tea pastries made just in case Miz Caroline want to do something civilized, like have afternoon tea."

"You two are worse than ever," Caroline chided, as she struggled to put away her own worries and join into the friendly quarrel between the older women. "What am I going to do with you?"

"Not a thing, darling," Aunt Kathleen gave her a little squeeze. "Betsy and I love things just the way they are."

"A cup of tea sounds wonderful, Betsy," Caroline admitted, "and I never turn down food these days."

"Well, that settles it," Aunt Kathleen agreed brightly. "We'll have a proper tea," she nodded at Betsy, "on the upper piazza, and then we'll have our stroll in the garden."

"Oh no, you's not gonna climb them stairs again," Betsy insisted.

"I told you that nothing has changed," Aunt Kathleen winked at Caroline. "Of course, I'm going to climb the stairs, Betsy. It's the only way to get to the upper piazza."

"Miz Kathleen, you's got to think of Miz Caroline now. She can't go running up and down them stairs. I's gonna serve tea on the lower piazza."

"But the upper piazza has a view of the harbor, Betsy."

"I know's that," Betsy declared as she stubbornly folded her arms across her chest.

"We'll let Caroline decide," Aunt Kathleen turned to Caroline. "What is your preference, darling?"

"Oh no, you're not putting me in the middle of this."

"Very well, Caroline. Let's reduce it to a medical decision then. Has the doctor told you to stay off of stairs?"

"No, the doctor hasn't restricted me in any way. He just told me not to do anything outrageous like horseback riding."

"There, Betsy. There's no need for Caroline to mount a horse to go upstairs."

"Humph," Betsy declared, turned her back and walked briskly away.

"What does 'humph' mean?" Caroline asked her great aunt.

"It means tea will be served upstairs on the upper piazza."

"Good. I can't wait to see the harbor from up there."

"Well, it's just at the top of the stairs. Let's go." Aunt Kathleen put her arm through Caroline's, and they walked to the foot of the staircase. "When we went up these stairs last spring, my dear, you were helping me. Now I'm not sure who needs the most help."

"I think we both just need to take our time," Caroline concluded as she accompanied her great aunt up the staircase.

"We can take all the time we need. That's one of the wonderful things about Charleston. There's no need to rush here."

"Oh, look at the harbor!" Caroline exclaimed the moment she stepped out onto the upper piazza. She immediately turned to her left and walked to the end of the piazza, the portion that faced directly onto Charleston Harbor. "Look at the sun dancing on those waves!"

"I've always thought of that harbor as being alive and capable of all the emotions of a person. It's a fascinating, unique being, dear. Every time I look at it, it seems to have a different expression."

"It's definitely very happy today, Aunt Kathleen." Once again Caroline forced herself to rise to the gaiety of the moment. "It's all smiles, and the waves are merrily playing tag with each other."

"Of course it's happy today. You're here, Caroline."

Caroline turned for an instant, gave her Aunt Kathleen a hug and pulled her closer to the railing. As they stood silently watching the waves, she kept her arm around the elderly lady's shoulders. "You know, every time I stand here, I think that anything is possible," Caroline's eyes filled with tears, and she paused to regain control of herself before going on. "I think I could fly. I could soar as high as I choose and be part of those gorgeous, fluffy clouds over the water, or I could dance on top of those waves."

"Anything is possible here. Anything is possible anywhere, Caroline. One just has to learn to keep the feeling, the faith, that anything is possible. This old house with its beautiful garden and its inspiring view of the harbor—it opens our eyes to the possibilities of life. Hopefully, we will take that special energy it gives us and that openness to creating the best possible lives, out into the world, wherever we go," her aunt concluded with the enthusiasm of an orator trying to motivate crowds gathered in the garden below.

"You're lucky to be able to live here, Aunt Kathleen," Caroline responded quietly, "to be inspired constantly by the beauty of the harbor and the garden and house."

The sadness in Caroline's voice prompted Aunt Kathleen to look up into her face. "Why, Caroline, you're crying. What is it dear?"

"Nothing special," Caroline lied. "I guess I just feel a little overwhelmed by the beauty. You are lucky to live here."

"That's true, dear. I am lucky to live here in this old house, as my mother and grandmother did before me. I can walk in the garden and stand here and look out at the harbor, but I still have to go out into the world, just like everyone else. The important thing to remember is that I can take the spirit of this place with me, if I choose to."

"You don't have to get caught up in the stress of the world?" Caroline questioned to encourage her aunt to go on.

"Absolutely not. I can live a happier kind of life—a life with fuller possibilities. Perhaps it's easier for me to choose that life because I see these inspiring surroundings every day, but still I have to make a choice, the same choice you have to make. There's no getting around it; life is a constant series of choices."

"You're right, of course." Caroline agreed, then fell silent as she once more struggled to keep back her tears. "I know I must keep choosing to be happy, but special places like this do inspire me, and I'm so glad to be able to come back here, especially now."

Aunt Kathleen stepped away from Caroline, looked closely at her face and seriously studied her for a moment. Obviously choosing not to probe into her niece's feelings at that time, she simply commented, "We'll have time to talk about that during your stay, I'm sure."

"But you don't even know what 'that' is," Caroline laughed nervously to cover her embarrassment.

"It's not so hard to guess, my dear."

"It's not? Does it show that much?"

"You do sound a bit strained, and the problems you're having were predictable—even inevitable."

"What do you mean?"

"I mean that it's just a simple human fact that it's much easier to talk than it is to act. It's much easier to plan than it is to carry out the plan. And especially if that plan involves changing one's way of thinking or one's life patterns. That is what you and David decided to do when you were here last spring, isn't it?"

"Yes, that's what we decided, but—"

"It was inevitable that there would be some degree of success and some degree of failure. So, here you are, back at Bradford House to refuel, and I'm almost glad you need to refuel because I get to see you again."

Caroline sighed, then asked, "Does age give you this kind of insight, Aunt Kathleen?"

"I wouldn't know," Aunt Kathleen quipped as she tried to lighten the mood. "I haven't gotten old yet. Come over here and look down at the garden." She took Caroline by the arm and pulled her gently back toward the center of the piazza. "Aren't the roses magnificent from up here?"

"Breathtaking. But what happened over there?" Caroline pointed to a section of the garden she hadn't noticed when she walked in. "I don't remember any dead area in the garden last spring."

"Oh, there wasn't one, but you see we had a terrific windstorm late in the spring after you left, and it broke off one of the major limbs of that large oak over there. Of course, I had a tree surgeon out immediately. He looked at the damage and declared that the whole tree had to come down."

"The whole tree?"

"Yes, the whole tree. Ridiculous, isn't it? One limb was gone, so this supposed 'expert' decided we should remove an ancient oak that was here before the house was built. Perfect nonsense, and I told him so."

"So what did you do?"

"I simply had him haul off the broken limb, but you see that created a new problem because that large limb was providing the shade for the azaleas that had been growing under it."

"And they died from too much sun," Caroline deduced sadly.

"Yes, at first I was quite upset to lose some of my azaleas, but then I realized there was another way to look at this situation. Actually, losing that tree trunk gave me a wonderful opportunity. Now that I have a new, sunny area in the garden, I can redesign that whole section. Think of it! A new path, perhaps. All new plantings to choose."

"Great Aunt Kathleen, that sounds like such a big project. Are you sure—"

"There you go with that 'Great Aunt Kathleen' stuff. You seem to think I have aged since you last saw me."

"You are a few months older," Caroline said gently.

"Only technically, dear, and I haven't seen the day yet that I couldn't tackle a new gardening project with enthusiasm."

"Of course," Caroline took her reprimand quietly. "And have you already begun to plan the new gardening project?"

"Certainly! I began to plan the moment that I realized I had a new opportunity, but I had to wait until this fall to start planting. It's so exciting! I have a whole new canvas to paint on. Think of it, Caroline. I know it's sad that some of the old plants are gone, but I have a new beginning here. And what a wonderful time for it to occur. Here you are, about to begin your new life as a mother and here I am, about to begin a new part of the garden. It's absolutely stimulating and so appropriate that it should all happen at the same time."

"Well, I never thought of a tree coming down as being an exciting beginning of a new part of life."

"But why not, my dear? When that tree came crashing through the drawing room window of your house last spring, your whole life took a new direction, a better direction."

"That's true. That was the beginning of major changes in my life. In fact, if that tree hadn't come down, I would never have met you." Caroline fell silent, unwilling to spoil her great aunt's high spirits by talking about her worries about David.

"But things have not proceeded exactly the way you had hoped?" Aunt Kathleen prodded Caroline to go on.

"No, they haven't."

"So your natural impulse is to be disturbed by what you perceive as failure, even to be depressed by it?"

Caroline nodded sadly.

"But you must not be immobilized by temporary difficulties."

"Well, I was at least mobile enough to get back to Charleston and back to you." Caroline nervously laughed again to cover the intensity of her pain.

"And there's plenty of mobility left in you to redesign, to replant a new part of your life, just as we're going to replant a new part of this garden. The important thing, dear, is don't give up. Keep going. That's what life is. Confronting obstacles, thinking through new options, making a choice, and then taking the first step toward the choice you've made. If one can see how exciting a new choice really is, instead of looking at it as a frightening change, then one can live a happy, productive life. Unfortunately, so many people see every change in their lives as a difficult hill they must climb, but it isn't. It's a wonderful opportunity to get to the top and see a different expanse stretching out before them. The old cliche is true, Caroline: life really is a journey, and a journey without hills—"

"I hear what you're saying, Aunt Kathleen," Caroline leaned tiredly against the corner pillar as the tone of her voice betrayed her despair. "I just don't know how to make the journey, and I don't think the rest of the world does either."

Aunt Kathleen peered at Caroline's strained face for a moment, then responded more quietly, "We will have plenty of time to talk, dear. Right now you need to rest from your trip and from your worries. Why don't you go lie down awhile? Perhaps this trip has been more tiring than you realized."

"I'm too keyed up to lie down. I think I'll just go freshen up a bit, and then a cup of tea really does sound wonderful."

"Let me walk you to your room."

"The blue bedroom I stayed in last spring?"

"Where else? It's your room whenever you're here."

"Sounds wonderful, but you just go ahead and sit down, Aunt Kathleen. I know my way, and I won't be long, I promise. I want to talk about that journey of life. I don't have a lot of time to find the answers I need." Caroline turned and began to hurry down the long piazza to the last set of French doors.

"Take your time, dear. You're in Charleston now." Aunt Kathleen called after her.

"Where Miz Caroline going?" Betsy demanded as she carried a heavily laden tea tray out onto the piazza.

"She's just freshening up, Betsy."

Betsy silently placed the tray on a wicker tea table, obviously biding her time until Caroline had closed the French doors behind her. "She need more than freshening up if you ask me," she whispered as soon as she dared. "They's tears behind that smile, Miz Kathleen."

"I know, I know."

"And she ain't just tired. She's real upset about something. Most likely that husband of hers, that Mr. David. He don't—"

"Hush, Betsy. Don't get started; she'll be back out in a minute. Just go ahead and arrange the tea table."

"Humph!" Betsy huffed as she began to arrange things. Aunt Kathleen, a rare, worried expression on her face, turned to stare out at the bay

"I'm ready for that tea," Caroline announced a few minutes later as she reappeared on the piazza.

"I got everything all set out for you, Miz Caroline," Betsy responded with excessive cheerfulness as she watched Caroline approach, "but I's warning you, I heard you and Miz Kathleen talking about a journey."

Aunt Kathleen left her musings behind and turned toward the tea table to join in Betsy's attempts to lighten the mood. "Oh no!" she exclaimed with mock horror, "we've been found out by Betsy."

"I's here to inform you, Miz Kathleen, that you ain't going on no journey. Your traveling days is over. You already been to Europe more times than I can count. And I's too old to go on any more trips."

"Oh, you needn't go, Betsy. Caroline is going with me." Aunt Kathleen winked at Caroline. "We have a wonderful trip planned."

"You and Miz Caroline can't go on no trip. She gonna have a baby! And you's no spring chicken."

"I'm not a chicken, young or old, Betsy," Aunt Kathleen settled on the wicker settee. "Sit down, Caroline and relax. As for you, Betsy, don't you get all bothered about what you think you heard Caroline and I talking about."

"Miz Caroline, you got to do something with her," Betsy insisted. "She ain't got no more sense now than she had when you was here last spring. She don't need to go no further than them garden gates."

"Now, Betsy," Aunt Kathleen picked up the teapot and began to pour tea into two cups. "There are needs, and then there are needs."

"What do that mean?" Betsy demanded as she put her fists on her hips.

"Look at these wonderful pastries that Betsy has baked, Caroline. Don't they look irresistible? Thank you, Betsy, I can handle the serving."

"I ain't leaving till you tell me what you means by 'there is needs and then there is needs.'"

"Now, Betsy, Caroline and I were just having a philosophical discussion. I'm simply saying that there are physical needs, and then there are needs of the spirit."

"Well, that be just fine with me as long as them needs of the spirit don't mean we have to go to Europe again."

"We are not going to Europe, Betsy."

"Humph," Betsy huffed as she walked out.

Caroline pressed her lips together to keep from laughing, and Aunt Kathleen solemnly sipped her tea, as they both listened while Betsy descended the staircase. Once she was obviously out of hearing, Caroline could contain herself no longer. She laughed quietly. "You two are something else."

"That's very well put, Caroline," Aunt Kathleen agreed. "We are something else, but heaven only knows what we are."

"In spite of the way you two carry on, you obviously care about each other."

"Oh, yes, my dear. Betsy has been in this house for over fifty years. I can't imagine life without her. We take care of each other. This little adversarial play that we put on for each other is simply a way of lightening our daily routines. You know, Betsy is a very intelligent woman. There have been many times in my life that in spite of her fussy tone, she has given me wise advice."

"And I'm sure you have helped her, too, Aunt Kathleen."

"I'd like to think so, dear."

"Tea on the piazza at Bradford House," Caroline sighed as Aunt Kathleen handed her a steaming cup. "I can't tell you how much I need to be here."

"Stay as long as you like, dear. Stay forever. Nothing would make me happier. I suspect, however, that it will be only a few days before you will be desperately missing your David."

"I'm not as certain of that as you are, Aunt Kathleen. I know that you are trying to distract me, to help me relax, but I feel a desperate urgency to talk to you."

"Then we must talk. What do you want to talk about?"

"I don't know exactly where to start, but I think—yes, I need you to talk some more about change. I'm facing some major changes right now, maybe more than I ever bargained for, and it's so frightening."

"I know, dear, I know. Change is frightening for all of us, but perhaps it would'nt be so frightening if we would just consider how common it is. For example, you walked out onto this piazza ten minutes ago, and you saw the harbor, and you were delighted with the fact that it had a life of its own, that it had changed since you last saw it, that it seemed to change from moment to moment. In fact, you stood there watching and eagerly awaiting the next transformation. Think how dreary it would be if every time you walked onto the piazza, the harbor looked exactly the same, as if it were painted in oil."

"That would be horrible," Caroline agreed.

"It would be horrible, dear, because it would be dead. And that's what life without change is; it's death."

"But change is still frightening, especially some changes, Aunt Kathleen."

"I know, but it's only frightening because we don't accept the fact that life is changing constantly, whether we like it or not, and we actually do have the resources within ourselves to adapt to change, to utilize change, to enjoy it."

"I just don't feel that way at all. That kind of understanding of life must come with age."

"Oh, Caroline, there you go again with the age thing. You don't have to be old to understand these things; you have to be willing to understand these things. You have to dare to understand these things."

"I don't know, I just don't know. It's one thing to make the changes I've made; you know, to choose to have my baby and to start working at the homeless shelter instead of partying all the time. But it's another thing to—well, I mean, what if—" Her lips began to quiver as her eyes filled with tears.

"Caroline, what change are you really afraid of?" Aunt Kathleen asked quietly as she leaned forward and took Caroline's hand. "It's not good for you to be so upset in your condition. If you can't put this problem aside totally, you need to state it bluntly so we can deal with it." When Caroline said nothing but continued to cry, Aunt Kathleen rose from the settee, went to her niece's side, and stroked her head. "Just say it, dear."

"My marriage is falling apart. David can't even stand to be around me. He doesn't want me; he doesn't love me. I know he's just waiting for the baby to be born; then he's going to leave me for good. That's the change I can't face. I just can't!"

"Why would David do such a thing?"

"Because I have changed, Aunt Kathleen. I've dared to change, just like you said. But what can I do if David not only hates the changes I have made but refuses to change himself?"

"I thought the two of you had come to an agreement last spring while you were here in Charleston."

"Supposedly we did. That wonderful week meant so much to me. It presented me with a brand new picture of how I might live my life, a beautiful picture. I thought David had received the same picture, but when we went back to Dallas, he just picked up his life and went on exactly like he always has. We have done nothing but lock horns ever since. Things have just gotten worse."

"Okay, Caroline, now you have said what is troubling you, and we can discuss it if you wish, but first I want you to calm down a bit. Here, take this hanky." Aunt Kathleen pulled an embroidered linen handkerchief from her pocket before returning to her seat. "Finish your tea, dear, and just listen to the birds. They are exceedingly happy today."

Caroline managed a small smile as she raised her tea cup to her lips. They sat there in silence, each lost in her own thoughts. Slowly Caroline calmed herself, and she reached for a tea sandwich.

"The truth is quite simple, Caroline. Because we are each unique and on a very individualized journey, we can't always walk in the lock step that marriage seems to require of us. When you came here last spring, you had reached a point in your personal life—not your married life, but your personal life—when you were ready to see things differently. Your grandmother had died, and you had learned the truth about her and her values. You also learned that her values, which you had adopted, were not serving you well. They were not producing deep contentment in your life. While you were here, you learned that there was another way to live. All of those revelations were intensely unique to you; David didn't receive those revelations."

"So how can I get David to change?"

"You can't. That's the simple truth. You can change yourself, but you can't change someone else. You can't change David. Only David can change David."

"Then it's hopeless."

"No, dear, it is not hopeless. God gives all of us chances to change—chances to move toward the light we need. He prods us all toward a better existence, and another thing, Caroline, God never gives up."

"I hope you're right, Aunt Kathleen, but David is so set in his ways, and he's older than I am. Psychologists say that people can't change—"

"Psychologists don't rule the universe, Caroline. God does. And the fact is, every living thing on this earth is changing constantly. All people, animals, plants—everything. We're all changing minute by minute. To be alive is to change. The real question is not, can we change or will we change? The real question is, will we choose to change to a better way?"

"There must be something I can do."

"There is. Know that God will continue to provide David with life experiences that will encourage him to choose the right path. Know that those life experiences will become more and more difficult to disregard until finally David will make changes that will make his life more like what God knows he needs. Don't you doubt it; as long as David lives, God will keep pushing him toward the changes that he needs to make in his life. He will never force him to change, but He will make it difficult for him to stay the same."

"How is he going to hear God? He won't listen to a word I say about our relationship."

"Then stop talking to him about it, and work on yourself. You are only partially into the process yourself. When you were here last spring, you were like that portion of my garden that lost the protection of the shade. You had lost your grandmother's overwhelming presence, that presence which protected you from the realities of life. You had finally confronted something drastic enough to make you know that you needed to change, and you were open to possibilities. However, in a way, you acted like I did in regard to the plants that were left after that tree trunk was removed. You went back to Dallas without a plan, just hoping things would work out. I left my shade-loving plants in a spot that no longer had shade, just hoping they would survive and of course, the hot summer has killed them. I should have known better. In fact, I did know better, but I didn't do anything about it. Looking back, perhaps I could have protected those plants, or I could have moved them, but I didn't do anything. Now the damage is done, and the dead plants must be removed."

"That's the part that frightens me. That dreadful change. In your garden it means removing dead plants. In my life it may mean divorce and becoming a single parent." Caroline could not force herself to go further and tell her aunt about her fears that David was having an affair.

"Whatever it means in your life, you will have to establish a new pattern, just as I must establish a new pattern in my garden. The question is how will we confront our fear of establishing a new pattern. I can't speak for you, but I can say what I plan to do. I'm sorry I lost those plants, but I'm not going to spend my time grieving over them, and I'm not going to spend my time wishing that things were like they used to be in that part of the garden." Aunt Kathleen's voice rose, powered by the strength of her indomitable character. "And I'm certainly not going to sit here and wish that somehow that dead area would just magically get fixed. I'm going to take what I'm tempted to see as a difficulty, and I'm going to choose to see it as an opportunity to create a new and very different space in my garden. I'm going to move forward and see to it that that area of the garden gets changed so that it will thrive again. I will not leave that brown, dead area in my garden."

Caroline stared at her great aunt, mesmerized by the intensity of her determination, the vitality of her spirit. Slowly she began to speak as a revelation came to her, "My garden is the environment I will be able to give my baby. I must focus on that fact; then I won't be afraid of whatever changes are necessary."

"That's right," Aunt Kathleen softly agreed, "and who can you change?"

"Only me. Oh Aunt Kathleen! How do you know these things about life? How did you ever get so wise? Whenever I'm around you, I realize that I'm just a tottering two-year old, fumbling my way through life."

"My dear, we're all two-year olds until someone teaches us,

sometimes directly through words and sometimes indirectly through actions. We all need models to follow. I fear your generation has fewer than mine did; as for me, I was blessed. I had my mother, your great-grandmother, Carrie."

"Yes, Carrie, of course." Caroline stood up and walked toward the piazza railing to block Aunt Kathleen from seeing the extreme worry that had suddenly flushed her face. "I remember the story of Carrie, of how she was so victimized by her father's deceit, of how she eloped with her beloved only to find out later that she had married her half brother."

"Talk about someone who had to make drastic changes in her life!" Aunt Kathleen exclaimed, "but Carrie, my mother, found the courage to turn her back on the love she had been so certain was her destiny and to reject deceit in spite of the costs to her own happiness."

"I confess I am in awe of her," Caroline commented, then as calmly as she could, she asked, "How did she ever do it? She must have felt so betrayed, so worthless because in spite of her lifelong attempts to be a good daughter and faithful to God, such horrible things happened to her."

"You must read her journal, Caroline. It is time. Last spring, you learned about my mother's heroic actions; now it is time you learned about her inner struggle. You see, my dear, that is where the battles are actually fought and where victories are really won—in the inner life. What we see, a person's actions—those are the fruits of that inner life."

"Yes, I want to read it." Caroline agreed. "In fact, I want to study it."

Silence reigned on the upper piazza as Caroline promised herself that she would learn everything she could about her ancestor, Carrie, and her heroic overcoming of her life's problems. Then she took control of herself, wiped the tears off her eyelashes, straightened her spine, turned and smiled at her great aunt. "You're wonderful, Aunt Kathleen. I treasure you. You're like a road map to me—a life map. I understand what you're saying, and I want to learn to be like you. I want to find the courage and resolve within myself to keep growing."

"Courage and resolve—we all need them. And a bit of a plan. So as we plot the new garden area, my dear, it will be a wonderful time for you to plot the new directions in your life, and after all the plotting is finished, we will both be further along in the journey of life."

"I can't believe the journey still continues for you. You seem to have arrived."

"Heavens, no! It goes on and on, and it's grand."

"If you say so. As for me, I'm ready to arrive."

"And be dead, Caroline?"

"Dead?"

"Whether you have actually quit breathing or not, when you end your journey, you're dead."

*   *   *

After supper that evening, Caroline automatically wandered back up to the second-story piazza to gaze out at Charleston Harbor. The big, fluffy clouds she had seen earlier that afternoon had increased, and they now caught the golden rays of light from the western sun and cast that light down onto the water. Caroline stood for a long time, leaning against one of the enormous pillars, watching the light from the sky darken to ever-deeper shades of gold and then rose and finally settle into a deep purple-blue.

As the light changed, the waves on the harbor picked up the different hues and gaily tossed them around. Someone on the block began to play a piano, and when Caroline heard a Strauss waltz from the talented fingers of the pianist, she turned her fancy free and imagined a ballroom full of early nineteenth-century ladies wearing silk gowns which matched the colors of the sky and water. In the extraordinary world of Caroline's imagination the ladies whirled around the ballroom, the ruffles and flounces of their dresses a kaleidoscope of color.

For Caroline, her hour on the piazza was a magical reprieve as the colors in the sky changed, the Strauss waltzes floated up to her, and lights began to come on all across Charleston. She sighed happily as she was reminded of the spring before, particularly the day when David had announced his decision to stay married to her and to raise the child that he had fathered.

What a glorious morning that was, Caroline thought. But how afraid I was at first. I stood here on the piazza and watched him march through the garden gate after being gone all night. I had no idea what he had decided, how he would ultimately react to the news that I was pregnant. Everything about his demeanor suggested that he was about to announce a separation and divorce. His stride was that of a man determined to get a distasteful task past him so he could get on with his life. But wonder of all wonders, the determination I saw in his face was a determination to go on with our marriage, to face the anxieties that he had and to deal with them. What a wonderful, life-changing day!

And what a wonderful evening that followed. Dinner in a cozy, quiet dining room overlooking the bay, followed by a long walk down the Battery under a full moon. The heavenly scents of spring flowers filled the night, and it seemed like every fifth house contained someone playing a piano. There were many couples in love walking on the Battery that evening, but we had an advantage. We could return to this piazza, stand right here, watch the moon and dream about our future together. I shall never forget the wonder of that day. In the morning I was so certain he was finished with me, but by evening, I never felt closer to him. And when every bit of light was gone from the sky, we walked the length of this piazza into our bedroom. David loved me that night with a gentleness, a tenderness that said quite clearly, "You are more precious to me than you have ever been." He was a changed man—a man much more able to express the depths of his emotions.

I shall never forget that night or the nights that followed for the whole week that we were here. Away from his business calls and my social responsibilities, we were on a honeymoon again, re-discovering each other and finding deeper love than we had ever known. A whole week of laughter-filled excursions visiting all the beautiful spots around Charleston, walking hand in hand, sometimes dining in quaint restaurants, sometimes picnicking on a beach, but always returning to this marvelous, old house and to our love-filled bedroom.

How I hated to board the plane back to Dallas! I knew that we had been suspended for a week in a special time that could not last forever, but I thought we had made some lasting changes in our relationship. I thought that we had learned to put our marriage first, that we had learned how much we could lose if we lost each other. And I thought that we were beginning the greatest adventure of our marriage, preparing for the birth of our first child. I knew that we would have a struggle ahead of us, a struggle to change the dynamics of our relationship, but I felt that we had a new unity of purpose that would carry us through the struggle.

Looking back now, I see that we lost the struggle the minute the plane touched down on the runway in Dallas. For David, it was business as usual once again. I started making changes in my life; I stopped accepting most social invitations, and I began to help Mother at the homeless shelter. In no time at all I discovered how much pleasure can come from helping people, so much more than there had ever been in my busy social life. I discovered that I actually had something to give, and it felt great to give.

David listened patiently to my growing enthusiasm for the social work I was doing, but he never would involve himself directly. Of course, I know he had to continue to run the business, but looking back now, it seems like the more I became involved at the shelter, the more David began to travel. Or did he began to travel because it became increasingly apparent that I was pregnant? Or—or—did he find someone else? Someone who could and would give him what he wanted?

I know he's not just afraid, like Mother thinks he is. I know he's hiding something from me, especially now that he's having those awful nightmares. I just don't think he loves me anymore, and I'm petrified that I'm losing him. How I long for him to put his arms around me the way he used to! To press me against his chest. I need him! Why doesn't he want me anymore? I'm having *his* baby, but I can't get close to him!

It's uncanny how similar my situation is to my great-grand-mother, Carrie's. She was prevented from being with the father of her child, and I can't be with David because he won't let me. We both have endured the emotional hurricane of separation from the man we love and need. It's an awful feeling!

Caroline shivered as a cold breeze blew across the piazza. She looked up at the sky and saw that the stars were especially bright. The wind must be changing directions, she thought. Oh, I hope it doesn't bring clouds by morning and make everything dreary. I don't need the weather to become bleak and mirror my feelings. I need sunshine; I need a lightness in the atmosphere to help me lighten inside.

The cold breeze once again wrapped itself around Caroline. I might as well go to bed, she decided. It has been a long day, and I'm very tired. Perhaps tomorrow will be better. At least I'll wake up here at Bradford House and spend time with Aunt Kathleen. I will definitely ask her to tell me more of Carrie's story. Yes, I must hear her story of victory over her agonizing circumstances, and Aunt Kathleen is right, I must hold on to the positive things I have. I'm here in a place where marvelous things can happen, where marvelous things have happened for generations.

Slowly she walked back down the length of the piazza to the French doors that opened into her bedroom, but before entering, she paused and turned back toward the harbor. The massive pillars of the old house stood like sentinels gleaming in the moonlight and pointing the way back down the piazza to the view of the harbor. These pillars have outlasted generations of Bradfords, Caroline thought. They have heard the ecstasies of lovers, the groans of women in labor, the cries of new-born babies, the last sighs of Bradfords before they entered eternity, and the sobs of those left behind.

They have watched the building of the city, the planting of saplings that have grown into vast havens of shade, the coming of carriages, trains, trolleys, cars, planes, and always—ships, all kinds of ships. They have cheered soldiers marching away certain of victory. They have resisted invading armies lighting their ways with torches. They have welcomed home soldiers returning from many wars—some chastened by defeat, some exhilarated by victory—but all, always, grateful to be home. Yes, these pillars have seen marvelous things, and tomorrow they will watch another sunrise and another opportunity for me. What will they see tomorrow?

F O U R

The next morning Caroline awoke to find sunlight dancing across her bed. "Fantastic!" she said aloud as she sat up. "I'm so glad it isn't dreary today." She threw the covers back and started to spring from the bed, but once again she was amazed at the bulk of her body. She laughed at herself. "I never seem to remember that my figure isn't what it used to be." Lovingly, she ran her hand across her stomach and thought of the reason for its swollen state. "Dear child," she murmured. "I can't wait to see your face. I already love you so much. I must take care of you, so I guess I must take care of myself." She stacked the pillows and leaned back against them, as she thought about what she had just said.

A sunbeam glinted off a silver frame on the bedside table and sent a ray of light into Caroline's eyes. She picked up the frame, which held an old, brown-toned picture of a woman holding a baby, with a man standing at her side. After studying the woman's face a moment, she recognized her from an oil painting in the dining room. "This is great-grandmother Carrie, and this baby must be her first child, so this is Robert's child. The man beside her is obviously older; he must be John Kendall, the man who tried to rescue her from public shame by marrying her." Caroline sighed and replaced the frame on the table. "I know she was very young when all this happened to her. What a courageous woman she must have been. All those months of waiting for her child to be born, wondering if it would be healthy. What was she thinking during those months? How did she get through them? Aunt Kathleen may know. Or Carrie may have recorded her feelings in that journal Aunt Kathleen wants me to read."

Slowly she slid down out of the high canopy bed, stood for a moment, and smiled as she thought of her baby. She pictured the two of them together. "As soon as possible," she said to her unborn child, "I want to bring you here to Bradford House—to Charleston. I want your earliest memories to be of this wonderful place, this place that has turned my life around and continues to move me in a forward direction." She stopped and thought about David and her fear that he might be having an affair. A shudder ran through her. "I don't think I can stand it if that's what's going on because—because I really will lose him, and I just can't stand that. I'm going to call him. I've got to make every effort to stay in touch with him; I've got to keep reaching out to him."

Caroline slipped into her dressing gown and walked out the French doors onto the piazza. The morning was inviting, cooler than the day before, but a cheery sun beamed down on her through crisp, invigorating air. She walked to the banister, looked down into the garden, and was not the least bit surprised to see Aunt Kathleen below on one of the paths close to the roses. She watched her for a few moments as the elderly lady walked serenely through her flowers touching blossom after blossom, bending to smell a few of the especially precious ones.

The enchanting power of the roses was obvious, and Caroline was suddenly desperate to be in their midst, to be a participant— not an observer. But I must call David first, she thought. It's only about four in the afternoon there, but he may be at the townhouse by now; at least that's where I'll start. Wherever he is, I'm going to find him. Quickly she returned to her room, donned warm clothes, and went to the drawing room to use the phone.

The housekeeper in London, Mrs. Watson, answered almost immediately after Caroline had dialed. "Oh, Mrs. Randolph," she exclaimed. "I'm glad you called."

Caroline immediately sensed trouble in the woman's voice, "You are? Any special reason? Mr. Randolph isn't sick, is he?"

"No, ma'am, but I'm a bit worried about him. He had the most awful dream yesterday morning. I didn't want to interfere, but he was actually shouting, so I took the liberty of entering the bedroom to wake him up."

"Mr. Randolph was actually sleeping during the morning? Do you mean he didn't go straight to the office when he arrived?"

"No, ma'am, he was too tired. He went to bed after I fed him some breakfast. I don't want to worry you, Mrs. Randolph, but I had to shake him awake. He was having quite a dream."

"I see," Caroline responded, "and I suppose he's not there now."

"No, ma'am, and he's not coming back for dinner."

"Thank you, Mrs. Watson. Please tell him I called."

"Of course." Caroline hung up the phone abruptly without giving the woman time to say more.

She paced around the room as she considered what to do next. *He's still having the nightmares, and they must be getting worse if Mrs. Watson had to go shake him awake. What is going on? David is definitely hiding something; I just know it. I might be able to catch him at the office, but what am I going to say if I do? I need time to think.* She stopped at the French doors that led onto the piazza and looked out at the treetops. *I need to be outside,* she decided and turned back toward the hall and the staircase.

When she stepped onto the garden path, the sunlight covered her like a mantle of hope and called her forward into the garden. The air, renewed by the breezes of the night, touched her face, stroked her hair and brought her its morning gift, the gentle scent of the roses. Surprising serenity blossomed in her as she began her walk down the winding path toward the rose garden. When Aunt Kathleen saw her coming, she waved excitedly.

"Good morning!" she called. "I hope you slept well."

"Wonderfully," Caroline called back. A moment later she

reached her Great Aunt Kathleen and gave her a hug.

"Isn't it a glorious day, Caroline? How could God have made a better day than this one?"

"It's marvelous. The air seems so changed from yesterday."

"We had a little cold front come through, or so Betsy tells me. She keeps up with the weather. I'm afraid I'm oblivious to what the weatherman says is coming."

"Oh, really? Don't you believe the weatherman, Aunt Kathleen?"

"Well, I figure God is going to decide what the weather is to be, and I'll just take whatever He gives me."

"That's probably just as well," Caroline agreed. "My experience is that weather forecasts are not that dependable."

"No, but these roses certainly are. Just look at them! My goodness, I declare I think they are going to bloom all winter."

"Could they?" Caroline struggled to allow herself to relax and be enchanted by the vision of roses so miraculous they bloomed all winter. "Could they actually bloom that long?"

"It's rare, but it has been known to happen in Charleston. Actually they need a dormant period, so we mustn't hope they'll bloom too long. I confess, though, that I don't want to give them any dormancy because I need their colors, their fragrances and the feel of their velvety petals. But then, I'm only being selfish. Let's cut a beautiful bouquet. What color shall we choose today?"

"Oh, I don't know, Aunt Kathleen," Caroline replied vaguely as she fought to keep her mind off David. "They're all so magnificent. Look at this one. There must be at least five different shades of pink and peach and yellow on this one."

"It's heavenly, but just look at this one over here," Aunt Kathleen pulled Caroline down the path. "Have you ever seen such drama in a rose? Like a petulant actress, it has refused to perform all summer, and now suddenly, it has decided, 'This is my moment. I shall grandly debut my ivory petals with their raspberry rims. I shall steal the show!'"

"Aunt Kathleen, as far as you're concerned, every rose in this garden has a personality They're all just like your children."

"Well, of course, they are. They're alive and developing, and they need nurturing. They are like children. They even have the thorns that sometimes come with children. So what color shall we cut, Caroline?"

"Now, Aunt Kathleen, I think you've already decided."

"You're too smart for me, Caroline. You're right. Since our raspberry-rimmed actress has finally decided to perform, I think we should give her the stage and sit back and enjoy."

"Sounds good to me."

"Now, you hold this bowl of water, and we'll get started." Aunt Kathleen was as excited as a four-year old turned loose on a playground. She snatched up her shears and snipped off a long stem, plunged it into the water in the bowl, and carefully keeping the stem under the water, she cut one-half inch off the bottom of the stem. Caroline was a bit startled as she watched her aunt plunge her shears into the water to cut the half inch off the end of the stem, but she said nothing. Great Aunt Kathleen cut another stem, turned to the bowl of water that Caroline held, plunged the stem under the water and once again plunged the shears under the water to snip off a half inch of the stem. "Now, be sure those stems stay underwater, dear," she gravely cautioned Caroline

"Yes, of course," Caroline was quite mystified by her aunt's behavior, but as she concentrated, trying to understand it, her anxiety about David lessened. She looked down into the water and saw two pieces of loose stem, each approximately one half inch long, floating around the bottom of the bowl. Her aunt repeated the procedure each time she cut another rose, and Caroline watched the short pieces of floating stem increase.

Suddenly it came to Caroline that she had seen all this before and that it had a special significance to Great Aunt Kathleen. "You did this last spring," she blurted out. "I remember now. The first time I ever laid eyes on you, you handed me a bowl of water; then you proceeded to cut roses, to stick the stem under the water and to clip off a half inch under the water."

"Yes, of course, that's exactly the way I did it," Aunt Kathleen said briskly.

"And you did the same thing when David came."

"Oh yes, my dear. He needed the lesson more than you did."

"Yes, I remember now. You taught us that a rose must be clipped underwater so that the water is always available to the rose."

"That's right, Caroline. Water is the basic sustenance of the rose once it is cut from the bush. Nothing must be allowed to block the passageways of the stem. That's why a rose should always be clipped underwater and kept underwater, so that it can have the fluid it needs to remain vital and to open into its full beauty."

"And you told us that people are like roses; they need constant nurturing too."

"They need to know that they are loved and valued. You embraced that truth more readily than David because you yourself were so needy when you arrived and so aware of your need. David did not want to make the changes in his self-centered lifestyle that would be necessary if he finally allowed himself to acknowledge that you needed his nurturing. He wanted to keep you static—frozen in development and time—as an eternal rose-bud, a thing of beauty in its youth where there is no danger because there is no change, no growth."

"But he finally did learn the lesson you were teaching us; he must have. Remember the morning after I told him I was pregnant? He had been gone all night—had just stomped out of here in a fury—but when he came back, rather than saying anything, he brought both you and me out into this garden. He clipped a rose stem from a bush, plunged it under water and carefully clipped off the end underwater and left it submerged. He did understand, didn't he, Aunt Kathleen. Didn't he?"

"My dear, you seem very intense for so early in the morning."

"Yes, I guess I am, but he did understand, didn't he?"

"I think he understood at the time, dear, but perhaps he needed to think more deeply about it. From what you've told me about his recent behavior, I would say that he wasn't really ready to make the commitment to fatherhood."

Aunt Kathleen took the bowl from Caroline and set it down

on the small garden table. "I think we have plenty of blossoms for a fabulous bouquet, but Caroline, if I take these roses into the house and put them into a vase full of water, in two days time that water will have been used up by the roses. Then what will happen to the flowers?"

"The flowers will droop, and eventually they will die."

"That's right, dear. I have to put fresh water into the vase everyday. Without their life-giving water, these roses will not live out their life-expectancy, and they will not become the beauties God planned them to be."

"And David and I have not been keeping the vase of our marriage full of water. Is that what you're saying?"

"That isn't for me to say; I can only say that people and relationships need nurturing. Whether it's a crisp, sunny day like today, a day when you feel that everything is possible, or a cloudy day, when your relationship seems hopelessly bogged down, the nurturing must go on. It must be a constant in every life. A single woman must nurture herself, and in a marriage, each mate must nurture the other."

"We haven't done a very good job of that, Aunt Kathleen." Caroline sat down in a chair next to the little table. "I've tried a little, but I haven't done nearly enough."

"These things don't come instantly. Last spring you and David understood, intellectually, what was needed in your marriage, but understanding intellectually and creating a habit of nurturing—those are two different things entirely. It takes time. It takes practice. It takes choosing, time after time, to put one's mate first. It isn't a fast process. It isn't an easy thing to learn." Great Aunt Kathleen sat down across from Caroline and fondly ran her fingers across the petals of a rose. "If both of you want a good relationship, both of you must understand what it takes and both of you must work at it."

"I've tried, Aunt Kathleen, but I can't nurture a relationship with David if he's halfway around the world. And it seems like since last spring, he has just moved further and further away. Emotionally and physically. He's gone more and more, and he stays gone longer and longer."

"And, why, my dear, do you think that David has not worked on your relationship?"

"I think the answer to that is obvious. He doesn't love me enough."

"And why doesn't he love you enough, dear?"

"I don't know. Perhaps it's what I did; my deceiving him into this pregnancy. Maybe that has changed his feelings. Or maybe it's because I'm not as physically attractive now that I'm pregnant. Aunt Kathleen, David has hardly touched me. In fact, in the last three months he hasn't touched me at all. I seem to be repugnant to him."

"And how does that make you feel?"

"Furious! What's wrong with losing my shape? I'm pregnant! Something wonderful is happening inside of me, but he's made it very clear that I'm not doing what he wants, and consequently, he doesn't want me."

"So you feel angry?"

"Yes, of course I feel angry!" Caroline slammed her hand down on the table. When the vase threatened to topple off, she remembered where she was, "Oh, I'm sorry. I shouldn't have brought this up. I don't know what's wrong with me. I woke up so happy and relaxed. Now listen to me! I came here to get away from all this, and I've brought it with me."

"Caroline, I don't think this is going to go away no matter where you go; you must deal with this. It's true that we don't need to mire ourselves down with discussion of this problem twenty-four hours a day, but occasionally, we need to discuss it—you need to discuss it. You need to come to an understanding of what's going on inside of you. And then you need to try to communicate that to David."

"David is in London, and heaven knows where he'll go next," Caroline said bitterly, "but it'll be somewhere he can avoid me."

"David will be back, Caroline. I think your goal needs to be to have more understanding of yourself, so that when he does return, you can speak more clearly and openly about what you are feeling."

"I do understand what I'm feeling, Aunt Kathleen. I'm furious with him. Why should he quit loving me because I'm not perfect all the time? It hurts to be treated this way."

"Now there's an important word."

"What? What word?"

"Hurts."

"Did I say 'hurts'?"

"Yes, you said, 'It hurts to be treated this way.' Your anger comes from the fact that you're being hurt. But why are you being hurt?"

"I just told you," Caroline retorted angrily because she was ashamed to tell Aunt Kathleen her real suspicions about David. "He only loves me if I look beautiful and am a social success. He has cast me off because I'm not beautiful anymore and I'm not doing what he wants me to do."

"And other than feeling angry and hurt, Caroline, what do you feel?"

"I feel worthless."

"Yes, I see," Aunt Kathleen nodded. "And are you worthless, Caroline?"

"I must be. I mean, look at what I've done that's wrong and what I keep doing that's wrong. I just can't please everybody all the time. I should be at the shelter helping Mother with the homeless women and children, but I also need to be what David wants me to be. And then there are all these things I need to do because I'm pregnant and I need to take care of my child. I just can't seem to please everybody."

"And so you feel that you're not worth anything."

"Yes, I guess that's it. It reminds me so much of a feeling I've often had before."

"When was that, dear?"

"It was when Grandmother was alive. You know how she was, so very demanding. I don't mean that she wasn't right to be demanding. She had very high standards, and as long as I was meeting her standards, she was loving and warm. I knew she loved me. But whenever I dropped the ball and didn't do what she wanted,

I felt like she didn't love me anymore, and I wasn't worth anything to her."

"And what about your mother, Marian?"

"Well, everything was okay when I was younger because Mother and Grandmother agreed on what I should be doing. They both wanted me to become a socialite, and that's what I was doing. But when Mother quit doing all the social things and started working with the homeless, then I felt like I wasn't pleasing her at all because I continued in Grandmother's way. I couldn't go down Mother's path—even though it seemed like a very noble path—without making Grandmother angry. So I always felt that Mother was disappointed in me because in her opinion I was shallow."

"And then you married David," Aunt Kathleen prodded Caroline to continue. "And David had another set of demands for you to meet."

"Well, yes, of course he did. He was my husband. He had a right to make certain demands of me, and I was eager to please him. I was glad to do whatever he wanted, but now, no matter what I do, I can't please him, and now he's—"

"He's what, Caroline?"

"I don't know. I just know I've got to get this worked out before this baby is born. I've got to do the right things for this baby. I want to be a good mother."

"And what does that mean to you, Caroline, 'to be a good mother'?"

"It means doing a great job of taking care of the baby so it will know I love it and it will love me."

"Caroline, are you listening to yourself?"

"What do you mean?"

"My dear, what you do or what people think of you is not the source of your worth. Apparently you've spent all of your life trying to please people. Of course, we all do that to some degree because we want to have good relationships with those around us and we want their approval, but we must not confuse their approval of us and our actions with our worth. Caroline, your worth doesn't come from whether your grandmother liked what you were doing, whether your mother approved, whether David approves now or whether this baby will love you. You were born worthy. Your worth comes from God."

"I'm sorry, Aunt Kathleen. I know that you are a very spiritual person, and you're probably right, but right now I have all these real problems to take care of, and I don't think I have the mental energy to worry about spiritual things."

Aunt Kathleen said nothing for a few moments. She simply reached up and stroked the petals of a rose. "You're right, dear," she finally responded. "It's not time to deal with this yet. We can talk about this another time. Today we shall just enjoy ourselves. We shall do whatever we want to do, whenever we want to do it. Of all your possible choices here in Charleston, Caroline, what do you want to do most?"

"Take a walk on the Battery, feel the sunshine, smell the sea breeze, and just be with you."

"That's the ticket!" Aunt Kathleen declared. "We'll cut a few more roses, take them in and arrange them, and by that time, I'm certain that Betsy will have a big breakfast ready for us." Aunt Kathleen rose from her chair. "And let's do a little shopping, Caroline."

"Shopping?"

"Yes, for baby things. I want to find the perfect gift for your baby."

"Are you sure you're up to a shopping spree?"

"Of course! I wouldn't miss if for the world. What could be more fun than planning for a new baby? Let's just enjoy today." She picked up the bowl of roses and started back to the house.

Long after midnight David threw the pen down on his desk in his London office and abruptly stood up. He walked to the large plate-glass window and stared out at the bright lights of London, but he didn't really see what lay before him. His eyes felt scratchy, and as he rubbed them, he thought of Caroline. *I can't put it off any longer. I haven't talked to her in two days. Now, according to Mrs. Watson, she's calling me. I'm sure she's furious and probably* has her feelings hurt, and I don't blame her. I just don't want to hear what she's probably going to say. She's so demanding these days, so impractical and irrational.

He sighed heavily and shook his head as he sternly but silently reproached himself, you know that's not true. You ought to at least be honest with yourself. She's not the problem. You're the problem. You're failing her, and you know it. He thought about that a minute before he began defending himself. I just don't know what to do about it. If I could just quit thinking about Danielle and what happened all those years ago. If I could at least quit dreaming about Danielle, I could get a decent night's sleep. Between the jet lag and the nightmares, I'm exhausted, and on top of that I've had these endless business meetings. In fact, I've got another important one tomorrow. Why can't Caroline understand that part of it? I know she doesn't know the truth about Danielle, but surely she sees that I've got to run this business. I've got to travel. I've got to be in touch with everything, be in control of everything. He crossed his arms on his chest and tightened his jaw as a flash of anger toward Caroline tore through him. Why can't she understand?

Then he answered his own question. Because it's not true. I know it's not true. I could delegate a great deal of what I'm doing. I want to travel. I want to be absorbed in this business because I don't want to think, and I don't want to feel. I sure don't want to remember, but I don't seem to have any choice about that. Every time I fall asleep, my subconscious reminds me of everything I ever did wrong, of how weak I was, and I hate myself for it. Still, I've got to call Caroline. I can't let any more time pass. He turned back to his desk and took the report he had been studying, stuffed it into his leather briefcase, and headed toward the door of the office. I'd rather call her from home, he told himself. Then I've got to get some sleep.

When David reached his townhouse, he went upstairs to the master bedroom and settled down in his favorite chair to call Caroline. He gathered his thoughts for a few moments before reaching for the phone and dialing their home number in Dallas. Their housekeeper, Hannah, answered, and when David asked for Caroline, she paused before responding in bewilderment.

"But, Mr. Randolph, she's not here. She's gone to Charleston."

David felt like a fool. He hated it when his employees knew more than he did. "Oh, of course," he lied. "I forgot. She's at her Aunt Kathleen's." It was a guess, but a pretty accurate one he was sure.

"Yes, sir," Hannah replied. "She called me after she arrived and said it was real pretty there."

"Thanks, Hannah," David wanted to get off the phone as quickly as he could. "I'll give her a call there." He hung up the receiver, sighed in exasperation, and rubbed his forehead which was beginning to ache. What kind of a husband am I? My wife is in the last stages of a pregnancy, and I don't even know what city she's in. I hope I have Aunt Kathleen's telephone number. I sure don't want to have to call anybody in the family and ask for it. He got up from his chair and walked heavily across the room toward the desk where he had left his briefcase. After much frustrated fumbling through his papers, he finally pulled out a thin, leather book and flipped pages until he found a number for Aunt Kathleen. "Here it is," he muttered, "Good."

He placed the call and listened to the phone ringing far away in Charleston. "Get ready," he warned himself. "She's probably going to be upset." Betsy answered and quickly went to find Caroline. Whatever she says, David thought, just agree with her this time. Try that for a change. Try telling her she's right; maybe that'll at least get her off your back and give you more time to work this out. It seemed like an eternity, but finally Caroline picked up the phone.

"David?"

"Hi, honey," he said, "how are you?"

"I'm fine," her voice was cool, distant and very controlled, and once again he warned himself to tread lightly. "How are you?" she asked.

"Fine. Everything's fine. Lots of meetings. A really busy trip. Not a free minute." David realized he was simply throwing phrases at his wife and struggled to think of a complete sentence. All he could come up with was a question that would put the ball back into her court. "How's Charleston?"

"Lovely." She only uttered one word before she fell silent again. David couldn't think of anything to say, and for a few moments there was dead silence between them. Finally he remembered to ask her about herself.

"How are you feeling?"

"Really well," she responded. Her tone was still quite cool, but it began to warm as she continued. "It's so easy to feel good here in Charleston, of course. It's as beautiful as ever. You should see the garden, and oh, David, it's so wonderful to stand on the piazza and look out at the harbor."

"Yes," he filled his voice with false enthusiasm and agreed, eager to get her off onto the subject of Charleston and away from the subject of his absence. "It's a special place all right."

"It's a magical place," Caroline's enthusiasm was obviously beinning to grow, so David relaxed a bit, confident he had control of the situation. "It's so peaceful, and I can't seem to drag myself away from the piazza. I just want to stand and stare at the harbor forever no matter what time of day it is. Oh, David, do you remember how beautiful it is? Last night I was there watching the sunset, and I thought about the week we were here last spring. It was like a second honeymoon. Do you remember?"

"Yes," he encouraged her to go on. "It was great."

"The colors in the sky were so beautiful last evening around sunset," she exclaimed. "And of course they reflected on the water, and someone was playing a piano down the block. It just made me think of all those wonderful evenings last spring when we sat on the piazza or walked along the Battery. Oh, David, I wish you were here. If you were here in Charleston, I just know we could settle things between us." David's muscles tensed as he realized that Caroline was turning the conversation into an inevitable verbal collision.

"Well, I'd sure rather be there with you than here with all these meetings," he lied, "but, of course, I'm tied down here."

Caroline, wondering if he was tied down with another woman, grew angrier with him and said nothing.

When she made no response, he hurried on, "What are you and Aunt Kathleen doing with your time?"

"Not much," she answered curtly.

"You must be doing something."

"After breakfast we're going to take a walk on the Battery, and then later today we're going to do a little bit of shopping."

"Shopping?" David asked eagerly to keep her on any subject other than their relationship. "What are you going to buy?"

"Aunt Kathleen says she wants to find a perfect gift for the baby."

"Oh, she doesn't need to do that," David protested mildly because he knew he was expected to.

"She wants to do it, David." Caroline's tone took on a sharper edge. "She *wants* to buy something for the baby. She said she couldn't think of anything more delightful than planning for a new baby." David was caught off guard, so he sat helplessly listening to the painful silence that once again fell between them. Finally Caroline broke the silence in what he considered the worst possible way. "Most people like to plan for a baby, David. Most people like to shop and plan special things like a nursery for their baby—" she broke off suddenly, and he heard what he thought was crying. He waited, not knowing what to say. Finally Caroline added, "I just wish you would tell me the truth, David. Whatever is going on, I have a right to know and—" He knew she was definitely crying now because she stopped talking abruptly and couldn't go on.

I've got to say something, he thought frantically, but I can't tell her the truth. "Caroline," he began tentatively, "I don't know what you mean—"

"David," she interrupted him, hesitated, then charged ahead, "are you seeing another woman?"

"What?" he demanded.

"I think you're having an affair—"

"That's ridiculous!" he exploded. "Why on earth would you think that?"

"You haven't touched me in months!"

"So it follows that I'm having an affair? Caroline, where are your brains?"

"My brains are working just fine, David Randolph. You obviously haven't wanted me since you found out I'm pregnant. You're always running off somewhere, and you're having nightmares all the time."

"I'm not having nightmares all the time; I haven't had one in several nights—"

"Now you're lying! Mrs. Watson told me she had to shake you awake yesterday morning." Caroline slammed the receiver down.

FIVE

When David heard the phone line go dead and realized that Caroline had hung up on him, he muttered a string of profanities and slammed the phone down too. "Where did she get the idea I'm having an affair? When do I have time for an affair? Women are absolutely the most irrational—" He stopped himself, leaned back in the chair, and warned himself, "Get a grip on yourself; you've got to think this through." He tried to relax his neck muscles, which felt like they were in the crushing hands of a wrestler, but his muscles just ignored him, so he flung himself up out of the chair and began to pace the floor.

"Is this nightmare ever going to end?" he demanded. "Is that baby ever going to get born? Why did she have to do this to us? And where could she possibly get the idea I'm having an affair?" He paced a few more minutes before announcing resolutely to the empty bedroom, "There's nothing I can do about Caroline. If she chooses to think I'm messing around with another woman, that's just her choice. I've given her everything any woman could possibly want. If she won't accept it and be happy, then there's no more I can do about it. I'm going to get some sleep. That meeting tomorrow is crucial. I haven't got time for these woman things. The economies of the whole Pacific Rim are in trouble. Caroline can think whatever she wants to, and she can certainly handle this pregnancy. It was, after all, her idea. Besides, after tomorrow's meeting, I'll probably have to fly to Hong Kong."

As his temper began to cool, he began to worry, "I don't like her being this upset. I sure don't like her thinking I'm having an affair, but I can't tell her the truth about the nightmares, so what am I doing to do?" He thought another minute, "There's nothing I can do. Caroline's fine. She's down there with her Aunt Kathleen. They'll work it all out one way or the other. They're not going to listen to me anyway. Maybe after that baby's born, things will settle down."

David jerked the covers back on his bed, sat down, removed his shoes, and stretched out full-length, gratefully relaxing his head onto a soft pillow. She'll be okay, he thought one last time as he began to drift into sleep. She's there surrounded by the beauty of Charleston. She's about to go for a walk and stare at the harbor. She loves all that. It will be good for her. She'll be fine. He drifted deeper into sleep—the sleep of a man who desperately wants to avoid reality and is burning himself out with work in order to do just that. Soon he was dreaming.

David jogged lightly through the dark woods north of Seattle, his strong, young legs carrying him easily toward the lake. Filled with intense excitement, he was thinking only of the pleasure he was running toward. He was heedless of the dark, looming hemlocks as he stared straight ahead toward the end of the path where it opened into the bright sunshine. When he broke through the trees, he ran to the edge of the lake and started out onto the pier, scanning the water from side to side looking for the object of his desire.

"David!" a happy female voice called his name. "David, David, over here." He turned to the right and saw Danielle bobbing in the lake, happily waving her arm over her head. "Come on in. It's wonderful!" she shouted.

"Looks cold to me!" he shouted back.

"It is cold, but I'm not, and I'm waiting for you. Come on in, you chicken." Suddenly she turned over in the water and dove down toward the bottom of the lake. Mesmerized, he watched as her sexy, long legs skimmed the surface of the water for an instant and then slid beneath its dark surface. He needed no more encouragement; he dove into the water. Heedless of the cold, he swam eagerly toward the spot where she had disappeared. By the time he arrived at her side, she had bobbed back up to the surface and was paddling around laughing. He grabbed her and gave her a passionate kiss as they sank together beneath the water. A moment later, his lips still clung to hers, but he began to kick to propel them back up to the surface. When they broke the surface of the water, she pulled away from him and laughed happily. "I missed you," she declared.

"And I missed you," he said. "There's nothing worse than wearing a business suit on a summer day and knowing your new wife is frolicking in the water, far away from you."

"Poor baby," she cooed mockingly, "Having to go back to work to support his spoiled wife. If only he had a woman in his life worth coming home to." She giggled, tore away from him, and dove under the water again. Extravagantly happy, he floated on the surface waiting for her to re-emerge. When she did, she slung her short brown curls around and wiped the water from her eyes.

"I've never seen anybody who likes the water as much as you do, Danielle. I think you must be part fish."

"Of course I'm part fish," she replied flippantly, "I'm a mermaid." She swam toward him, and he opened his arms and clasped them around her when she arrived. She pressed her lips against his, then drew back coyly and asked, "Do you want to see my mermaid tail?"

"I'd rather see it on the beach or in the woods."

"But mermaids can't leave the water," she teased as she pushed him away and dove again. This time he dove after her, and with his eyes open he searched through the dark water until he saw her white legs and arms. She was beckoning him to come closer, and as he approached, she held out her arms, a smile on her face. Just as he was about to embrace her, her expression suddenly changed. Total panic swept across her face. Her eyes grew wide with fear, and she seemed paralyzed in the water. Afraid that she was out of air, David swooped her into his arms and pushed them both up to the surface.

"What happened?" he demanded. "Are you okay?" She was hanging her head, so her short, dark hair covered her face. He lifted her chin back and brusquely pushed her hair away from her face so he could see her. "Are you okay?" he demanded again. She began to sob. "Danielle, what's wrong?"

"Take me home. I want to go home!" she cried.

"But what's wrong?"

"I just want to go home," she sobbed. "Take me home, David."

"I don't understand—"

"Take me home!" she screamed. "Get me out of here."

"Okay, okay," he agreed. "Just be calm. Can you swim?"

"No, no! Get me out of here, David!"

"Okay, okay, calm down; I'll get you out. Don't worry." He put his arm around her and began to swim back to the shore. She lay limp in the water as he pulled her along, and he would have thought she was lifeless except that she continued to sob. When they reached the pier, he pushed her up the ladder ahead of him. As soon as her feet were on the warm, wooden boards, she suddenly collapsed into a sitting position and sat there all crumpled up. David pulled himself up onto the pier and squatted down next to her.

"Honey, tell me what's wrong. Please tell me."

"I don't know," she cried. "I don't know."

"Did you run out of breath?"

"No."

"Did you feel weak or have a cramp or something?"

"No."

"So what happened?"

"I just suddenly felt so sad."

"Sad?"

David couldn't imagine sadness turning into the sobbing scene he had just witnessed, but she continued to cry quietly in front of him. He didn't understand her, but he loved her desperately, and he was her husband—a young husband—but still a husband. He supposed this was one of those times, those unexplainable times, when women just became very emotional, and it was his job to be strong and take care of her until she was quieter and steady again. "Take control!" he heard his father's voice echoing from the past. "Be a man! Take control!"

"I'm taking you back to the house," he announced. He stood up, leaned over, and with his strong, tanned arms, he swept Danielle up off the warm boards. "Put your arms around my neck," he ordered. She did as she was told, buried her face in the crook of his neck and cried quietly as he carried her back to the house. As he walked back through the dark woods carrying his beloved, he wished that their cottage was not so deserted, that there would be someone there to guide him through this new experience, but he knew he was on his own. He carried Danielle into the cottage and laid her on the bed in their bedroom. He sat down beside her and held her close. She became calmer, relaxed in his arms, and stopped crying. When he was sure she had control of herself again, he pushed her slightly away to look into her face. He started to ask her what had happened, but before he could speak, she said, "Make love to me, David. Make love to me now."

Startled, he protested, "Danielle, we need to talk—"

"No!" she exclaimed. "Make love to me." She grabbed him around the neck and fiercely pulled him down on top of her. All his resolve to take control of the situation disappeared as his own passion overwhelmed him.

He threw his arms around her, but instead of feeling her in his embrace, he heard the sound of shattering glass. A sharp pain in his left hand caught his attention and began to drag him back to a semi-wakeful state.

Slowly he perceived that he had been dreaming he was embracing Danielle, but instead he had broken a china lamp and cut his hand. He struggled to sit up in bed, finally cleared his head by shaking it, and managed to walk across the room to the light switch without cutting his feet. In the glare of the overhead light he examined the china shards, then mechanically returned to pick up most of the pieces. All the time his mind replayed his dream about Danielle, so when he had finished, he didn't try to go back to sleep. Instead he sat on the edge of the bed and thought. It's obvious I can't sleep this problem away. Maybe I need to just sit here and think about it. Maybe I need to let my mind remember what it seems to insist on remembering; then I can move on.

I should have known that something was seriously wrong with Danielle. Why didn't I see it? Why didn't I recognize what I was looking at? Over and over she kept suddenly losing control of her emotions over absolutely nothing. Like that day she came in from shopping. Her behavior was so bizarre. David sat and intentionally allowed his mind to drift back in time.

"I'm so glad you're here!" Danielle burst through the door of their brand new home in Seattle. "And oh, David, look what I just bought. I hope you're making tons and tons of money because I've spent millions of dollars." She staggered under the weight of an enormous pile of dress boxes. They were piled so high he could hardly see her face. He stepped forward to help her, but before he could reach her, she dropped them and they fell all over the new carpet with many of the lids coming off and the clothing scattering across the floor. Danielle giggled happily. "Just look at it all." She threw her arms around David's neck, gave him a passionate kiss, then released him and said in a high-pitched voice, "Aren't they gorgeous? Isn't the house wonderful? Isn't it the most beautiful day you ever saw? Oh, I've never been so happy in all of my life!" Then she ran from David to her father, Philip DuBois. "Daddy, I'm so glad you're here. I want you to see everything I bought, well, almost everything. There are a few things that are only for David's eyes." She threw her arms around her father's neck and hugged him. Then she whirled back toward David and demanded, "Why don't you say something?" although she'd given no one a chance to speak.

"Hi, baby," her father quickly filled the silent void. "It looks like you've had quite a day."

"Oh, it's been wonderful, just splendid!" Danielle began to whirl in circles across the carpet until she reached David and threw herself into his arms. "I went to all my favorite stores," she told them, "and if I wanted something, I bought it. I feel like I own the whole world. Here, let me show you what I got, David." She raced to a box that had spilled open on the floor and snatched up a dress and held it in front of her. "What do you think? Isn't it gorgeous? Can't you just see me in it going to the country club? The women will be green with envy, and the men's eyes will pop out." Before David could get a word out, she threw the dress on the floor and snatched up a suit. "And look at this. When I wear this, I'll be the model of propriety, my nose in the air." She walked across the floor holding the suit in front of her pantomiming the way she would act when she wore the suit, but her eyes fell on another box and she threw the suit to the floor and ran to the box, jerked the lid off and turned around with a slinky satin night gown. "This, darling, is for only you to see me in. What do you think?"

"Well," David finally realized he had a chance to say something. "They all look fabulous, Danielle, but of course they'll look even better on you."

"I should hope so," she exclaimed, "but what do you think, David, really what do you think about what I bought?"

David looked at the jumble of scattered boxes on the floor, paused a moment in bewilderment, then glanced back at Danielle. The bright light in her eyes was fading; he was instantly afraid for her, so a surge of panic propelled him to speak. "Super choices, honey, really great! I can't wait to see them on you." Danielle nodded eagerly up at him like a hungry child still waiting to be fed, and when he said no more, she whisked around and looked at her father.

"What do you think, Daddy?"

"Oh, baby, you've always had fabulous taste, and it looks like you've done it again," he answered enthusiastically.

"So you both like what I bought?" she demanded.

Practically in unison they agreed enthusiastically with her choices. "No one can put a wardrobe together like you can, Danielle," her father said.

At the same time, David was saying, "Super choices, honey." He took her in his arms and looked down at her earnestly. "Of course, you're already the most beautiful woman in the world."

Danielle smiled happily up at him her eyes sparkling again. "Did I really do a good job?" she asked eagerly.

"Fantastic," David insisted and leaned over and gave her a quick kiss. When he straightened up and peered down into her face, he was startled to see that the sparkle was once again fading from her eyes and her upturned, smiling lips were now quivering. In an instant her eyes filled with tears, so many tears that they began to flood her cheeks, and she began sobbing. Desperation overwhelmed David; he felt a frantic need to help her, to fix her, but before he could even ask what was wrong, she cried, "Oh, I wish I were dead!" and ran out of the room.

Speechless and as paralyzed as a stone statue, David watched her go. Once again, he was drowning in the kind of shock, followed by fear that he had only learned to feel since he had married Danielle. Finally he regained enough control of himself to issue a quick command to her father, "Don't leave, Philip. I want to talk to you," before he ran after Danielle. He found her in their bedroom where she had thrown herself across the bed and was sobbing into the pillows. The experiences of their first year of marriage had quickly taught him that he could do nothing when she behaved like this, nothing but wait. No matter how he posed the question, "What's wrong?" he would receive no answers. So he simply took her in his arms and held her while she cried and heard himself repeating over and over, "It's going to be okay. It's all right. Just have a good cry." All the time his mind was full of one relentless question—why? Why does this keep happening?

Eventually she lay still and silent in his arms, and he knew that once again she would fall into an unexplainable, deep sleep. Gently, he laid her back on the pillows. Her eyes were closed, and her breathing had changed to the rhythmic breathing of sleep. David knew that the episode, whatever it was, had passed. He covered her with a light blanket, stood for a moment looking down at her, his love-filled heart wrenched by this experience that had been so often repeated in the last year. Then resolve overwhelmed his pain, and he turned on his heel, left the room and marched back into the living room.

"I want to talk to you, Philip," he said firmly to his father-in-law. Philip, obviously hoping to avoid the conversation, silently turned away from him and looked out a window. "Something's terribly wrong with Danielle," David raised his voice slightly. "We have to do something."

"She's just high-strung," Philip answered quietly. "She's always been high-strung."

"She's always been like this?" David demanded.

"Like what?" Philip asked cautiously.

"Well, one minute she's on top of the world, incredibly happy and in total control of herself and everyone around her. The next minute she's plunged into some kind of emotional hell, and I want to know what's going on."

"I told you, she's just high-strung." Philip still would not turn around and meet his gaze.

"Look, Philip," David lost his temper and grabbed his father-in-law's shoulder, "I don't know anything about young women. I've never been married before, but it doesn't make any sense to me that a beautiful woman like Danielle who has everything her heart can desire should be going around saying, 'I wish I were dead.' I mean, maybe, occasionally a woman might say something like that if she's upset about something, but Danielle just suddenly blurts out, 'I wish I were dead' in the middle of her happiest moments. It's just like flipping a switch. What's going on?"

"She's just always been like that."

"You mean she was like that when she was a little girl?"

"Well, it wasn't quite as extreme when she was a little girl."

David was keenly aware that his father-in-law was hedging, hiding something, but with the confidence so typical of youth, he was absolutely certain that whatever the problem was, he could fix it. Danielle was his wife; it was his responsibility. He glared down at Philip and commanded, "I want some answers, and I want them now."

Philip glared back at him and made no comment.

"You're not telling me the whole story," David angrily raised his voice.

"I've said all I have to say."

David walked away and tried to steady himself. When he spoke again, he kept his voice level, "Look, Philip, I don't want to argue with you. I sure don't want any bad feelings between us, but I can't stand by while the woman I love is in obvious emotional trouble. You know what's going on, and I need to know. Now tell me everything you know." When Philip continued to remain defiantly silent, David's temper rose even higher. His first impulse was to throw his father-in-law against the wall until he got the answers he wanted, but he clamped down on himself. He paced around the room until he could cool his temper, then as calmly as he could, he said, "Look, Philip, we're not going to sweep this under the rug anymore. I've been watching this for a year, and she's getting worse. You know things that I need to know. What's wrong with Danielle?"

"I told you."

"No!" David insisted, "She's not just high strung. She's sick somehow, and we have to fix her. I'm going to call a psychiatrist."

"Oh no you're not!" Philip shouted, his face contorted with anxiety. "Don't call a psychiatrist, don't do that."

"Why not?" Once again Philip fell silent, and David threatened, "If you don't give me some answers and give them to me now, I'm going to call a psychiatrist. I'm going to get her help; I'm not going to stand by and watch my wife go down the drain."

"You'll just be throwing your money away; they can't help her," Philip shook his head sadly. "I've thrown thousands away on psychiatrists for her."

"I don't care about the money!"

"Do you think I do?" Philip demanded, "I would spend millions to help Danielle; I would spend every penny I have, David, but it wouldn't help her. We just have to keep her steady."

"What is it?" David demanded. "What is making her act this way? Don't you get it? If I know what the problem is, I can fix it."

"I wish it were that easy, son, but it's not. Life just doesn't work that way. Some things just can't be changed."

"Are you saying Danielle was born like this?"

"No, she wasn't born like this. She was a very happy, well-adjusted child. Terribly spoiled, I'm afraid. She was, after all, the only child my wife and I had."

"Look, a spoiled child may very well grow into a spoiled woman and throw temper tantrums when she doesn't get her way, but Danielle is not throwing temper tantrums. She just suddenly changes, and she becomes desperately unhappy—dangerously unhappy."

"I know. Believe me, I know."

"Well, when did this all start?"

"It started when her mother died. The trauma of her mother's death seems to have pushed Danielle into this extreme behavior. At least, that's what the psychiatrists say, and that's what I've observed too."

"But lots of kids lose their mothers. I mean, it can't be easy, but it doesn't end up like this every time."

"Well, it's like I told you," Philip started to step around David. "She's just very high strung, so her mother's death hit her especially hard."

Determined not to accept defeat, David grabbed Philip's upper arm and thrust his face close to the older man's face. "I'm not going to accept that anymore," he coldly informed him. "You won't just push me aside again. You are going to tell me the truth. I have to live with this. I love her; she is my future. I want the truth, and I plan to get it now."

Philip stared steadily into David's eyes, trying to intimidate the younger man with his solid, silent presence, but David refused to blink or look away. Finally Philip looked down at the floor and muttered, "Yes, I guess you have to know."

"So tell me," David insisted, still grasping the man's arm.

"It's very simple really, and yet it's so complicated no one seems to be able to unwind it."

"Just say it!"

"Danielle's mother did not die in an accident; she killed herself. I made up a story about my wife falling and hitting her head to explain the fact that she died in our room in the resort. I was able to buy off the investigators to keep them from pursuing the case, but I was never able to fool Danielle because, you see, she was the one who found her mother. And she found her in a bed littered with empty bottles of pills."

David muttered a string of angry profanities, released his hold on Philip and held his own head in his hands. "Poor Danielle! How old was she?"

"She was twelve. Plenty old enough to understand what her mother had done, but totally unable to understand why her mother had chosen to leave her."

"And you just covered it up?"

"Certainly! At least, publicly. I saw no reason for our family to endure the shame of suicide. I saw no reason for Danielle to bear that burden, to be stigmatized publicly."

"But you got help for Danielle, didn't you?" David demanded. When Philip said nothing, David exploded, "What kind of a father are you?"

"Not a very good one. I told myself that Danielle would go through a certain amount of grieving, but that if I could divert her mind on to happier things, she would heal, so that's what I tried to do. I took her all over the world on my business travels. I gave her everything she wanted. I thought if I could just get her away from it—"

"And get yourself away from it," David added angrily.

"Yes, David, that's true. I wanted to run away."

"Did you talk to Danielle at all about her mother's suicide?"

"No, we never mentioned it. It was always there between us, but we never talked about it, not until she started to behave so strangely. I even managed to avoid dealing with her erratic behavior for far too long, I'm afraid, but, David, believe me, when I knew she really needed help, I did get her the best help."

"It doesn't seem to have worked," David retorted acidly.

"I know it seems like that to you, but believe me, she's much better than she was when she was fourteen."

"You should have told me this, or Danielle should have told me. Somebody should have told me!"

"I just wanted to believe that if she was happily married and establishing a family of her own, she would be stable. And you're so strong; you're so well grounded, I knew you would be good for her."

"Me? I don't know what's good for her! How could I possibly know? Especially if no one even bothers to tell me what I'm dealing with." David paced around the room before adding, "She wants to have a baby. Did you know that?"

"Yes, she told me. How do you feel about it, David?"

"I want a family some day, but not now, not with Danielle acting like this. She's under enough strain; a baby would be too much for her."

"David, you're not looking at this from the right perspective. Danielle needs normalcy. She needs something that will keep her from thinking about herself and the past all the time. A baby is something she could give herself to, something that would encourage her to live in the present and think about the future. Doesn't that make sense to you, David?"

"I don't know. I really think she needs help first."

"You're the only one who can help her, David. She worships you, and having your baby will be the thrill of her life. It will set her on a new course, a positive course. You can save her, David. You're the only one who can. What do you say, son? Do you love her enough to risk it?"

David walked away, well aware that he needed time to think.

"Do you love her enough to give her this chance?" his father-in-law challenged once again.

"Of course, I do! I would do anything for Danielle."

"Then do this one thing—just this one thing."

David waited, knowing he should definitely not commit to

anything, but he wanted Danielle fixed, and he was more than pleased to think he had the power. "Okay," he finally agreed.

"You won't be sorry, son." Philip walked over and patted him on the shoulder.

"How could I have ever been so stupid?" David demanded of himself as his mind returned to the present. He stretched out on the bed. "How could I have ever been so egotistical? Philip was the ultimate con man, and he sure suckered me that day." David sighed deeply. "He loved his daughter; I know that much, and he would have sold anybody, including me, down the river to help her. And I was more than willing to be sold because I just wanted Danielle, and I wanted her happy and staring up at me with those adoring eyes of hers. Stupid, totally stupid. But I've got to be smart now. I'm not a kid anymore, and I can't let my past ruin my present with Caroline. I've got to figure a way to satisfy her without telling her what happened to Danielle. And if she's so upset with me she's slamming down the phone and hanging up on me, I better figure out something good, and I better do it soon."

Caroline sat down and had a quiet cry after she hung up on David. When she returned to the breakfast table, she was composed, and Aunt Kathleen wisely made no comment about her red eyes. Half an hour later they were ambling along the Battery, the sidewalk atop Charleston's sea wall. As they gazed out at Charleston Harbor, a slight breeze caressed their faces, invigorating them and creating small waves that kicked up their foamy heels in the blue-gray water and made the sailboats bob.

"Look at those sparkling white, billowing sails," Aunt Kathleen pointed toward the boats. "They remind me of old-fashioned cotton sheets hung on a clothes line blowing in the wind. How I used to love to see those when I was a child!"

"I can't imagine a world without electric clothes dryers," Caroline responded, her mind still very much imprisoned in her anger with David.

"Oh the great joys you missed, my dear!" Aunt Kathleen chuckled. "I suppose young people get tired of hearing us old folks say things like that, but you know, there is something very special about sheets that have been washed and hung on a line to dry. They smell wonderful, and they feel so nice and crisp and cool when you slip between them at night."

"I bet they didn't seem so wonderful when you had to iron them," Caroline countered cynically.

"That was a chore," Aunt Kathleen admitted, "but, of course, we had help in the house in those days, and to tell you the truth, my dear, I've never actually washed a sheet, so maybe I shouldn't be so sentimental about them. And now that I think about it, I spent a ridiculous amount of time trying to keep the children from getting the wet sheets dirty before they got dry and back in the linen closet."

"Somehow I can't imagine Cousin Kendall going out to the clothes line and throwing mud on clean white sheets," Caroline commented. "I know he's your son, Aunt Kathleen, and I shouldn't say this, but he seems kind of stodgy or formal, if you know what I mean."

"Oh, he is, my dear, he is. He takes after his father. He doesn't know what to do with me most of the time. You're quite right; Kendall would never have gotten the sheets dirty intentionally. The problem was that the children always wanted to play under items hanging on the clothes lines. You know, a blanket over a clothes-line makes a wonderful hideout or an Indian teepee or something like that." When Caroline expressed no enthusiasm for the idea, Aunt Kathleen demanded, "You have played under a clothes line draped with a blanket, haven't you, Caroline?"

"Well, no, Aunt Kathleen, actually I haven't."

"Mercy me!" Aunt Kathleen threw one of her hands up in the air. "I almost feel like running home, throwing a blanket over the clothes line behind the house and making you play under it right now. But I guess that wouldn't work out too well considering your shape."

"No, I don't think so," Caroline smiled weakly at her aunt as she struggled to join in her light-hearted tone.

"Well, at the very least, Caroline, promise me that you won't let your child be impoverished by a life full of television and computers—those things children do now instead of living."

"Oh, Aunt Kathleen!" Caroline couldn't resist her aunt's cheerful mood any longer, so she started laughing in spite of her worries.

"Well, I mean it," Aunt Kathleen insisted indignantly. "Your child will have no imagination. Thank goodness I grew up in a time when we didn't have such silly distractions. We really played, but even if such distractions had existed, Mother would have seen to it that we played. She was very keen on the three of us being outside or on the piazza, making up stories and acting them out. In fact, she, herself, took part in the plays we put on."

"What about your father?"

"Well, he was a good twenty-five years older than Mother, so mostly I just remember him sitting on the piazza swing and laughing at our antics. He was our audience and a very supportive one. He also read to us a great deal. We had wonderful evenings, sitting on the piazza in the summertime or sitting around the fireplace in the winter, as Father read to us. Since he was older and less energetic, he was less of a playmate to us than Mother was, but he was very involved in our lives."

"I saw a picture of your parents next to my bed when I woke up this morning, a small picture in a silver frame. I recognized Carrie, and I assume the man was your father, John; they had a little boy with them in the picture."

"Yes, that was taken about five years after their marriage. The little boy was Carrie's child by Robert Montgomery. You remember the story I told you last spring."

"How could I forget it? It's not often that a person finds out her great-grandmother eloped with a man who turned out to be her half-brother. And worse still, that she discovered she was carrying his child after the annulment. Her father, James Bradford, tried to make her marry a wealthy planter, didn't he?"

"Yes, he did, but as you know, John Kendall stepped in and asked Carrie to marry him."

"He had always loved her, truly loved her, hadn't he?" Caroline asked wistfully.

"Yes, he had, and he was happy to have her in his life under any— Caroline, why are you asking me these questions?"

"I feel like—that is, I hope—" Caroline stopped as unreleased misery began to clog her throat and prevent her from speaking.

Aunt Kathleen took her arm and suggested, "Let's go sit down on that bench over there under the live oak. I think we need to talk, dear." Caroline nodded as she tried to hold back her tears. When they were comfortably seated, Aunt Kathleen said quietly, "Now we're out here where no one can hear us, and whatever you say we can just leave here and let the sea breezes blow it away. Answer my question, dear, as honestly as you can. Why are you asking me about your great-grandmother Carrie?"

"I feel a strange kinship with her and also with her mother, Mary."

"I see," Aunt Kathleen murmured. "Let's begin with Mary. Why do you feel a kinship with her?"

A great anguish overwhelmed Caroline as she struggled to say the words she feared so much. "Take your time, Caroline," her great aunt advised. "I wish we didn't have to talk about this at all, whatever it is; it's obviously excruciatingly painful to you. But I cannot help but notice that you are thinking about it all the time, and I know that you will never be able to relax, until you talk about it."

"I agree," Caroline said, then took a deep breath before continuing, "Aunt Kathleen, I think David is having an affair."

"Do you?" Aunt Kathleen asked calmly. "Why do you think so?"

"He hasn't touched me in months, and he's making every effort to stay away from home, away from me."

"That doesn't seem to me to be conclusive evidence to prove he's having an affair, Caroline, but let's not argue that point. Why does your suspicion make you feel a kinship with your great-great grandmother, Mary?"

"Because her husband had an affair, and she had to go through her pregnancy and the birth of her child knowing that he didn't want her or the child."

"And you think you're in that situation?"

"Yes, I do. At least I think I do. I know David doesn't want our baby; he's made that plain from the beginning."

"Yes, he has been plain about that, but he couldn't give you up when he found out about the baby, don't you remember?"

"I know," Caroline agreed, but added, "He's able to give me up now."

"My dear, at this point I have to tell you that I think you're mistaken about David. Something is definitely going on with him, and I think it's far more serious than we know."

"What do you mean?"

"I mean that he's not just worried about losing you in childbirth the way he lost his first wife. There's more to it than that."

"He's hiding something, Aunt Kathleen. I know he is. I don't know how I know, but I'm sure of it."

"I agree, dear. He is hiding something, but it isn't another woman."

"What do you think it is?" Caroline asked.

"I don't know, but my counsel to you is to put away the idea of an affair. Whatever is bothering David strikes me as being more deeply rooted than secrecy about an affair."

"What do you mean 'deeply rooted'?"

"I mean psychologically disturbing. I would say he's engaged in a life-shaping battle with something from his past, something that is deeply buried and comes up in these nightmares he's having."

"'Life-shaping battle' sounds very serious to me, Aunt Kathleen. Shouldn't I be helping him if that's what's going on?"

"What can you possibly do?" Aunt Kathleen asked quietly. "These battles, and we all go through them at various times in our lives, can only be fought alone. The only ally David *can* have is God; the only ally David needs is God. And God *is* with him, whether David knows it or not."

"So I just stand by?"

Aunt Kathleen nodded, "You do just that. You stand by; you stand by him in the only way you can, Caroline."

"How? How do I stand by him if he pushes me away?"

"Refuse to leave. It's that simple. He may not let you close to him physically, but you can still stand by him spiritually. Caroline, just believe in David and pray for him. God will do the rest. God will bring him through this rough spot in his life, maybe not in the time frame you prefer, but He will do it. God never loses."

"I accused David of having an affair and hung up on him this morning," Caroline confessed.

"And how would you evaluate that behavior now?"

"I was wrong. I let my hurt feelings dictate my behavior. I was selfish."

"You don't have to continue existing in that space, in that self-ishness, Caroline," Aunt Kathleen gently prodded.

"I know, I know. It's just that he's hurt me so much—"

"Well, you think about it. I'm sure you'll do what's best. Now," Aunt Kathleen suddenly switched the subject, "tell me why you have your great-grandmother Carrie on your mind."

"It's simple really. I know Carrie's story, so I know that when all the confusion of her two marriages was over, she ended up carrying and giving birth to a child that no one wanted, a child that was considered a burden. I just want to know how she found the courage to deal with her pain because I feel like I'm in the same situation."

"First of all, I need to state emphatically to you that there are many people who want you to have your baby. I don't think you really need me to name your supporters for you. There is really only one person who has objections—"

"The father of the child, the man I love," Caroline countered sadly.

"And he's the only one you're worried about, and I don't blame you. He's certainly the important one, and his behavior is hurtful, to say the least. Still there are others who want your child in their lives, and the same was true for Carrie. Although she certainly had fewer supporters than you do, she had her mother and John Kendall."

"That just doesn't seem like enough support to me. How did she do it, Aunt Kathleen? I have to know! I just don't have the resevoir of confidence to get through this, and the thought of the future scares me to death!"

"Caroline, I could tell you about Carrie's life and her faith, but it won't have the impact on you of simply reading her journal. You need to read her own words."

"Yes, I see the wisdom in that."

"Then you can ask me anything you want, and I'll try to help, okay?"

"Okay." They both stared out at the water for a moment, then Caroline asked, "So what shall we do now?"

"Do you still want to go shopping for the baby?"

"I'd love to," Caroline said as enthusiastically as she could because she knew her great aunt was looking forward to the adventure.

"You'd rather go read Carrie's journal, but I think you need to get away from your problems for a few hours before you start, so let's go shop and have lunch out. We won't be gone too long."

As Caroline drove her Aunt Kathleen's car carefully up the narrow drive to the back entrance of the house, she once again insisted, "I shouldn't have let you buy all those baby clothes. David is going to kill me for letting you spend so much money."

"What else am I supposed to do with it? Besides, do you realize that this child will be my very first great-great niece or nephew?"

"You mean you're finally willing to admit that you're my great aunt?" Caroline teased. "You know that's what you're doing, don't you, if you call my baby your great-great niece or nephew?"

"I have never denied my age," pretending great indignation Aunt Kathleen staunchly defended herself. "I simply reject all ideas that I should either think of myself as old or act old. In my heart and head I'm still in my twenties. That's what counts, Caroline, and don't you ever forget it."

"Well, get ready to think young, Aunt Kathleen, because here comes Betsy, and she looks pretty worked up."

"I should say she does. She looks like a thunderstorm ready to blow hail on us. Prepare for a diversionary tactic, Caroline."

"What diversionary tactic?"

"We'll get her excited about the baby dresses we bought," Aunt Kathleen quickly suggested, but when Caroline looked doubtful, Aunt Kathleen nodded, "You're right. That's not good enough. Wait, I know what we'll do. We'll tell her about that monitoring device you bought. She'll have a fit about that, and I do mean a fit."

"You two's been gone near all day," Betsy began scolding the minute she reached the passenger side of the car. "I knew you was going shopping, but I didn't know you was going to buy all of Charleston, and I bet you ain't had nothing to eat," she fussed as she helped Aunt Kathleen out.

"Oh we had the most wonderful lunch, Betsy," Aunt Kathleen insisted, "at the Courtyard. How I love that place, and you should have tasted their she-crab souffle! Really, Betsy, we must find a way to get you that recipe."

"I don't need no recipe for she-crab souffle. I got my own, handed down from my mama, and everybody who's anybody in Charleston society done said it be the best in Charleston. Besides, you ain't gonna get me off the subject that way, Miz Kathleen. You should have been home hours ago."

"Here, help me with all these packages, Betsy," Aunt Kathleen ignored her housekeeper. "We bought the sweetest dresses—"

"I's coming back later for them packages. I's gonna get you and Miz Caroline in the house and lying down for a nap." Betsy started ushering Aunt Kathleen toward the house as she turned her attention to Caroline. "What you be thinking, Miz Caroline, the two of you gallivanting all over Charleston, and you in your condition, too. I can't trust—"

"Caroline, do you think we should leave the baby monitor in the car?" Aunt Kathleen abruptly raised her voice. "I wouldn't want anybody to steal it."

"Ain't nobody gonna steal—baby monitor? What's a baby monitor?" Betsy demanded.

"Oh, it's the latest thing in baby care," Caroline insisted as she joined her aunt's diversionary action. "With a baby monitor, Betsy,

I can leave the baby alone, but still be able to hear any sound it makes. Why I can even go outside for hours without checking on the baby—"

"Leave your baby for hours? Not while I's still breathing you ain't!" Betsy exploded. "Where's that thing. I want to see it, and I want to see it now!"

"It's in the back seat," Aunt Kathleen volunteered as Betsy turned toward the car. "It's a wonderful gadget for modern mothers, Betsy."

"I's moving to Dallas before I lets any baby in this family be watched over by a machine!" Betsy went looking for the alien gadget while Aunt Kathleen and Caroline hurried inside.

"Let's get up the stairs, Caroline, before she catches up with us," Aunt Kathleen urged.

"If we can, you mean. I don't know about you, but I'm exhausted, and I feel as slow and clumsy as an elephant."

"We must, darling! We're in enough trouble for staying gone most of the afternoon, and you know how Betsy can go on about the stairs."

They helped each other up the circular staircase as speedily as they could, but when they reached the top, they both needed to stop to catch their breath. "I hate to admit it," Caroline said, "but Betsy is right. We did wear ourselves out. Those stairs felt as steep as a mountain."

"Don't you dare let her hear you say that. Sh-h-h! Here she comes. Quick, let's go out on the piazza and try to look rested."

"I hope you're a better actress than I am," Caroline turned toward the French doors that led onto the piazza. Once outside, she settled gingerly into a wicker chair as Aunt Kathleen sat on the adjoining settee.

"Let's have some tea, darling. That'll bring us to life."

"I'll take the tea, but nothing but a nap is going to revive me for long, I'm afraid."

"A nap does sound good," Aunt Kathleen tried unsuccessfully to stifle a yawn just as Betsy came through the door.

"I knowed it, I knowed you wore yourselves out," Betsy fussed.

"You both gonna go take a nap right this minute, and I ain't gonna take no for an answer neither."

"Perhaps you're right—" Aunt Kathleen began.

"And as for this baby monitor thing, Miz Caroline, I don't like it, and we ain't gonna have one around our baby." Betsy stood with a fist planted defiantly on each hip. "You and Mr. David got lots of money, and you can get our baby a nurse to take care of it if you don't want to. Though how you can turn your baby over to someone else is more than I can take in, but you sure ain't gonna turn it over to no machine."

"You're probably right, Betsy," Caroline agreed in order to bring peace to the piazza.

"I ain't probably right; I is right."

"You usually are, Betsy," Aunt Kathleen tried to save Caroline from further scolding. "And you're definitely right about a nap being in order." She rose from the settee, "I'm on my way to my bed right this minute. How about you, Caroline?"

"Me too," Caroline rose awkwardly. "Just put the baby monitor back with the other packages, Betsy. I promise to return it."

"If you don't, I's gonna send it to a watery grave at the bottom of Charleston Harbor," Betsy threatened melodramatically before turning and stalking away.

Aunt Kathleen came over and kissed Caroline on the cheek. "Rest well, darling. I had a wonderful time shopping, and part of the fun is knowing that I'm being naughty."

As Caroline crawled into the high, canopied bed of the blue room, she saw the old, leather-bound volume that was her great-grandmother's journal lying on the bedside table. Aunt Kathleen had given it to her before they left to shop. From the moment she spotted it, she knew that sleep would be impossible, that she would never be able to drift off while the undiscovered territory of her great-grandmother's life journey lay so near by. She plumped up the pillows behind her head and reached for the volume. As she ran her hand over the cover, she thought about her conversation with Aunt Kathleen that morning. I listened to every word she said, Caroline thought, but I still feel so anxious about David and about our future. I hope this young woman, Carrie, who is long dead can give me a clue about how I can get through the present and deal with the future.

Suddenly it occurred to Caroline that much of the pain and anxiety that Carrie had lived through had occurred in this very room. In fact, in her moments of desperation Carrie had flung herself on this very bed. She had buried herself in its soft comfort as she grieved over the loss of Robert and the selfishness and deceit of her father, which had brought her such suffering. Caroline reached over and touched the tall, ornate post of the bed which rose to support one corner of the canopy. She felt an uncanny closeness to Carrie, her great-grandmother.

She must have been quite an extraordinary young woman, Caroline thought, to have endured so much and not have been broken by it or allowed it to sour her view of life. If my father had acted as James Bradford did and treated me like a commodity to sell to the highest bidder, I would have felt like dirt. David's behavior, which is far less damaging than what Carrie endured, makes me feel worthless enough. She must have known something I don't know; she must have possessed some handle on life that helped her find victory over her situation. When I compare the difficulties of my life with those of Carrie's, I feel ashamed of my weakness. It's true that David and other important people in my family, like Grandmother, have always made it plain that I had to earn their love by being the person they wanted me to be. Still, no one has ever tried to sell me to the highest bidder. What defenses did Carrie have that I don't have? I must know! Caroline opened the journal and held the aging pages closer so she could read the faded writing.

April 2, 1890

"My mind is reeling so wildly from the onslaughts of my recent life that I know no remedy except to turn to my journal. As kind as Mother is and as willing as she is to listen, there is a limit to what I can say, even to her; so many of my feelings are too shameful. I have no other recourse except to return to this journal which

I have kept for so many years—during the happy, peaceful times of
my youth and during the difficult years as I waited for Robert to
finish school and fervently hoped that my father would approve
our marriage. Can it actually have been only a few weeks ago that I
lay in his arms and felt that I had finally found the haven where I
was destined to spend the rest of my life? In spite of my father's
disapproval and the necessity of our elopement, I was filled with
such hope only a few weeks ago because Robert and I were finally
one. And I believed that in time my father would forgive us for
marrying without his consent and that I would be reunited with
my family. Now I find myself married to John Kendall in a hastily
arranged marriage because—oh, I can hardly bear to write it—
because my father has lied to me all my life and Robert is, in fact,
my half brother.

"How could Father have done such a monstrous thing? Why
did he not tell me the truth years ago? He knew how deeply in
love with Robert I was. He must have known; I made it perfectly
clear that I wanted to marry Robert. Oh, I can understand that
Father made mistakes in his youth. I can understand that the
War destroyed his world and confused his values temporarily. Yes,
I can understand all that and forgive him. I can even understand
his decision to hide his affair with Cousin Diana and to keep his
relationship to Robert a secret. No doubt he believed it was the
best way to protect everyone. But how could he keep silent once
he knew that Robert and I were falling in love? Did he reject the
validity of my feelings? Perhaps he did at first. A young girl in love—
such a love would surely pass, but when it did not, when my love
remained strong and Robert asked for my hand, why did Father not
speak then? Was it his pride he had to protect? Was he so arrogant
that he believed he could control everything? Did he care nothing
for my feelings? Was I worth so little to him? Was I only a piece of
goods to use to bargain with another rich man and thereby double
the Bradford wealth? Am I so worthless?"

"No, no!" Caroline protested aloud as she slammed the journal down on the covers of the bed. "She wasn't worthless! How

could she have felt worthless? Just because her father didn't have the common decency to treat her like a human being with feelings? Her worth didn't depend on her father's evaluation of her or on his approval. I wouldn't let anyone make me feel worthless just because—" Caroline stopped as an image of her own pattern of behavior seeped into her mind. Her throat tightened; she stared at the mantel across the room.

"That's exactly what I've done," she whispered. "I set my sights on David the minute I met him because I knew that I had finally met a man Grandmother would approve. I knew she would be ecstatic at the thought of his wealth and position. And every time I gave up on catching David, Grandmother's anger drove me to try again. I even agreed to his absurd demand that we have no children. God forgive me, at Grandmother's insistence, I even considered aborting my child rather than losing David." Caroline felt her baby move, and she placed her hand on her extended stomach, attempting to come as close as she could to stroking her child. "Oh how could I have even thought of doing such a horrible thing for any reason?"

Caroline sighed and shook her head. "When I married David, I let him decide whether I was worth anything." She thought of David's most recent trip to London. "Every time he leaves now without an obvious, pressing business need, I feel dumped. I feel like I'm not worth loving. I have done something that doesn't please him, so I'm worthless to him and just plain worthless in general. And he could make our child feel the same way." She stroked her stomach again. "I won't let him!" she angrily exclaimed. "He's not going to make you feel that way, my precious child. No one is ever going to make you feel worthless!" Caroline's eyes filled with defiant tears. "But how am I going to stop him? How am I going to stop myself from feeling worthless? Dear God, I hope there are some answers in this journal because I have to know how she learned to deal with her situation. I have to know for my sake and for my baby's sake." She picked up the journal and began reading again.

April 5, 1890
    "I cannot stop thinking about Robert. I cannot stop loving

him. What a dreadfully sinful person I am. I understand that it was not possible to go on being Robert's wife. I understand that to do so would be wrong. Why can I not take control of my feelings and stop longing for him?

"I feel immeasurable gratitude to John Kendall for wanting me. What other man in the world would want a woman who is carrying another man's child? Still, I do not love John; I cannot love him. I cannot extinguish my love for Robert as if I were blowing out a lamp. I cannot forget that deep inside of my womb, it is Robert's child who is growing. I love that child so dearly because it is Robert's. It was only my desperation to protect my child that has made it possible for me to marry John. I would never have married him to protect myself or my father's good name, but for this unborn, innocent child I would do anything.

"My life has changed so drastically so quickly; my mind and my heart—especially my heart—cannot catch up with all the changes that have occurred. I know I am not treating John well. I keep to myself. I cling to the bedpost and cry for hours on end. I have always been able to exert my will and to do the thing that I thought was right. This is the first time I cannot control myself. My behavior disturbs me greatly. What is wrong with me? I must be a weak, worthless creature to lose control of myself and especially to treat John so. He has done nothing wrong. Indeed, he has done something honorable beyond words, yet I cannot love him. I am not even comfortable around him. I am so torn in my affections; I am grateful to John, yet, God help me, I still love Robert. How could I continue to love a man who is my half-brother? How could I persist in this sin?

"Oh, dear God, what have I done that such a fate should come to me? All my life I have tried to be Your child, to follow Your commandments. Now I feel that You have cast me away from You, that You do not love me. Can all of this pain really have come because I disobeyed my father and eloped with Robert? Can You, oh God, have turned Your back on me because I did not honor my father in this one thing, after so many years when I was faithful to Your commandments to the very best of my ability? Even now I strive to abide by Your commandment that we forgive. I seek to forgive my father for the deception that led me down this path. I would never have allowed my heart to love Robert as a woman loves a man had I known he was my half-brother. I would certainly never have married him. I would never have conceived this child in such sin. Am I so responsible, even though I was ignorant of the facts? God, how can You allow me to be victimized by this deceit which was not of my making?

"Even as I ask this question, I beg You to forgive me for asking it, for I do not feel worthy to question Your motives. But is it not better to ask the question, honestly and openly, rather than to harbor it in my heart? After all, You know all that I feel and all that I think. Yes, it is better to write it in this journal. Perhaps by doing so, I can find some resolution.

"Mother advises me to give myself time, and I am sure that is very good advice, but at the moment, time seems to be passing very slowly. I not only feel my own pain; I agonize over John's pain. And even though Robert is out of sight, I can well imagine what he must feel, for I know he loved me deeply for many years; this dreadful ordeal must hurt him so. I pray that he understands why I have married John Kendall and that he can somehow find peace. I thank You, my God, for even allowing me to approach You, for I must be a very great sinner, very unworthy of Your love to be in such a predicament. Please, please have mercy on me and on Robert and John."

"Why does she keep blaming herself?" Caroline demanded aloud, even though she was alone in the bedroom. "She didn't do anything wrong, not intentionally. She made one mistake out of ignorance, but her father committed the sins. He was the adulterer, the liar. Why does Carrie blame herself? Why can't she just step back and see the bigger picture? It's so obvious that it's not her fault. It's not like she did what I did. I lied to David; I tricked him into fathering a child he didn't want. That's why he's so upset with me. That's why he's avoiding me. Even though I complain bitterly, it is, after all, my fault that our marriage is in trouble.

David hasn't done anything wrong. And Aunt Kathleen is right, as much as I hate to admit it. David is not having an affair with another woman. That was just an easy rationalization for me. If I could convince myself he was sleeping with someone else, I wouldn't have to face my own guilt. And I wouldn't have to deal with the fact that David is struggling with something very important, something I probably brought on by lying to him in the first place and becoming pregnant. I've got to call him later, once I can get my thoughts together." Caroline sighed, brushed her hair back from her forehead, and returned her attention to the journal.

April 9, 1890

"Mother came to visit me, and John, knowing that I had a great need to talk to her in private, left for the afternoon. Poor Mother. She has suffered so much at Father's hands. She has lived with the knowledge of his adultery with her cousin for twenty years, and now she must watch the consequences of that unfaithfulness unfold in the pains of my life. It is so unfair of me to talk to her about my pain, yet she insists that I need to talk. So I did—for hours. I told her how convinced I am that I have sinned greatly, that I have not honored my father's wishes, as the Bible commands, and that I am being punished for breaking that commandment. She said just what I knew she would say—that the sin that I have committed is minor, that what I endure now is the result of Father's sin, of his deceit all these years. And she, too, takes the blame, for she allowed this deceit to go on.

"Oh, I cannot help but look back and wonder about my own honesty; perhaps I was too secretive in the early stages of my relationship with Robert, especially the first year that I corresponded with him while he was away at school. If only I had talked more openly about the depth of my feelings, surely someone would have told me the truth. So once again, it comes back to a mistake that I have made. Oh dear, I just seem to be going in circles; I cannot take it all in, but I need so desperately to understand. How else can I find the peace I need to go on?

"I am very angry with my father; this much I know, but I also know that even though this anger is justified, I must forgive him. But how? How can I forgive him? It is easy to forgive Mother; she, too, was victimized by what Father did, but Father's behavior has been totally selfish. If only once Father had said, 'No, Caroline, you must not allow yourself to love Robert. He is my son.' If only once he had told me that truth, how different my life would be now! How different Robert's life would be! How different John's life would be! Most importantly this child that I carry would not be in danger of living its life as a social outcast. When I think of this innocent child suffering, I think I shall lose my mind. My child must be my first priority; I must lay aside my own losses for its sake. I must accept the position I have been forced into, and some-how, I must become a good wife to John Kendall.

"John seemed so miserable this morning at breakfast. His eyes betray that he has slept little, if any, for days. I hear him in his study most of the night. I do not know what he is doing, but I know he is suffering. Why should this loving man be made to suffer, and how can I help him? Mother said that I could ease John's suffering if I allowed him to share in my own. I do not know. It seems cruel to ask him to share in what I feel because so much of what I feel is love for Robert, my yearning to be Robert's wife and my grief that Robert is gone. So much of what I feel is love for Robert's child and agony over what will happen to Robert's child in the future. Can it truly be good for John Kendall to discuss these things? Surely no man wants to hear such things, but Mother argues that John chose to marry me because he loves me, and that the worst thing I can do is to exclude him. It just seems too much to ask any man to bear. For his sake I should never have married him. But what else could I do? I could not bear my child out of wedlock; I could not ask my child to endure a lifetime of society's rejection. Oh! I am trapped in an iron vise forged by my father's actions and choices. But perhaps I trapped myself by defying my father. I am so confused."

"How can she keep blaming herself?" Caroline demanded as she once again lowered the journal to the coverlet. "She is such a good person, so loving, so self-sacrificing. Her mother is right; she's got to talk to John. I know she doesn't want to hurt him; I know she doesn't want to reveal her secret feelings, but she has to. He's just hanging around, loving her and waiting for her to share her pains from the past with him. He needs her to talk to him, just as I need David to talk to me, but he just won't open up and— *Wait a minute!* Could he be protecting me? Carrie is trying to protect John; maybe David is trying to protect me. But from what? I already know what happened to him in the past. Don't I? Maybe not. Maybe there is something he's not telling me. That's what Aunt Kathleen was talking about this morning. There's something going on with David that is so deeply buried and so painful that he can't talk about it. He can't even face it himself. That's why he's having those nightmares."

A surge of anxiety rushed through Caroline. "But what can I do to help him? Nothing. Absolutely nothing, but wait." Caroline fumed, and in her frustration she snatched the pillows out from behind her and beat them into a plumper shape. When she settled back down, she was finally able to acknowledge more of the truth of her aunt's words. "She didn't say 'just wait.' She said 'stand by him and pray.' Okay, I can see how I can stand by him; I can call him and apologize for accusing him of having an affair. I can tell him I know he's struggling with something and that I'll give him the time and space to deal with it. I can do those things, and I will. That leaves prayer. I've never been very good at prayer, and I don't have a clue how to pray for someone who has hurt me so much. On that I'm definitely going to need help. I hope it's in this journal." She quickly snatched up the journal and began reading again.

April 12, 1890

"After dinner last evening, when John sat down to read in front of the fireplace, I joined him. He looked up from his book and smiled at me, yet his eyes were full of sadness. For a moment I thought I would not be able to open my heart to him. I struggled with my thoughts, trying to decide where to begin. Finally, I just began with the raw truth.

I said, 'John, dear, Mother has suggested that I speak to you about some things that are torturing me in mind and heart. I am not sure it is a kind thing to do, for my thoughts and feelings may hurt you.' He leaned forward with a slight eagerness in his eyes and begged me to continue.

'It is difficult to be honest with you,' I continued, 'because I cannot speak honestly without speaking about my feelings for Robert, and such words must surely pierce you like a sword.'

'Such words will be difficult to hear, Carrie,' he admitted, 'but in any marriage, there must be intimacy—intimacy of heart and mind and even—at the appropriate time—physical intimacy. I know that at this time in our marriage we cannot relate to each other in the usual fashion of newlyweds, but if we can at least share our thoughts and feelings, we shall be growing closer to each other. I want to grow closer to you, Carrie, even if it is painful to do so.'

I took a deep breath, and although I was quivering inside, I told him that I still loved Robert, that I could not forget that Robert had fathered my child, that I felt terribly battered by what my father had done, and that I was certain that God had deserted me because I am a great sinner.

He said, 'Your feelings about Robert, your child and your father do not surprise me, Carrie. They are not feelings I would choose for you, but you should not feel guilty for having them. They are justified under the recent circumstances. No one's feelings are like a candle that can be lit and then blown out on a moment's notice. As for your feelings that God has deserted you or that you have committed a great sin, those feelings are wrong, Carrie, and you must fight against them.'

'But if I had obeyed my father, I would not be in such a mess,' I argued.

'If your father had not been deceitful, you would not have been put in this situation at all. Your father is the great sinner, but only he can do anything about that. You, Carrie, made a quick, impulsive judgment that turned out to be a bad judgment. Please remember, however, that you made that judgment to elope with Robert because you were ignorant of crucial facts that were being

withheld from you. God judges our intentions, Carrie, not the out-
come of our acts. Your intention was to marry the man you love
and be faithful to him the rest of your life.'

'Oh, John,' I cried. 'How do I begin to untangle this mess?'

'I think you and I both need to begin in the same place,' he
answered, 'and it will not be an easy place for either one of us to
begin. We need to begin by forgiving your father. I confess, I find
it much more difficult than I thought it would be. For now that we
are married, Carrie, I want you to be my wife. I do not want to see
you distraught day after day, crying and feeling hopeless. I want
you to be happy; I want to be able to make you happy. And all of
the things that I want are thwarted by what your father has done.
I hate him, Carrie.'

'Oh, no,' I protested. 'You must not hate him. You can be
angry with him, John, but you must not hate him.'

'You see, Carrie,' he answered, 'you are more spiritually
mature than I am, even though you are twenty-five years younger.
You, at least, do not hate. What little spiritual maturity I do have
tells me that forgiveness is where we need to begin. I honestly do
not know if I can forgive James Bradford, but I do know that there
can be no peace in your heart or in mine or in our relationship if
we do not forgive.'

'How do we forgive, John? How do we do it? I do not feel
forgiveness for my father.'

'And I have confessed to you that I hate your father.'

'Then how do we forgive?'

'I once heard a very profound man talk about forgiveness, and
he insisted that it had nothing to do with feelings, that forgiveness
is simply a choice that one makes and that every time the
unforgiveness rises in one's mind, one has to choose, once again,
to forgive. I think he is right, Carrie. My own life experiences tell
me he is right. After the War, there was much to forgive. I came
home and found that my family had been destroyed; some had
been killed by Yankee soldiers, and the remainder had died from
the malnutrition the War caused. Carpetbaggers owned my land; I
had been stripped of everything I had except my education, but

for a long time, I was not even allowed to teach. I cannot tell you how bitter and angry I was. I hated the Yankees. I lived in unforgiveness, Carrie, for many years, but I was blessed because one day a visiting pastor came to my church. He came to talk about forgiveness. I almost got up and walked out; I had heard all the sermons on that subject that I ever wanted to hear; however, something about this man's quiet but direct way caught my attention. He said that forgiveness was the basis for peace and that, in spite of what we Charlestonians might think, we could forgive if we chose to. I went to speak to him later and told him that I didn't know how to choose forgiveness. He looked at me and said, "just do it. It is an act of will. Just do it intellectually until you feel it."'

'Did it work, John?'

'Yes, eventually it did. I chose to say, "I forgive them" thousands of times in the next few years until finally I actually felt forgiveness toward them.'

'And that is the way I must forgive my father,' I said after reflecting on John's words. 'I must just choose to do it, and every time the pain comes back up, I must choose to forgive him again. And what about you, John? How will you forgive Father?'

'My words to you, dear Carrie, have shown me the path I must take. I, too, must choose to forgive James Bradford, even though I know that there are many moments of pain ahead of me that he has caused and that I will have to forgive him again and again.'

'Oh, John,' I cried as I leaned toward him. 'This is something we can do together. Finally here is something good that we can share.'

'I had not thought of it, Carrie, not that way,' he responded. 'But it is a very special kind of intimacy, to join together in forgiveness.'

Through my own tears, I saw that there were tears in his eyes, but that a certain joyfulness had permeated his countenance. He held out his hand to me, and I clasped it, and he said, 'We choose to forgive James Bradford for the pain he has caused us.' I said the words that he had just spoken, and we clasped our hands together tightly in agreement. For the first time, I felt more than friendship toward this wonderful man who has rescued me from such disgrace and saved my child's future. I stood and leaned over and kissed him lightly on the lips. Then suddenly I felt quite overcome with exhaustion. Seeing my weakened state, John rose and escorted me to my bedroom. After I had slipped into my bed, I lay there and thought. I felt certain that we had turned some important corner in our relationship, that somehow the first building block was in place for our marriage. I slept better last night than any night since my father took me away from Robert."

"I could never forgive anyone who hurt me like James Bradford hurt her," Caroline said emphatically. "No way! I wouldn't even want to. I would just want to get even. I know that the amount of pain David has caused me in the last six months is nothing compared to what Carrie's father caused her, but he has hurt me! He's made me feel like dirt, and I want him to be sorry for the way he's acted. Then I want him to change. If he doesn't, I don't want to go on in this marriage. After all, I've got plenty of money of my own; I can take care of myself and my baby. If David doesn't want me and our baby, it's his loss."

Having vented her anger verbally, Caroline immediately felt ashamed of herself. "What am I saying? I'm right back to being totally selfish again. I've got to work on myself. I can't just dump David from my life because he's not making me happy right now or even because I think he's mistreated me in the past few months. If I do something like that, I'm saying he's worthless, and he's not. He's caused me a lot of suffering, but that doesn't make him worthless. If he's worthless, so am I. After all, I've caused him a lot of suffering.

"So what do I need to do? I need to forgive him, but how? John Kendall told Carrie to choose to forgive intellectually until it became a part of her heart. Boy, that sure sounds familiar. Aunt Kathleen is always telling me to choose a better way. 'Just do it.' That's what the preacher told John Kendall. Just do it. That's a choice. Okay. I can do that; I can choose to say I forgive David, and I can choose to tell him I forgive him. Can I choose to ask him to forgive me? That needs to be done too, and I know it. I've asked him to forgive me for lying to him, but I've never asked him to forgive me for only counting his worth in terms of what he could do for me. That's what I've really done to David, and I need to ask his forgiveness, or nothing good is going to come out of this marriage. Do I have the courage to do that, to ask for that forgiveness?"

SEVEN

Caroline placed Carrie's journal on the bed beside her while she silently considered her own marital predicament and compared it to Carrie's. I'm glad I know from Aunt Kathleen that Carrie eventually worked through all her confusion and pain, that she was ultimately able to create a good marriage with John Kendall. Those facts give me hope for myself and my marriage, and, of course, that's why I've had Carrie on my mind so much lately. I thought my connection to her was just the result of our similar anguish over being pregnant when so few people wanted the babies we were carrying. Now I see that she and I have another thing in common; we both think we can earn our worth by doing what those around us want us to do. I see the problem intellectually, but I'm not sure I know how to solve it.

Caroline picked up Carrie's journal and began reading again.

June 1, 1890

"Mother came to our house early this morning with news that will change my life forever. It is obvious now that my child and I will never escape condemnation by the citizens of Charleston. Late last night the coachman who was driving the carriage on the night Robert and I eloped became intoxicated in a tavern and told the story of my elopement. Gossip about Robert and me is rampant in the city, and I have been so upset I have not left the house all day. John insisted that he must go and teach his classes as a way of showing that we will not give credence to the gossip, but he came home early.

"Father has, of course, involved himself. For the first time since our marriage, he came to our house and insisted that we deny the story the coachman has told in order to protect the Bradford name. Father plans to run for the legislature this year, so he is adamant that the Bradford name not be sullied. Since it was deceit that produced our problems, I am determined not to use deceit to extricate us from this new dilemma. John is in agreement. Mother insists that we have a right to our privacy, that it would be best to simply go on with our lives in a normal fashion and allow this gossip to die down. I think she is right. I am, after all, expecting a child, and that child must be my most important consideration. I must not allow myself to be too upset by this.

"No matter how brave I try to be, I am not fooling myself. I do not think society here in Charleston will ever forget this scandal. The fact that I married Robert and then, a month later, married John is simply too fertile a field for their gossiping tongues. They have concluded rightly that my child is Robert's. Of course, they do not know the circumstances that led me to leave Robert and have my marriage to him annulled. They do not know that Robert is my half-brother. To tell them that truth might very well save my own name and clear John's name, but it would certainly hurt my father. More importantly, it would hurt my child. It is one thing for society to think that my child was fathered by a man other than John, that he was fathered by Robert Montgomery, but if they discovered that Robert is my half-brother, my baby would be a total outcast.

"Oh, is there no way to unweave this web of deceit that we are all caught in? I wish that John and I could leave Charleston. I would miss my Mother terribly, but it seems like the best thing for my child. John insists that we will not run, that we have done nothing wrong, and that while society may not know the truth, we do, and so does God. What a horrible day this has been! Why has God allowed me to be the prey of my father's mistakes? I must have offended God greatly to be found so unworthy of His love. I am horrified at what my baby, once it is born, may well suffer all of its life. How could God let a totally innocent child suffer? I admit I have broken a commandment. I did not honor my father, but must my child pay for my sin, as I paid for my father's sins of adultery and deceit?"

Caroline slowly lowered the journal to the coverlet and stared straight ahead as tears gathered in her eyes. She wondered, would God really let Carrie's child suffer just because she didn't obey her father and reject Robert? It doesn't sound like that much of a sin to me, but it's true that she wouldn't have been pregnant if she hadn't eloped with Robert. Did God really let her innocent baby pay the price? Oh dear! I might as well be honest with myself. Of course, I care about Carrie's child, but what I really want to know is, is my baby going to have to pay for my mistakes? I admit that I deserve to pay a penalty for lying to David, and I will freely pay any penalty David imposes. I just want to get it all paid for before our baby is born. I can't bear for him to hurt our child by keeping his distance from it or acting unloving toward it. If he does, it will be my fault, not the baby's, but the baby will have to pay the price. I can only do so much to make things right with David, and I will do what I can regardless of my pride, but ultimately I have no control over David's response to anything I do. Is God going to allow my innocent child to be hurt no matter what I do?

I guess I already know the answer to that question. I haven't spent all these months working down at the shelter for homeless women and children and learned nothing. That place is filled with children who are paying dearly for sins they didn't commit. And they are probably the lucky ones. Think of all the children who live on the streets all over the world. Dear God, if you won't help them, why would you protect my baby from my sins?

A wave of anxiety washed over Caroline. *What am I going to do? Why does God allow innocent children to suffer? I know great thinkers have tried to figure that out for centuries and have come up with no answers, but I don't care. I need answers.*

She paused a moment, then swung her legs over the side of the bed and settled on her feet. "If anyone knows anything, it's Aunt Kathleen," she mumbled. "I hope she's awake because I have to talk to her." She left her room and started down the hall.

As she knocked softly on Aunt Kathleen's bedroom door, she asked, "Are you awake, Aunt Kathleen?" Cautiously, she opened the door and peeked in. Aunt Kathleen was sitting in a chair in front of the fireplace looking up at a portrait over the mantle. She turned and smiled at Caroline.

"Come in, Caroline dear. I'm afraid I'm being a little lazy. That nap was quite a bit more needed than I wanted to admit. Don't tell Betsy."

"Oh, I won't," Caroline agreed as she entered the room. "I hope you didn't make yourself sick shopping too long."

"Oh, no, dear. It was exhilarating. What a wonderful day!"

"It was a beautiful day," Caroline agreed automatically. Aunt Kathleen peered up at her with a questioning look on her face. "Sit down for a moment, dear. I've just gotten up, and I decided to sit here and reflect for a moment."

Caroline sat in the chair opposite her aunt. "It's a little stuffy in here, Aunt Kathleen," she observed nervously. "Would you like for me to open the French doors?"

"Oh, no, dear, we'll go out on the piazza and have some tea soon."

"Right." Caroline fell silent, unsure how to bring up the subject on her mind.

Aunt Kathleen smiled absentmindedly and continued gazing at the portrait above the mantle until Caroline grew concerned, "Is everything okay, Aunt Kathleen?"

"Yes, dear. Everything is fine."

Caroline was mystified by her aunt's distant behavior and even less certain she should ask what she came to ask. She looked at the portrait above the mantle that her aunt seemed to be studying. There she found the picture of a glowingly beautiful young woman, a blonde with sky-blue eyes and a very fair complexion, who was wearing a stunning, white ball gown. Caroline recognized a great likeness to Aunt Kathleen in the young woman's face. Judging by the young woman's hairdo, Caroline guessed that the picture must have been made in the early sixties.

When Aunt Kathleen continued to be silent, Caroline asked, "Who is she?"

"That's Allison, my daughter, at the time of her debut."

Caroline felt even more uncomfortable then when she had fled her own room; all she knew about Aunt Kathleen's daughter was that she had died in some kind of accident. Unable to think what to say, she made the obvious comment, "She was very beautiful."

"Yes, on the inside as well as the outside," Aunt Kathleen paused and studied the portrait another minute while Caroline struggled to think of what to say next. "But you are troubled about something, Caroline; I can see it in your face. What is it?"

"I wanted to ask you about something, but now doesn't seem like the right time. Perhaps I should leave you alone with your thoughts."

"No, dear, my thoughts can wait until I don't have the pleasure of your company. Now what is bothering you?"

"I was reading your mother's journal, about the time when Charleston society found out about her elopement with Robert."

"Yes?"

"Well, I just don't understand why she blames herself so much for what happened. It really wasn't her fault that she married her half-brother, but she's convinced that everything happened because she sinned by disobeying her father. She's even blaming herself for what may happen to her unborn child."

"She made a mistake, an innocent one, and certainly I agree she's over-reacting in her self-condemnation." Aunt Kathleen grew quiet and watched Caroline's face a moment. "You seem quite overwrought, Caroline. Are you sure it's my mother's self-condemnation that is bothering you so much?"

"It's more than that. She keeps writing about how her child will have to pay for her sins, and I—well—I wonder if my child will have to pay for my lie to David. It's so hard to explain, Aunt Kathleen. I never thought very deeply about the part that God plays in things, but Carrie keeps worrying about how her sin is going to ruin her child's life."

"And what do you think about that?"

"It seems like an overreaction to me; I'm not sure I believe in that kind of thing, but then I remember all the kids at the shelter, and there's no denying that they are paying for their parents' behavior, or sins, if you want to call it that."

"We do seem to be bound together some way, don't we?" Aunt Kathleen observed. "The different generations, I mean. Whatever we do does impact those who come after us."

"I guess there's no escaping that conclusion. But Carrie factors in God in such a specific way. I don't know; I just never thought about His part in it, I guess."

"When you do think about it, what do you conclude?"

"I don't understand Him. He's supposed to be all powerful, but He's also supposed to be love, so it's really hard to understand why children are allowed to suffer." Caroline laughed nervously, "I guess I was supposed to figure all this out in college, but frankly I was too busy partying. Maybe we should just drop the subject."

"If you like, Caroline," Aunt Kathleen murmured, but she sat perfectly still and watched Caroline's face.

Caroline couldn't resist going on, "I mean, Aunt Kathleen, you've always had such great faith; you've probably never even been tempted to ask such questions."

"I've asked them many times, but never more vehemently than when Allison was killed."

"Aunt Kathleen, I feel so selfish. The truth is, I don't even know how your daughter died."

"In an airplane crash. She had just been married to the most wonderful man, and they were flying to Canada for their honeymoon."

"Oh no! Why did the plane crash?"

"Pilot error was the official designation, I believe. You see, the pilot was called back to do extra duty, and he had been drinking. I'm sure he thought he was capable of flying the plane, but he wasn't." Aunt Kathleen stared at the portrait of her daughter for a moment while Caroline struggled to think of something—anything—to say. "Caroline, you can be sure I had a lot of questions for God, not the least of which were why did He let such a pure-spirited, young woman die and why did He let my daughter die."

"Oh, Aunt Kathleen, I'm so sorry I brought this subject up. Let's just drop it; surely you don't want to relive all that."

"Only if it will help you, and I think it will. Yes, I asked the questions you are posing now. My daughter was a loving, spiritual being who was just beginning her life. Why did God allow her to die? Why did he allow such a horrible thing to happen to me? And what about the other members of my family, like Carrie, my mother, who had already been so hurt by her losses? From her journal you can see what kind of person my mother was and what she had already suffered. Why did God allow her granddaughter to be killed in a plane accident?"

"Did you ever find any answers?"

"I struggled with those questions for years, Caroline. I kept demanding answers. Maybe God answered me immediately, and I just didn't want to hear it because I didn't want an answer, any answer. I just wanted to blame someone. Maybe He waited to answer, I don't know. But it was several years before I understood why God had not given Allison special protection and saved her life—why He had not given me special protection and saved me from the immeasurable pain I suffered. All my life I've been very close to God, very dedicated to being His child, and I had an overwhelming reaction to her death which is just the reaction you're describing. I understood that the accident had occurred because the pilot was drinking. I knew what I have told you so far, but it didn't lessen my pain. It didn't even keep me from being angry with God because as you say, He could have saved Allison. And I felt somehow that since I had always loved Him so much—well, it was several years before I found answers that gave me some peace."

"Tell me, Aunt Kathleen, if you're sure you won't be too upset talking about all this."

"I'm fine, but you need to realize that any understanding you have now will just be intellectual in nature. Eventually, when some catastrophe occurs in your life, you will need to take this intellectual idea and apply it to your heart. Do you understand?"

"I think so."

"Okay. About three years after Allison died, one of our friends had a fine teenage son who was killed by a drunk driver. When I heard of his death and attended his funeral, all the feelings that I had about Allison's death were magnified to an unbearable degree. The same old questions demanded answers. Why did God allow this wonderful teenage boy to be killed by a drunk driver? How could He allow this wonderful woman to lose her son so senselessly?

"I went to visit my friend; I wanted so much to offer her words of consolation, but there was so little I could say, except to say that I had suffered the loss of a child too. My words were useless; she looked at me and angrily demanded, 'why did God allow this to happen to Jason?' She went on to give me a long list of all the wonderful things that Jason had done already in his life. What a fine, godly young man he was. And she was right. He was everything she said he was. Her distress was so obvious—so hard to watch, and she kept coming back with the same questions, 'Why Jason? Why me?'

"I started answering her first question with the only answer I had ever been able to find for myself. It was a very intellectualized answer, and I knew she wasn't ready to accept it, but I needed to say it. I explained to her what I had come to know, namely that when God creates us, He really does give us autonomy. He really does give us freedom to choose. So we go about our life choosing, and when we make a bad choice, sometimes innocent people pay. He won't step in and take our freedom to choose away from us because if He did, we would no longer be the creations He made. We would be robots. Does that make any sense to you?"

"Yes it does, but I don't feel any better about it."

"I understand, Caroline, but the fact is that when God creates, He does not simply produce an extension of Himself. He creates a whole new individual. That individual is not all good like He is, nor is that individual bad. That individual is free to choose between good and evil. Without that choice we would be mere extensions of God, not truly unique creations."

"I still don't feel any better about the possibility of my child being hurt by what I have done or what David may do."

"I know, and I can't make you feel good about the possibility—no, inevitability—that your child will suffer at some time in its life from other people's bad choices. I can only tell you that the ability to make free choices is worth a great deal to all of us. And when we learn to think about the inevitability that our bad choices will harm someone else, we start making better choices."

"I guess we at least hope we will," Caroline mused aloud. Both women sat, lost in their own thoughts, for a few moments. When Caroline roused herself, she asked, "You said there was a second question you wanted answered.

"Yes, I wanted to know why God had allowed this tragic thing to occur in my life. I guess I thought I should be immune from such pain because I had always been close to God."

"And you found an answer to that question also?"

"When I went to see my friend who had lost her son, she voiced the same question I have just mentioned. Much to my surprise I heard myself responding to her question by asking her a question. And the question startled me. It was as if it did not come out of my own mind, but there I was, voicing it."

Caroline leaned forward, "What question?"

"What mother does God love less than He loves you?"

"I don't understand, Aunt Kathleen."

"Neither did she. It wasn't an answer that she could take in at that time; so of course, she responded angrily, 'What on earth are you talking about, Kathleen?' And somehow, I had this knowledge, quite suddenly, and I said again to her, 'What mother does God love less than He loves you? Don't you see, don't you see, Janice? God gives all of us free choice. This man chose to drink. He chose to get behind the wheel of a car and to drive while he was drunk. His choices caused the death of your son. Someone was going to be killed, and whoever that someone was, he or she had a mother who would grieve. What mother did God love less than you? You're asking me why God let this happen to you? It was going to happen to someone—to some mother. And since He loves us all equally, regardless of our bad deeds or the good things we have done, what mother would He have chosen to put in your place?"

"God loves us all the same?" Caroline demanded.

"Yes, He does. He loves every human being the same."

"Then, why do we try to be good? Why do we try to do what God wants us to do? What's the point?"

"The point of doing things God's way is to love God back and to bring great joy into our own lives, Caroline. We don't have to earn God's love by being good, by being holy. We are loved. The most holy person and the least holy person on the face of this earth—God loves both of them the same. If we are going through our lives trying to make good choices in order to gain God's favor, we're missing the point entirely. We already have God's favor. He loves us, and nothing can change that. The question is, will we love Him back? Will we live lives of joy while we are here on earth because we are living with God and living in God's way?"

"So you suddenly knew why God had allowed Allison to die?"

"I suddenly knew that Allison died because of the pilot's choices, and God did not give her special protection, nor did He protect me from the inevitable grief because in order to do that, He would have had to substitute someone in Allison's place. Someone was going to be sitting in that airplane, and there was no one in the whole world whom He loved less than He loved Allison. There was no one He was willing to sacrifice to save Allison. There was no mother He was willing to sacrifice in order to save me my pain."

"Somehow this makes me feel terribly insecure," Caroline said bluntly. "If striving to do the right things doesn't make God love me, I feel helpless because I have nothing else to give."

"You're looking at the situation from the wrong side, Caroline. You feel insecure because you cannot earn God's love, but you don't have to earn it. You are loved by God no matter how many mistakes you have made in your life or how many more you may make. You will always be loved by God. When all is said and done, is that not the ultimate security?"

"This is very difficult to take in, Aunt Kathleen."

"I know, dear. As I said, it is an intellectual answer; it takes time to take it into your spirit. Hopefully, you will understand it long before you need it to cope with great difficulty in your life. But do try to remember it, even on the intellectual level. And please, Caroline, I know that you and David are having difficulties and that you're facing the delivery of your baby, but please remember, Caroline, the bottom line is that God does love you and He will stay with you no matter what comes your way—whether it is the result of your choices or someone else's."

"I'll try to remember, Aunt Kathleen. Frankly, if anyone else had told me what you have told me, I don't think I would have paid any attention. I think I would have said, 'This is absurd,' and rejected the idea totally. But I have seen your life in action, especially the peace and the joy you have inside. Now I know that you have that peace and joy in spite of the horrible pain of losing Allison. Knowing these things, I cannot ignore what you are telling me because I know that you are speaking from wisdom gained from life experiences, not from theological theory. So I will think about it, and I will try to apply it to some of the things that have happened to me already."

"That's a good idea. Apply it to what you have already experienced, and it will become your own, and it will be there for you should you ever need it. Now, Caroline, this has been a very heavy conversation. Why don't we go have a cup of tea and a light supper on the piazza."

"Sounds great."

"You know, Caroline, a good life comes from balance—from balancing the difficult times and the good times. From balancing the painful thoughts with the happy thoughts. Let's bring out some happy thoughts."

They had a quiet supper, and Aunt Kathleen told family

stories—funny stories—incidents that had become legendary in the
family. And then they both went off to bed, but Caroline's spirit
was still disturbed by what she had learned about Allison's death,
and Aunt Kathleen's words about dealing with tragedy still haunted
her. She wandered out onto the upper piazza and walked the length
of it to stare out at the harbor. She leaned against one of the massive pillars and tenderly ran her fingers across her extended abdomen—the safe-haven for her unborn child. Love welled up in her
for her child who would soon be born into the world. She felt
fiercely protective of it already, and she was bothered considerably
that even a woman such as Aunt Kathleen had not been able to
protect her daughter. She continued to stroke the haven of her
child and stare out at the lights across the harbor, seeking some
peace that would lead to a good night's rest. She felt her child
kicking, and she smiled as she thought, it won't be long before I
will be able to see my child's face.

But how much harder it will be to protect it once it is outside
of my body. I thought that if I did everything right, then everything would be all right. This story of Allison is very disturbing. I
think for the first time, I have a glimpse of how David must have
felt when he lost his child, and I understand a little bit more about
his fear of having children, of risking that painful loss again. I must
call him in the morning. Perhaps I should tell him some of what I
have heard tonight. Perhaps I should tell him that I understand a
little bit more about his fears. I still don't know what's really going
on with him. I think Aunt Kathleen is right; there has to be a deep-
rooted reason that he's having those dreadful nightmares.

"Is you all right, Miz Caroline?" Caroline was startled out of
her thoughts by Betsy who was walking slowly toward her down
the piazza.

"Yes, Betsy. I'm fine. I'm just thinking over some things that
Aunt Kathleen said."

"You's been talking about Miz Allison, hasn't you?"

"Yes, we have, and I feel so many disturbing emotional
responses to what I heard. I feel very self-centered because I never
knew about this pain in Aunt Kathleen's life. And I feel very

disturbed that such a thing could happen to a spiritual woman like Aunt Kathleen. And I guess most of all, I feel very mystified about the way she's been able to handle it. Anyone looking at the way she lives her life now would never guess that something so tragic happened to her. But she must have lived through a devastating time when she lost her daughter."

"It was a bad time, Miz Caroline, a real bad time. But Miz Kathleen, you know, she ain't the type of woman to just give up and give in. She don't let herself just get angry or just get sad and stay that way. She gonna work her way through it somehow. She was good and mad at God, but she didn't break off her relationship with Him. She was grieved. My how she grieved! But she was also determined to live the rest of her life. She did battle with the thing. You know what I mean? She didn't let it beat her. She just kept insisting that if she kept asking, God would give her some answers that would give her some peace, and He did. And she been able to help lots of people since then. Yes ma'am, they's lots of people in this city who would have given up after their own tragedies and lived in anger or lived in sadness if it hadn't been for your Aunt Kathleen. I knows what I's talking about, Miz Caroline. When my grandson was killed in Vietnam, it was Miz Kathleen that help me get through that."

"Oh, no, Betsy. I didn't know about that either."

"There ain't no reason for you to know all these things, child. Don't beat yourself up over that. You ain't been here in Charleston. You been back there in Dallas. Your grandmother, Miz Judith, she separated you entirely from this family. There ain't a reason in the world for you to know what's happened here. And it ain't even important now that you didn't know. What's important now is that you take what you're learning and you make it yours and you use it in your own life."

"I hope I never need this information."

"Hard times come into every life, Miz Caroline. You's already had some hard times, and sure as you's living, you's gonna have more. Take this information Miz Kathleen give you and store it up, and you use it when you need it, and you pass it on. That's what family is all about. That's what community is about. We gots to learn from those who come before us. 'Cause life don't really change that much, not the big things—not the joys and not the griefs. They don't change. It don't matter if it's one hundred years ago or now or one hundred years from now. Human life is human life. We gots to learn from those who walked before us—how to enjoy life and how to deal with the hard parts of life."

"It must have been very hard for Aunt Kathleen to talk about her daughter."

"I'm sure it was, but she want you to have this information. She's willing to go through this story one more time 'cause she knows if you lives, you's going to eventually face suffering. And you's going to face joys too. And Miz Kathleen, she want you to face those sufferings with all the ammunition you can possibly have. And she want you to take those joys and cling to them to balance out your life."

"Yes, she said life was about balance."

"And it is, Miz Caroline, it is. We don't get everything we want in this life, but God, He always make sure we get enough of what we want, as well as a good dose of joy. You got to notice that joy, He give you, Miz Caroline."

"I'll try, Betsy. I'll try very hard. I'm sorry to say that, for me, in the past, the joys have been pretty superficial things—parties and dresses and that kind of thing."

"Your life ain't over, honey. It ain't over by a long shot. It's just beginning, really."

"I'm very blessed to have Aunt Kathleen and you, Betsy. I'm very blessed to have learned that there was another legacy in my family, that my grandmother's legacy was false, that life is about more than social position and money."

"Now that's what I's talking about, see, right there. You's looking at the blessings—at the joys in life. You's seeing that you's raised by your grandmother and she sent you down the wrong path, but God, He intervened, and He brought you here last spring, and He brought your husband here, and you two learned something. You learned there's another way. Now you's trying to live it, and it ain't easy. It ain't easy to change. And I figure, you's a little ahead of Mr. David, but you gotta remember you's a little younger than Mr. David. It's easier to change when you's younger. But he gonna come around. He gonna understand."

"If he chooses to," Caroline added.

"That's right, Miz Caroline. He gonna have to choose. We all got to choose. And right now, you got to choose to go to bed and rest."

"I think you're right, Betsy." Caroline put her arms around the dear old woman and gave her a big hug.

"You got to take care of that baby. Now you get on down to your room, and you go to bed, and you have a good rest and think about joyful things. Just store up this other knowledge about dealing with bad times for when you need it, but you go to bed thinking about the good things. Then you sleep real well."

"I will, Betsy. Good night." Caroline returned to her room, but after she had settled in bed, she lay there a long time thinking about Aunt Kathleen and Allison. I wonder if I will ever have to face such a tragedy, she thought, and if such a tragedy comes, will I know how to handle it?

EIGHT

Caroline awoke suddenly from a fretful dream, turned over and checked the time. "Five o'clock," she muttered, "I'm not getting up at five o'clock in the morning." She lay flat on her back and stared at the underside of the canopy of the bed. Filled with a vague sense of foreboding she couldn't identify, she tried to remember what she had been dreaming, but she could remember no specifics. "I just know it was something about Aunt Kathleen and the death of her daughter," she murmured. "And something about Carrie too."

The thought of Carrie reminded her of the journal lying on the bedside table, and once she remembered it, she knew she would not fall back asleep. She pulled herself up in bed, turned on a lamp, and plumped up some pillows to lean against. "I've got to know the rest of Carrie's story because somehow her story and my story and Aunt Kathleen's loss of her daughter—they all fit together." She picked up the journal and opened it. "I don't know how, but they do."

June 4, 1890

"It is Sunday afternoon, three days after the news of my elope-ment with Robert was made public. I have received two notes from hostesses whose dinner parties John and I had been invited to. They have cancelled the parties. I cannot help but believe that it is because they do not want us to come. Mother picked me up yesterday to go shopping, and wherever we went, the fine ladies of Charleston left. As we walked along the sidewalk, the ladies actually crossed the street to avoid meeting us. When we entered a dress shop, the previous customers left, rather than be there with us. Through the entire ordeal, Mother insisted that we keep our heads held high and repeatedly reminded me that neither one of us has done anything wrong. If she had not been there to give me the strength, I would have fled back to my house to hide.

"The ultimate insult came when John and I entered church this morning and sat in our usual pew. Those who were already seated got up and moved away from us, and those who came in later refused to sit close to us. Obviously Charleston society intends to shun us, just as they shunned the Yankee soldiers who occupied the city after the War. If this is my fate, what will be the fate of my child? I cannot sleep for worrying about it. I am totally confused about God's silence, His lack of protection in the midst of all that is happening. I thought I had such a strong faith, but I find that I am shaken to the core. I cannot even think of a reason to continue this journal. Nothing can help my misery now."

Caroline felt sickened when she glanced at the date of the next entry. "Almost seven months," she thought, "seven months with almost no emotional support. How did she get through those months? I just don't have that kind of courage; what could possibly give anyone that kind of courage?" Caroline glanced at the next entry and murmured, "at least she did eventually continue," as she started reading.

January 1, 1891
"I cannot imagine why I am picking up this journal and writing in it again. I guess it is because I have no one to talk to. Poor mother has listened to me for such a long time, and I do not want John to know how desperate I feel.

"The new year has begun, but we seem to be mired in the past. Our social situation is worse than ever. Father has paid the coachman to lie and say that he made up the whole story, but no one believes the coachman's lies. They believe his original story. Once again, deceit has not served us well. To reveal the entire truth would free me from some of the scorn that I now endure as Charlestonians would understand that I was victimized by my father's actions twenty years ago. But I cannot defend myself because it would worsen the plight of my child.

"It is a dark, rainy time here in Charleston, a colder winter than we are accustomed to, or so it seems to me. Perhaps it is just the state of my mind and spirit. I stay very much at home now. And given the bad weather, I am not even able to go out into the garden. I am big with child, but do not expect the birth for another six weeks. Mother encourages me to rest and keep a serene spirit as much as I possibly can. She comes to visit me daily and sometimes takes me over to Bradford House to give me a change of scenery. She and Father are very much at odds with each other, so she stays here in town.

"How I would love to go out to the countryside to be away from the prying, gossiping people here. How I would love to give birth to my child in the serenity of the countryside where there are no judgmental faces or pointing fingers! I cannot leave the city, however, until after the birth, because to do so would be to admit to society that I have reason to hide myself away; and I have no reason to hide! I may not be able to go out much now because of my condition, but when I do go out, I shall hold my head high. I am John Kendall's wife and soon to be the mother of a precious child.

"There are those who say that this child should be stillborn or that both the child and I should die at the birthing. It is hard to believe that people could have such cruelty in their hearts. And it is harder still to forgive them for it. I do not think I shall ever be able to forgive them for the suffering they are causing all of us. The only thing I can think of to be grateful for is that Robert is far away. No, there is more to be thankful for—something very important—

and that is that this crisis has created a bond between John and me that, I think, will never be broken."

"Thank God for John Kendall," Caroline whispered. "And thank God for her mother. Aunt Kathleen is right; I have much more support than Carrie had, but somehow she made it through this horrible time. And apparently it is the difficulty of this time that created the strong marriage that she and John ended up with. I wish David and I were using our difficulties to draw closer; how can I make that happen? I guess I can't until he wants the same thing, but will he ever want it?" She sighed and turned back to the journal.

January 3, 1891
"My time is near. The birth of my child is only days off, and I am afraid. I think my fear is natural. Mother assures me that it is, for all childbirth places the child's life and the mother's life in danger. How I wish that my child was my husband's, a child produced from our love. The unnaturalness of all that has occurred in the last nine months has totally disrupted the serenity of my spirit, and I find myself in a state of confusion and anger. I am still angry with my father. I know that I must choose to forgive him and that forgiveness is an act of will. I try to make that act of will everyday, but I know in my heart that I still have not forgiven him. I am also angry with myself for disobeying my father and eloping with Robert.

"I feel that my present pain is a just punishment for what I have done, but I totally reject the idea that my child should suffer from my bad choice. I do not understand a God who allows innocents to suffer from the wrongdoing of others. I had hoped that in all these months of thought and prayer and counsel from my mother and John that I would have resolved some of these issues by now. But I still find myself asking God, 'Why do you allow the innocent to suffer?' And even though it seems especially selfish of me, I find myself angrily demanding of him, 'why have you allowed this to happen to me? I have never been an immoral person. I have always loved You, God. Why have you allowed this to happen to me?' Part of me thinks that I must deserve this punishment, that I'm unworthy because of my sin, but part of me feels that the punishment is entirely out of proportion to my sin and that God is not being just to me. Why am I singled out for this dreadful situation while others who have lived immorally are allowed to live in happiness in spite of their sins?"

Caroline lowered the journal. "She's asking the same questions that Aunt Kathleen asked when Allison was killed and the same questions that I am asking right now. Why should my baby come into this world unwanted by its father, perhaps required to live its life knowing it is unloved by its father? I'm the one who lied to him; my baby is innocent. Why does God allow these things to happen this way? Aunt Kathleen finally found some peace in the fact that God creates us with choice and that having the ability to choose is worth the pain resulting from bad choices. I don't know what I think about that." She picked up the journal again.

"My personal pain has truly softened my heart for the suffering of others around me! All my life I have been concerned about the underdogs of our society, particularly the ex-slaves. The war did not free them, not really. They have been despised and brutally used, and I have watched their suffering with great anguish. I have often wondered how God could allow such suffering for these people simply because of the color of their skin or their lack of education or any other reason society determines. Now I feel their pain and suffering even more intently. They do not deserve the treatment they have received. In most cases they are more godly than those whom God allows to mistreat them. I find there is a new and deeper bond between me and such people. I now am an outcast of society, and I feel worthless as a result of the behavior of others toward me. I am considered a scarlet woman, and were my maiden name not Bradford, I fear that John would lose his job. Sometimes I wish he would be dismissed. Then we could go elsewhere to live. At other times, I am infuriated by society's response, and I am determined to stay and fight because the fight is for more than my child. The fight is for all of these thousands of good, but outcast people around me."

"I see the worry in John's eyes, but I also see a strength in him that I have never seen in another man. I need his kind of strength now, so last evening I asked him how I could learn to be as strong as he is. He simply replied, 'Strength is the courage to love in spite of all obstacles, and whether you know it or not, you have that kind of strength, Carrie.' I hope he is right.

"Mother has incredible strength too. She insists that God will keep His promise and make good things out of bad things. I do not see how she could possibly think that or how it can possibly come about that way, but she has walked this road ahead of me. She has known of my father's infidelity all the years of her marriage. At this point, I can only stand on my mother's faith, for my own faith is so shaky. It is hard, indeed, to face childbirth without the reassurance of my faith.

"I am so keenly aware of the possibility that my child may be disfigured or crippled in some way because of my close family relationship to its father. A year ago I would have said that God would never allow such a thing to happen to an innocent child. But now I believe He would. I want to throw myself at the feet of God and beg Him to bring my child forth in a healthy state, unmarked by my mistakes or those of my father, but how can I beg God for anything when I do not think that He values me enough to hear my prayer? Mother says I must relinquish myself and my child to God, and depend on Him. But how can I do this when I cannot understand what God has allowed to happen so far?"

January 4, 1891

"My child was born early this morning and though I am weak from the delivery and the emotional reaction I had to it, I must write down the wisdom I have heard from my mother's lips this day, so that I can cling to it for the rest of my life. My labor was easy for a first birth, and much quicker, I am told, than is normal. I gave birth to a boy, but when the doctor showed me my son, I saw that his left foot was deformed. I cried out, 'Oh, God, no!

Punish me for my sin. Do not punish my innocent child.' I became hysterical at the thought that my child would suffer all his life because I had married Robert. I shall be eternally grateful that my mother was present, for she took immediate and decisive action. She shook me roughly by the shoulders and spoke to me in the sternest voice I have ever heard from anyone.

"'Carrie, stop this at once!' she commanded. I was so startled by her tone and her actions that I stopped sobbing and stared into her eyes. 'Look at your child.' She held the baby up for me to see. 'Look at him. He is perfectly formed except for his left foot. He has one fault in the world's eyes—a malformed left foot. Will you, his mother, condemn him to a life of suffering?'

"'No,' I exclaimed. 'Of course not!'

"'Do you think he is worthless, Carrie, unworthy of your love because his foot is deformed?'

"'Mother, how can you ask me such a question?' I was becoming angry with her.

"'Because, Carrie, you are insisting that God, who is love itself, is rejecting you and punishing you for one mistake. Do you not think that God can be at least as loving toward you, His child, as you are toward your child?'

"I broke into tears again, but they were much quieter as I saw the truth for the first time in all these months. I would never reject my child for one fault nor cause it suffering. I would not reject my child for a million faults. How could I have thought that God had rejected me? People had rejected me, but God had kept me and my child safe, and now He had placed my child in this world for me to protect and love. I reached out my arms, and Mother put my baby boy into them. I knew with a certainty that my feelings for him were like God's feelings for me.

"God's ways are still a great mystery to me, but tonight I feel much more at peace with God than I have in nine months. I believe that a new door of understanding has been opened to me, and I need only to walk faithfully and patiently through it toward greater security with God's ways. Security with God's ways is what I need, not understanding. No one understands God. I see that now. How could I ever have thought I could—or should—understand God? I can only trust Him with my life."

"God loves us," Caroline said as if it were a completely new idea that she was the first to discover, "He loves us in spite of our imperfections, our bad decisions. He love me in spite of my superficial values and my lying to David. He loves me so much He actually gives me choice. And I took my choice and used it badly when I lied to David. But Carrie's mother is right; God loves us even in our mistakes, and He can make something good out of our mistakes. I see that in Aunt Kathleen's life. I see that, through the pilot's mistake which caused the death of Allison, God increased Aunt Kathleen's spirituality, and she started helping others here in Charleston and she's helping me now. And going even further back in our family, Aunt Kathleen is who she is because her mother had to endure the results of her father's deceit."

January 12, 1891

"My son is thriving, and we have baptized him. It was difficult to choose a name for him. John insisted that he wanted the boy to be named after him, but I felt that he was merely being generous and that in his heart, he preferred to wait until he had a son of his own. My father insisted that for the sake of appearances my son must be named Bradford, but I do not want my son to carry the Bradford name or to be part of the legacy that my father has created. I was in quite a quandary about what name to give my son until the day before the baptism. On that day my mother brought over the exquisite baptismal gown that she had made over twenty years ago for my baptism. As we prepared it for the ceremony, she suddenly looked at me and asked, 'Is there any possibility that you and John would consider naming your child after my side of the family? I know it is selfish of me to ask, but I would dearly love it if you would name your child Patrick Fitzgerald Kendall.'

"'After your father?' I asked.

"'Yes. As you know, dear, my parents died when I was a very small child, and the only close family I had left was my Aunt Verité, who raised me. I would dearly love to think that the name Patrick Fitzgerald would not totally disappear from my family.'

"I knew from the smoothness of Mother's tone that she had given much thought to the difficulty of naming my son and had come up with a family name we could all be comfortable with.

"'I will speak to John about it,' I agreed. And the next day at the church, with only my mother and father and John and I present, my son was baptized Patrick Fitzgerald Kendall. It was not the festive occasion that a new mother dreams of, but I am counting my blessings that things have turned out as well as they have. And now that my baby is here, for some reason I cannot explain, I care very little what people are saying about me. I care only for the future of my child and, of course, for my husband, John, who has stood so faithfully by my side through this whole ordeal.

"As we were leaving the sanctuary, John stopped in the foyer and insisted that he wanted to carry the baby outside. I placed my son in my husband's arms—grateful that he was so eager to make this public profession that my child is his, for I have no doubt that while Charlestonians would not attend the baptism, they were watching.

"Now I look forward to a quiet life of raising my son and supporting my husband in his professorship. I pray daily that I will grow to love John Kendall more and that at the appropriate time, we will establish the intimacy that a married couple should have. I want Patrick to have brothers and sisters and John to have sons and daughters that are totally his own.

"Spring will begin in Charleston in another six weeks, and while it has been a long, dark period of suffering and waiting, I believe that the birth of Patrick and the new bond that I feel with John will make the spring magnificent. I plan to live each day, caring for my family, noticing my many blessings, and seeking to aid those around me who are suffering. I have learned a difficult, but vastly important lesson. Life does not deal out to us what we deserve. Thus, when I look at unfortunate people around me, I must remember that they may very well not have created their own misfortune. They may very well be the victims of other people's wrong decisions. I am sure that reaching out to help the less fortunate of this city will encourage Charlestonians to ostracize me even more, but I do not care.

"From the moment I learned that Robert is my father's son and found myself cast into a seemingly bottomless pit of deceit and despair, I have wondered how to stop the destructive cycle of self-ishness that Father began. I now know the answer. I have looked squarely at the self-serving lies of the past and the grasping for material wealth at any costs, and I have chosen not to continue the lies or to make material comforts my primary goal. I will not con-tinue my father's pattern of life. Thanks be to God I have found the courage to insist that the false values stop here with me."

"The courage to insist that the false values stop here with me," Caroline repeated the last lines of her great-grandmother's journal entry aloud. "Courage—there's the key element. After you know what's wrong, you have to have the courage to make it stop by taking control of yourself. But oh! It is so much easier to keep moaning about what others have done to you, about what others are doing to you. It is so much easier than changing yourself. So much easier! For the most part that's what I've been doing, but my life will stay right where it is if I don't find the courage to change me. I know David is hiding something, but I can't make him talk about it. I can't make him do anything, but I can make myself change. I can quit whining and start acting, but where do I find the courage I need?"

Caroline absent-mindedly stroked her enlarged stomach, as she thought. Finally the moment came when her thoughts became connected to the action of her hand. She looked down at her stomach and thought of her unborn child; in an instant she recognized the wellspring of her courage. "Love," she whispered. "Love," she spoke more emphatically. "Love is the source of my courage; my love for you, my child, and God's love for us both. He will show me the way, and He will make me able to see it. I will believe that, and I will watch for His way with all my might. I can do it, my precious child, for love of you. John Kendall was right: strength is the courage to love in spite of all obstacles. I can do that."

*   *   *

"Book me a flight to Tokyo for tomorrow evening," David ordered his secretary as soon as he returned to his office.

"Yes, sir, but before I do, you may want to talk to Stefan. He called an hour ago and said he needs you to come to Zurich."

"Zurich?" Startled, David stopped reading the memo in his hand and finally made eye contact with her. "Don't you mean Geneva?" Before she could answer, he was already working to calm his nerves by assuring himself, I'm not going to Zurich. I don't care what Stefan needs. I'll never go to Zurich again. An image of a gleaming, white room flashed through his brain, and he struggled not to shudder.

"Stefan said Zurich, Mr. Randolph."

"You're mistaken!" David responded far too curtly. "Stefan handles Zurich. Call him and tell him—no, just get him on the line. I'll tell him."

As soon as she left the room, David sprang from his chair and paced. He tried to think of the Tokyo market and the collapsing Japanese economy, but the image of the white room had taken his brain captive. Finally he stopped at the window and stared at the building across the street, but its white awning sent his mind back to the white room, and he remembered what he most wanted to forget. The white room was not empty. A woman was huddled in the corner, her back to him. He approached her, and at the sound of his steps, she turned and looked up at him out of Danielle's eyes—

"Stefan is on line one, sir," his secretary interrupted his thoughts.

Unspeakably grateful, David welcomed the interruption and took the call. "Stefan, what's this about—" he couldn't even say the word, Zurich— "what's going on? What's the problem?"

"I can't get the loan through, David. The Japanese stock market has caused the bankers here to draw back from Pacific Rim investments."

"Offer them more collateral."

"They won't touch it, David. They want to see you."

David's heart pounded as his brain yelled, No! He placed his hand over the receiver and took a deep breath. "Tell them I'm on my way to Tokyo tomorrow. I want some first-hand information. Better for all of us."

"They'll like that. I'll tell them and wait to hear from you."

"Good." David hung up the phone and buried his head in his hands. I can't come unglued. I can't! First the past just kept coming up in my dreams, but now it's taking over my thoughts in the middle of the business day. I've got to stay in control. Remember what happened to Danielle because I didn't control things. Besides, Caroline will never forgive me—especially not now. Not after I came down so hard on her for lying to me, for getting pregnant. I've got to control things this time—can't mess up like I did before. If I hadn't been so weak before, I wouldn't have this hell to live with now.

A light tap on the door made David jerk his head up before his secretary entered. "Everyone's assembled in the board room, sir."

"Right," David answered sharply although at that moment he had no idea who "everyone" was or why they were waiting for him. "Did you get my Tokyo reservation?" he demanded to cover his confusion.

"No, sir, not yet."

"Well, get to it," he dismissed her as he stared blindly at the memo in front of him. How did my life get so messed up, he asked himself as soon as she had left. Why do I keep asking the same question when I know the answer? I'm in this mess because I lost control of things. I didn't act like a man. Well, I won't do that again. He forced himself to focus on the memo. Fortunately it was the agenda for the meeting. He snatched it up, straightened his tie, adopted a composed look, and strode from the room.

"Call my housekeeper and tell her I'll be dining at home tonight," David ordered his secretary as soon as he returned from the meeting which, because of the financial crisis in Japan, had

lasted twice as long as anticipated. "And call me a cab." He continued on into his office and began gathering papers and stuffing
them into his briefcase. *The sooner I get away from here, the better,* he thought. *I could hardly concentrate in that meeting. I've
got to have some space to push the past back where it belongs.* He
turned to leave his office, stopping before he reached the door to
adopt the body language of a composed man.

"Stefan called again from Zurich—" his secretary began.

"And?" David demanded without letting her finish.

"He said the banks would await your call after you return from
Tokyo." She stared at him, obviously aware that something was
wrong with him. His mind was flooded with profanity, so he dared
not open his mouth. He gave her a curt nod in reply and proceeded past her.

"And your flight to Tokyo leaves at 7:00 tomorrow evening,"
she called after him.

A good, quiet meal and a sound sleep, he thought as he hurried to the taxi. *That's what I need. All these ghosts from the past
will just have to get back in their graves. I have no time for such
nonsense.*

As David entered the dining room of his London townhouse,
Mrs. Watson began profuse apologies, "I'm so sorry, sir. Dinner
won't be ready for an hour. I wasn't expecting you, sir. I'm just
setting the table now." Suddenly she snapped a folded, white linen
tablecloth and made it sail across the table. David jumped at the
sight of the large expanse of white cloth. "Are you all right, sir?"

"Certainly," he turned and walked toward his study, resolved
to break his iron-clad rule never to drink when he was stressed. He
poured himself a glass of Scotch, sat down at his desk, and slowly
sipped it as he intentionally forced himself to focus on the present
moment. He glanced around the room and took comfort in its
elegant coziness. A fire crackled in the fireplace, and its light made
the ruby-red Persian rug glow. A few moments later he opened the
top desk drawer to find paper to make notes for his impending
trip. When he tried to close the drawer, it would not slide shut.

His frustration boiled to the surface again, and he muttered an oath as he jerked the drawer from the desk. "Just as I thought, a piece of paper jamming up the works," he muttered as he snatched the crumpled paper out. Although it was no more than a blank sheet of his own stationery, it took complete control of his mind and cast him 25 years back in time.

"Don't call, Danielle," he heard his 26-year-old voice plead with his wife to put down the phone she had snatched up. "Just leave it alone. I'm sure it has nothing to do with us. Please, don't call."

"Something is wrong, David. I feel it," she insisted as she waved a crumpled paper at him. "This is a bill from a sanitarium in a town outside Zurich."

"So it's an old bill, just a piece of paper caught behind a drawer in your father's desk. Leave it alone, Danielle. Just put the contract in the drawer like I promised your father I would. And stick that old bill in the drawer too. It's none of our business."

"It *is* my business, and it's not an old bill. It's only three months old. Mother died in that town, and I want to know why Daddy is being billed from a sanitarium there."

"Was she ever in that sanitarium?"

"No, I told you. She died. You know what happened. She took an overdose and—"

"Please, Danielle, don't upset yourself by going back over all that past tragedy. Think of the baby; you can't afford to upset yourself now."

"I am thinking of the baby. Do you think I can have any peace if I don't check this out?"

"Then let me handle it. I'll call for you."

"When?"

"First thing tomorrow morning."

"I can't wait that long." She began dialing.

There was a soft knock on the door, and as David pulled his thoughts back from the past, Mrs. Watson entered with a tray. "I thought you might like some hors d'oevres, sir, just to tide you over until dinner. I always say a hungry man can't relax properly."

"Yes," David rubbed his eyes and tried to concentrate, "yes, Mrs. Watson. Relaxation is what I need. Been a long day."

She set the tray on a cocktail table and beckoned him toward the couch to enjoy the hors d'oevres. "I hope you don't mind my saying so, sir, but you look kind of upset. Why don't you come on over here and leave that desk behind you. You've worked enough."

"Yes, that's what I must do. I must leave it all behind me."

Mrs. Watson looked puzzled, started to speak, then thought better of it and obviously changed the direction of her comments. "Let me pour you another drink, sir," she offered as David threw the crumpled paper into the wastebasket and walked to the couch.

"No thanks."

"Just give me another half hour, and I'll have your dinner ready. You just relax," she encouraged as she left the room.

David took his shoes off and stretched out on the couch. Caroline in Charleston, he thought, that's what I'll think about. I can just see her sitting on the piazza staring at the harbor. And Aunt Kathleen working in her rose garden. Seems like a million miles away—another planet—another time—so far away. David drifted into sleep.

He walked out onto the piazza to look for Caroline, and he saw her with her chair turned away from him, turned to face the harbor. Her mass of auburn hair was piled up on top of her head, and flickering rays of sunshine glinted on it. "Caroline," he murmured as a great peace settled over him. He walked down the long piazza toward her. The bright sun softened the colors of the harbor and gardens but made the massive pillars gleam with inviting warmth. "Caroline," he called louder, and she turned her regal head, saw him, smiled and cried joyfully, "Oh David! You're here; now everything is perfect." She stood and began to walk toward him, her flowing dressing gown swirling around her ankles, her left hand resting on her protruding stomach, protecting the child she carried, his child.

"You look beautiful!" David called down the piazza. He walked briskly toward her, but no matter how quickly he walked, he came no closer to her. The piazza had never seemed so long before.

Slowly Caroline raised her right hand, and David saw that she held a phone in it. "I must make a phone call," she said.

"No, not now," he insisted. "I'm here. It can wait."

"Zurich can't wait, David."

Terror seized him when he heard Caroline utter the word "Zurich." "No!" he yelled. "Stop! You don't know what you're doing."

The whole world was reduced to slow motion as he tried to reach her. Caroline began punching the numbers on the phone and turning away from David as he tried to run toward her. He was panting with exertion, but no matter how hard he strained, he couldn't close the gap between them.

"Bookkeeping, please," he heard Caroline say. "Yes, I'll wait."

"No, Caroline!" he yelled at her. "Don't do it. Don't!" He ran faster, but he came no closer to her.

With maddening slowness, she turned to look at him. "I have to know, David," she said calmly, stringing each syllable out. "I have to know, and you won't tell me." She turned her attention back to the phone. "Hello, are you the bookkeeper? Yes, good. I'm calling regarding a bill sent to Mr. DuBois of Seattle, Washington. I think there's been a mistake. Mr. DuBois doesn't know anyone at your sanitarium." Caroline paused and listened. Still running, David watched as she trembled and staggered against the railing, obviously in great distress.

Finally he reached her and helped her into the chair as she mumbled into the phone, "Sorry, my mistake."

Her face buried in her hands, she shook uncontrollably as David fell to his knees in front of her. "Honey, please, take it easy," he begged. "Try to calm yourself."

"You knew!" Caroline cried. "All this time you knew!"

"You have to understand," he tried to put his arms around her, "Please listen to me!"

"No!" Caroline screamed as she pulled away from him. Then

she lowered her hands from her face, and David found himself confronted by a furious Danielle.

Desperately confused, David drew back and stared wildly around. The sunshine grayed as the gleaming white house turned to walnut paneling, and he realized he was in his father-in-law's library in Seattle.

"Where's Daddy?" Danielle demanded.

"He's in Vancouver."

"I want to talk to him. Now, David! Now!"

"Let me help you—"

"You can't. Daddy has been paying for the sanitarium to care for a woman named Madame Pontellier."

"So? Maybe she's a friend. I'm sure there's an explanation—"

"Mother's maiden name was Pontellier, David!"

"Then this must be a relative of your mother's."

"Who entered the sanitarium 12 years ago? In October? David, that's when Mother died."

David's mind leapt to the worst possible conclusion, just as he feared Danielle's had.

"Now, wait a minute," David desperately fought for time to control his own wild imaginings and to find a way to calm Danielle. "Let's not forget the facts. There is some reality to hang onto here. I know it's painful, honey, but your mother did die. You know that's true. You found her after—"

"After she took the pills. You might as well say it."

"You're right, honey. We might as well say it because it's history. Painful history, but history just the same."

"How do I know for sure, David? I have to know!"

"Of course you do." David folded her in his arms and said as gently as he could, "You know because you saw her, Honey. You saw the truth. It's awful, I know, but it's the truth. You saw her when you found her, and there was a funeral, wasn't there?"

"Yes, of course there was."

"And you saw her during the funeral, didn't you?"

Danielle drew back from his arms before replying, "No, the coffin was closed." Her eyes were enormous, brown reflections of dread as she stared up at David, silently begging him to make things all right again.

"That's not unusual, honey. The family often wants it that way. I'm sure you saw her after they—after they prepared her for the funeral. You had some private time with her then, didn't you? You know, to say good-bye."

"No, I just saw her on the bed with all the empty pill bottles, and I screamed, and Daddy came and called for help, and one of the maids took me away. Then Daddy came back from the hospital—I guess it was the hospital—and said she was dead."

"Okay. Now there's the truth. She took the pills; they obviously tried to save her, but they couldn't. Your father came to tell you the painful news. Danielle, your father would never lie about such a thing. It would be unspeakable."

"But who is Madame Pontellier?"

"I don't know, but I'm sure there's a reasonable explanation."

"I'm going to Zurich!" Danielle wrenched herself from David's arms and turned to go.

"No, honey, listen to me." He caught her arm and forced her to stop. "You just need to talk to your father."

"I have to see for myself; I'm going to Zurich."

"No, Danielle! No! You can't go to Zurich. You mustn't! I won't let you." He threw both of his arms around her to keep her from bolting from the room, but she melted into nothingness in his arms. Wildly he stared around the room, desperate to find her. She was walking out the door of the library. "Wait, Danielle, wait!" he shouted as he tried to follow her. Once again his world had turned into slow motion. His muscles churned, struggling to move him ahead, fighting for every inch of space he could gain. Finally he reached the door and slowly sailed through. On the other side, the warm sun of Charleston temporarily blinded him. He stopped, totally confused by the change in location. He closed his eyes and shook his head to clear it, but when he opened his eyes again, he saw Caroline standing at the end of the piazza turned to face him. She stood tall and straight, her chin in the air. She was the perfect portrait of the infuriated southern lady, and he knew that when she finally chose to speak, her words would be few, cool and totally intimidating.

He stopped and waited, a condemned criminal before the judge who would pass sentence on him.

"You have deceived me, David, to protect your adolescent ego. You are a failure. Your presence is no longer needed here." She turned her back on him.

"Caroline! No, wait!" David struggled toward her.

Suddenly he began to fall, and after he landed, he opened his eyes and realized that he was face down on a plush, ruby-red Persian rug. There was a fire in the fireplace; he was alone in his London study.

NINE

By the time Caroline had finished reading Carrie's journal and drawn her conclusions from it, the sky had finally lightened. As Caroline left the bed, she resolved, I'll call David again this morning. I don't know exactly what I'm going to say, but I want to talk to him. It's imperative that we keep talking regardless of what's going on with him. And then, for the rest of the day, well, I have a feeling that Aunt Kathleen and I will be working on the new garden plans. Strange, that sounds wonderful. A year ago I would never have wanted to work on any garden, but now a quiet day with Aunt Kathleen, looking for plants or arranging them in the garden— that sounds like heaven on earth. The only thing that could make it better would be to be at peace with David and to see my baby safely delivered, perhaps even playing in that garden. Now there's a wonderful thought! And I'm determined to concentrate on positive things. Well, I guess I better get dressed and get on the phone and see if I can locate David.

She walked barefoot across the warm boards of the wide, old, pine floor and opened the shutters that covered the French doors. The sunshine swept across her whole body with a welcoming warmth. She put up her hand to shade her eyes a bit, so she could look out into the garden. Far out toward the roses, as she expected, she saw Aunt Kathleen sitting with her Bible in her lap. From where Caroline stood, Aunt Kathleen appeared to be just staring at one blossom, deep in some kind of thought. But Caroline's experience with her great aunt told her that Aunt Kathleen was praying. "I wish I could do that," Caroline whispered. "I wish I could get up in the morning and say even a short prayer. It seems to give Aunt Kathleen such strength, and how I would love to have that strength!" She sighed and turned back toward the room.

Half an hour later Caroline joined her great aunt in the dining room. "Good morning, dear," Aunt Kathleen called from her chair at the dining room table. "How did you sleep?"

"Fairly well," Caroline chose her words carefully rather than upset her aunt. "I had a lot on my mind, so I woke up early and finished reading Carrie's journal."

"Was it helpful?"

"Yes, Aunt Kathleen, it was. There's still a great deal to think about concerning what we talked about yesterday as well as what's in her journal, but I feel more in control of things, especially myself."

"Well, good. After breakfast, we'll get out and do something interesting, as long as you're feeling well."

"I feel wonderful. Don't worry about me. I'm ready for anything."

"As you can see, Betsy has decided that we are having breakfast in the dining room," Aunt Kathleen cast a look over Caroline's shoulder at Betsy who was entering the room, "although I found the garden to be perfectly delightful and thought perhaps we might breakfast on the lower piazza."

"It be too cold on that lower piazza," Betsy declared. "It still in the shade. You was sitting out in a spot of sun in that garden of yours. Even so, you should have had a coat on."

Betsy put the tray of breakfast food down on the buffet.

"One of these days, Betsy," Aunt Kathleen said. "It is going to become too cool, and I will have to stay indoors more, but I shall

not give up my garden until I absolutely have to." With that proc-
lamation, she turned back to Caroline. "Are you hungry, dear?"

"Starving," Caroline answered as she seated herself.

"Well at least this is one time in your life when you can eat as
much as you like without having to make any apologies. As the old
saying goes, you're eating for two, dear."

"I think I'm eating for four, Aunt Kathleen, and I'm afraid I'm
going to hate myself after the baby is born."

"After the baby is born will be soon enough to worry about
that. You just do what your doctor tells you, and I'm sure he's
telling you to get plenty of food and rest."

"Yes, he is," Caroline looked up as Betsy put a plate of food in
front of her, "and Betsy is keeping me well fed. What about you,
Aunt Kathleen, did you sleep well?"

"I was a bit wakeful, off and on during the night," Aunt
Kathleen admitted. "But that's to be expected at my age, I think,
and I figure if I'm going to be awakened occasionally, I might as
well spend the time doing something useful."

Betsy abruptly demanded, "Does you need anything else?"

"No, Betsy, I think we have everything we need. Thank you
again." Betsy took her cue and left. "I'm glad you slept well,
Caroline. I was afraid I might have worn you out yesterday."

"We did visit quite a few shops," Caroline agreed, "but I
enjoyed it. There are so many darling specialty boutiques here. I
love the way they reproduce the old styles. I know my baby can't
wear batiste and lace all the time, but some of its clothes should be
more than basic cotton knits."

"Absolutely," Aunt Kathleen agreed. "What shall we do
today?"

"The way you ask that makes me think you already have a plan."

Aunt Kathleen smiled mischievously, "It has occurred to me
that we might go check out the nurseries. I am eager to get started
on replacing that dead part of the garden."

"Count me in," Caroline replied as she eagerly consumed her
breakfast. "That is, if you can drag me away from this food. I feel
like eating all day."

"Well, take your time, dear, and have as much as you want."

"When I get back to Dallas," Caroline said between bites, "I'm going to take a serious look at the garden around our house. I've always just left it up to the gardener, but I think he does rather unimaginative things. Of course, I didn't realize they were unimaginative until I started talking about gardening with you, Aunt Kathleen. Now you've really sparked my interest in plants, and I think, I'll take up gardening as a hobby."

"It would be good for you, dear. Gardening is good for everybody."

"I don't think David would agree with you," Caroline laughed. "I doubt David has ever actually touched the soil."

"Well, he's not too old to begin," Kathleen joined in Caroline's laughter.

"That's true, if we can get him back to Texas," Caroline said a little more soberly, "and keep him there long enough to do any gardening."

"I think David is going to do a lot of changing after the baby comes. Maybe not instantly, but that man's going to become more of a homebody. You mark my words. He's going to want to be at home. And from what I hear about technology these days, he ought to be able to run that business from Dallas, at least a good bit of the time."

"I'm sure he could," Caroline said sadly, "if he wanted to, but I don't want to think about that today. It's so beautiful outside, and the idea of shopping for plants sounds like a wonderful activity for the day. There is one thing I wanted to ask you, Aunt Kathleen."

"What's that, dear?"

"This sounds like such a stupid thing to ask. I don't know why I don't know the answer already. I'm supposed to know the answer. After all, I've been going to church all my life."

"Church?" Aunt Kathleen looked a little startled. "I thought we were talking about gardening."

"Well, we were, but I saw you out in the garden this morning, and I know you were praying. I know you pray every morning, often in the garden."

"And you want to ask about prayer?"

"Well, of course I've prayed a lot of times in my life, but somehow it doesn't seem to produce the same results in me that you have. So I was just wondering if I'm doing it wrong."

Aunt Kathleen took a slow sip of tea and settled the cup back in its saucer before answering. "I don't think there's a wrong way to pray, Caroline, but you may be stopping short of the possibilities of prayer."

"What do you mean?"

"Well, it's been my experience that we often raise children to formalize prayer a great deal. There's certainly nothing wrong with the beautiful prayers that have been written down and oft repeated, but if we stop there, we don't have the personal relationship that our soul really hungers for."

"Well, what should we do, other than say formal prayers?"

"Just talk to God, Caroline, just like you talk to me. Simply tell Him what you're thinking, tell Him what you're feeling—the good and the bad. Tell Him what you think you need and what you want. Tell Him your dreams. Tell Him your sorrows. Tell Him whatever's going on inside of you."

"But doesn't He already know that?"

"Of course He does. You're not telling Him because He's uninformed. You're telling Him because you need to tell Him and you need to know He's listening."

"Why would He listen to me?"

"Because He loves you, dear, without any reservations. He loves you more than you can ever imagine. I know that when things are not going well in your life, it's hard to imagine that God does love you, but we talked about that last night. When things aren't going well in our lives, it isn't God's doing. It's our doing. What a comfort it is to know that we can always talk to Him about it and that He can help us to change or to deal with whatever has happened to us. Don't complicate prayer, Caroline. Just remember that you are talking to God—and He is the Almighty, but He loves you. And He wants you to talk to Him."

"I'll try," Caroline agreed and made her private resolution to pray that evening. After the women had eaten in silence for a few moments, Aunt Kathleen asked, "What do you think David's doing right now?"

"Well, let's see," Caroline turned her head to look at a clock on the mantel. "It's almost 9:00 here, so it's about 5:00 in the afternoon in London. I hope he's coming back to the townhouse. I hope he isn't having one of his business meetings that last until midnight. But even if he is, he often returns to the townhouse about 4:30 to freshen up and have a snack before he goes out again. So I'm going to try to call him after breakfast and see if I can catch him somewhere. Our last conversation ended on a bad note, to say the least, and I don't want to leave things like that."

"I think that's a good idea," Aunt Kathleen agreed. "You and David need to keep talking, even if you're only talking about the weather. In fact, sometimes, dear, it's best to just talk about the weather. Don't make every conversation you have with David a difficult conversation. Sometimes if you give problems a little time, a little space, you both can get a better perspective and come back able to resolve things."

"I hear you, Aunt Kathleen. I won't fuss at him."

Aunt Kathleen laughed. "That's what I'm talking about. Fussing at men has never done much good, Caroline—at least, that's my experience with my husband and my son."

"I think most men would agree," Caroline also laughed. "But it is a great temptation to fuss. This morning, however, I shall just talk about the weather."

"And tell him how much you miss him," Aunt Kathleen added.

"Oh, of course, because I do miss him. And I also plan to tell him how much I love him."

"Good. Then we'll go nurserying and plan that new garden area." Aunt Kathleen lowered her voice and whispered, "And Betsy will have a wonderful morning fussing at us."

"I'm sure she will," Caroline agreed. Finished with her breakfast, Caroline stood up from the table and asked, "Is there a convenient telephone on the first floor of the house, or do I need to go back up to the drawing room?"

"There's a phone right across the hall in the library, and you'll have plenty of privacy there."

"Good, excuse me just a few minutes. I'm going to try to get David on the phone."

"I'll probably be right here discussing future menus with Betsy and when you're finished, we'll get on with our day. In fact, I may try to sneak in another cup of tea."

Caroline went across the hall, but left the door to the library open because she did not want the kind of privacy that would enable her to get into an argument with David. I just want to hear his voice, she thought, and let him know that I'm thinking about him and that I miss him. Nothing heavy. No nagging, as Aunt Kathleen said. Just let him know that I care, and I want to know that he cares. She sighed, sat down at the desk and picked up the telephone, then dialed the appropriate numbers to reach the townhouse in London. As she expected, the housekeeper answered the phone. But much to her joy, the housekeeper said that David was relaxing in the library, waiting for her to prepare dinner.

When Caroline finally heard his voice, he sounded unmistakably upset to her. "Caroline," he demanded. "Is everything okay?"

"Yes, David, everything is fine. I wanted to call you this morning just to hear your voice, and I wanted to tell you that I miss you."

"Don't start that, Caroline."

"I'm not starting anything, David. I'm having a wonderful time here in Charleston. I just wanted you to know that I'm thinking about you and that I love you and that I'm looking forward to seeing you when you come home."

David seemed to be startled by the gentleness in Caroline's voice. "Oh," he finally said. "Well, I'm glad you're having a good time, and I can't say exactly when I'm coming home, but I miss you too. I'm afraid there's a bit of a financial crisis brewing in Japan. I'm not sure how that's going to impact Randolph Industries, so I've been meeting with a lot of my advisors over here and trying to get ready in case there's any kind of collapse in the Japanese market."

Caroline was usually mystified by most of David's business comments. "I don't understand. What has Japan got to do with Randolph Industries?"

David obviously struggled to take the irritation out of his voice. "It's a complex thing, honey, but basically the problem is that Randolph Industries has invested heavily in Japan and other Pacific countries, and if their economies go bad for some reason, then we stand to lose a lot of money."

"Oh," Caroline said. "I guess I didn't know that."

"Well, you really don't know anything about the business, honey, but you don't need to worry about it. That's my arena, and I'll take care of it."

"I'm sure you will, David. I just hope you're taking care of yourself too. You sound kind of tense."

"Well, I'm a little tired. It's been pretty nonstop since I got here. I really don't have a choice at this point. If the Japanese market collapses, we're going to be in a lot of trouble, and I've got to make contingency plans."

"So, do you have more meetings tonight?" Caroline asked anxiously.

"No, I'm going to bed. Tomorrow's a long day—" David couldn't force himself to mention his scheduled flight to Japan the next evening— "we'll see what happens after that." It was obvious to Caroline that David was being evasive, but she bit her tongue so that she wouldn't say more.

"Please just take care of yourself, David, and know that I love you."

"I love you, too, and I want you to have a good time in Charleston, honey, and don't worry about anything."

"You won't believe what we're doing today, David. Aunt Kathleen and I are planning a new garden here."

"Planning a new garden!" David suddenly sounded alarmed. "Caroline, you're not doing anything too physical, are you?"

"Not at all. I promise. Aunt Kathleen wouldn't let me overdo. We're just going plant shopping—you know, wandering leisurely through nurseries."

"Sounds good, enjoy yourself."

"I plan to. Bye now." She held the receiver to her ear a second longer as she listened to David say "Good-bye" from the other side of the Atlantic. Then she replaced the receiver and congratulated herself. "Well done, Caroline. You didn't gripe once." She returned to the dining room door and said to Aunt Kathleen, "I think I'll go back upstairs and change into something more appropriate for nurserying. Can you stand to wait a few more minutes?"

"No problem, dear. I'll just gather up my purse and things."

Caroline hurried to the staircase and began the steep climb. Part of the way up she suddenly bent in half and clutched her stomach. "Oh, dear God!" she cried as she sat down on the narrow stair. Another pain seized her, and this time she screamed, "Aunt Kathleen!"

Aunt Kathleen came hurrying to the foot of the staircase, "Caroline, what's wrong?" She began to climb the stairs to Caroline's side even as she asked.

"I don't know," Caroline gasped. "I just suddenly had these horrible pains. Oh, Aunt Kathleen, here comes another one." She grabbed the banister and clenched it tightly.

"Hold on, Caroline, I'm coming." Aunt Kathleen encouraged her niece as she struggled to reach her. "Betsy! Betsy!"

"I's here, Miz Kathleen," Betsy answered irritably as she came through the door, "and there ain't no need—oh, my Lord have mercy!" She paused just an instant before starting up the stairs.

"No, Betsy," Aunt Kathleen commanded. "Get on the phone and dial 911 and have them send an ambulance here immediately."

"Yes, ma'am," Betsy turned and hurried to the library.

"I've got to lie down," Caroline gasped.

"Do you think you can walk, dear?"

"I've got to. I've got to lie down." Caroline's face was grim with the pain she was feeling.

"Caroline, it would be best to wait for an ambulance—"

"I can't! I've got to lie down. Oh, Aunt Kathleen, I can't lose this baby!"

"Don't even think that way, Caroline," Aunt Kathleen commanded. "Betsy!"

"I's here," Betsy rushed back in.

"We've got to get Caroline down."

"I's coming," Betsy flew up the stairs faster than she had in years. "Now, Miz Kathleen, you get yourself down. I's gonna get Miz Caroline down."

"You'll need help," Aunt Kathleen insisted.

"There ain't room but for one of us to help her, and I's the one," Betsy heroically took charge of the situation. "Now get on down them stairs outta my way, Miz Kathleen. I's got a job to do here."

Aunt Kathleen obeyed.

Slowly Betsy helped Caroline rise from the step, then she slung Caroline's left arm over her own shoulder. "Hold on to that railing, Miz Caroline," she ordered, "We's going down."

Caroline gritted her teeth, and together they took the stairs one-by-one. "We's gonna put her over there on that little couch," Betsy directed Aunt Kathleen who grabbed Caroline's right arm to support her as soon as they reached the last step. "Then we's gonna elevate her legs."

"What's happening?" Caroline cried as soon as they had her lying down. "What's going on, Aunt Kathleen? Why am I having these horrible pains?"

"I don't know, dear." Aunt Kathleen leaned over her and stroked her head. "They may be premature labor pains."

"Now?" Caroline demanded. "But it's two months before the baby's supposed to be born."

"Some babies comes early," Betsy insisted. "You just lay still. That ambulance be on the way. I's gonna get a cold cloth."

"That's a good idea," Aunt Kathleen agreed as Betsy rushed out of the room.

"Oh!" Caroline started moaning again as she grasped Aunt Kathleen's hand.

"Just try to ride the top of the pain, Caroline," Aunt Kathleen said. "I know it hurts horribly, but try to see yourself riding on top of a wave or something."

"Oh, Aunt Kathleen," Caroline gasped. "You don't think

something's wrong with the baby, do you? I don't care about the pain. I can stand the pain; just don't let anything be wrong with the baby. I couldn't stand it if—"

"Caroline, I insist you stay calm. You're not going to do yourself or your baby any good by getting hysterical. I know this is frightening, but help is on the way, and there's no reason to think that the baby's in trouble. Most likely you're just having a premature delivery."

"Premature?" Caroline cried. "Premature means the baby can die!"

"It doesn't have to mean that these days, dear. Now, lie back. Try to relax between pains."

Betsy rushed in with a basin of cold water and some cloths and began to wash Caroline's perspiration-covered face.

"I can't bare to lose this baby," Caroline cried. "I can't stand—"

"We ain't gonna lose this baby," Betsy broke in. "If this baby gonna come now, it don't mean nothing except that God done decided this baby gonna come early. Why them doctors got all kinds of ways to save babies these days."

"Betsy's right," Aunt Kathleen insisted. "Caroline, don't even think such things, just rest between the pains, and know that everything is going to be fine."

"Oh, God!" Caroline cried as she doubled up again in pain.

"Hold on, Caroline. Hold on." Aunt Kathleen gripped her hand. When the pain had passed, Betsy commanded Caroline, "Lie back down. Lie back down and relax every muscle in your body."

"Betsy, where is that ambulance?" Aunt Kathleen demanded.

"I don't know. I'll go out on the piazza and look." Betsy scurried out of the room as Aunt Kathleen continued to put cold cloths on Caroline's forehead.

"Remember, God is still here, dear," Aunt Kathleen comforted. Caroline nodded weakly as she struggled to release the fear inside of her.

Betsy hurried back into the room. "The ambulance just pulled up to the garden gate, Miz. Kathleen. They's coming in with a stretcher now."

"What about a doctor?" Caroline asked. "Oh, why did I leave Dallas?"

"There's no point in even asking such questions now," Aunt Kathleen insisted. "We'll get you to the hospital. There are plenty of doctors there at the hospital."

"But I wanted to have this baby with my own doctor in Dallas."

"Caroline, let's just get this baby here in the best shape we can, if that's what's happening. Don't jump to any conclusions. Many women have false labor, and then it stops, and they go full term, and their babies are born just fine. Don't assume anything now, dear, except that we are going to get you to the hospital, and you and the baby are both going to be fine."

Caroline clutched Aunt Kathleen's hand again as another pain began. "Pray, Aunt Kathleen," she begged. "Please pray."

"Betsy and I are both praying, dear."

"And we ain't gonna stop for a second until you and this baby be just fine," Betsy added. "I's gonna go get those men."

Betsy hurried off. "Hold on, Caroline." Aunt Kathleen put her arms around Caroline and held her tight. "Hold on. It's going to be okay."

Three hours later, Aunt Kathleen once again had her arms around Caroline as she lay in a hospital bed crying.

"Go ahead and cry," Aunt Kathleen encouraged as she stroked her great niece's hair. "But gently, dear. All the hard work is over, now. You have a baby girl."

"But she's in desperate danger," Caroline sobbed.

"She's in danger," Aunt Kathleen agreed, "but she is not beyond help. The pediatrician has assured us that she has a very good chance of surviving and being a normal baby. She's just going to have to survive the last two months of this pregnancy outside of you, in an incubator. But, darling, you've got to remember how far the medical profession has come in dealing with premature births. Even more important, God is still here; He's the one who has brought us this far."

"He ain't gonna leave us or your baby," Betsy encouraged from the other side of the bed.

"But why did He let her be born premature?"

"I don't know, Caroline, and I don't need to know. Neither do you. Just do your part now; don't wrack yourself up, Caroline. You're going to need your strength. That baby's going to need you."

Caroline did not seem to hear a word. "Oh, dear God, I can't stand it if my baby dies," she started sobbing.

Aunt Kathleen held her close and looked across the bed at Betsy, and the glance they exchanged communicated a great deal. Betsy nodded her agreement. Suddenly Aunt Kathleen took Caroline by the shoulders and shook her hard as she hardened her voice, "Caroline, stop that sobbing at once! I forbid you to think of the worst when there is so much hope surrounding you."

Caroline was so startled by her aunt's tone that she suddenly stopped crying.

"Now, lie back on the pillows," Aunt Kathleen commanded, "and relax." Caroline did as she was told. Aunt Kathleen took a deep breath, held Caroline's hand and looked her directly in the eyes. "Here are the realities, young lady. You have given birth to a beautiful little girl. She has some health problems because she has been born prematurely, but she is in the safest possible place she could be. She is in the hands of God, and she is in the hands of a very competent, very skilled staff at this hospital. You are a blessed woman. Your baby is alive. Your baby has a good prognosis for developing normally. It's not going to be easy. It isn't a certainty that your daughter will make it, but her chances are very good. You, Caroline, are going to have to play a very major role in your baby's survival. And you can't do that if you reduce yourself to a sobbing child. Now, take control of yourself. You have a new responsibility in your life—a responsibility much more important than your feelings."

"Yes, Aunt Kathleen," Caroline agreed meekly. "I'll do the best I can."

"Of course you will, dear," Aunt Kathleen lightened her tone. "We're all going to do the best we can for that child."

"What about David?" Caroline asked. "What does he know?"

"I'm not sure, dear. When they took you into the delivery room, I called Marian, and she has called David. I don't know much more than that. I'm sure he's making plans to come to Charleston, and Marian said she's coming. But we have to realize that it's only been about three hours since you had that first pain."

"Has it really?" Caroline asked. "It seems like an eternity."

"I know, dear, but it's actually only been about three hours."

"Does mother know that the baby is born?"

"Oh yes. I called her again as soon as the doctor came out and told me. She knows she has a granddaughter, and I'm sure she's called David and told him. Everybody is doing what everybody needs to do. The doctors and nurses are taking care of the baby. Your mother's on the way, and most importantly, I'm sure David's on the way."

"I wish I could talk to him," Caroline said.

"We can try to call him, if you want to, dear."

"Yes, please."

"There's a phone right here. Now you just lie quietly and tell me the number, and I'll dial it for you, and we'll see if he's left the house yet."

Caroline told her the number and listened as her great aunt spoke to the housekeeper in London. David had already left for the airport, but the housekeeper was obviously promising to reach him if she could. Aunt Kathleen gave the housekeeper the hospital number and Caroline's room number. When she put the phone down, she said to Caroline, "David will call you if the housekeeper can reach him, but he's hurrying to catch the first plane to the states, so all we can do is wait."

"I can't bare to just lie here, Aunt Kathleen. I want to do something for my baby."

"There's nothing you can do now, dear. The doctor's going to come by in a few minutes and update you."

"What did he say right after she was born, Aunt Kathleen? He talked to me then, but I was so confused I don't remember the details."

"He told me that the baby was in good shape considering the

fact that she is eight weeks premature. He said she has weak lungs," Caroline looked frightened, "but he assured me," Aunt Kathleen went on, "that is perfectly normal for a baby at this stage of development. So they have the baby in some kind of safe situation—on a respirator, I'm sure."

"So, her condition is stable?" Caroline asked.

"That's my understanding, dear. Her condition is stable, and the doctor is with her now. He didn't want to leave her to come talk to you until he felt sure that she was safe. So we'll just have to wait."

"Yes," Caroline agreed. "Are you sure they know what they're doing?"

"I's sure," Betsy broke in. "That Sister Angelica, I think she run the place. She come out and she told me in no uncertain terms that everything been taken care of."

"Sister Angelica?" Caroline asked.

"Yes, Miz Caroline. That Sister Angelica, I tell you, she could run the country. We ought to elect her President. She don't take no foolishness off of no one. She's my kind of woman."

"And she's in charge of the unit?" Caroline asked hopefully.

"You better believe it. She gonna be in charge of any place she is. Don't you worry about that baby. She gonna get the very best from that Sister Angelica and everybody else around. I likes that woman."

TEN

By the time David finally settled into the seat of the jet bound for the states, he was actually praying, and for David Randolph, a self-described independent thinker, this was radical behavior indeed. He had long ago given up any belief in God's involvement in his life and had proceeded to structure his attitudes and behaviors to please his appetite for power and pleasure. However, the thought of losing Caroline had jolted him so forcefully into the reality of his own powerlessness that he was engulfed in panic for the first time in two decades. No amount of practicing the mental control mechanisms he had taught himself over the years could hold back the flood of sheer terror that gripped his mind and body. Physically he was actually twitching and felt compelled to wrap his arms around himself in an effort to hold himself in his body. His brain had turned into one of those hideous commercials that verbally and visually assault one with 20 images per second.

God, don't let me go crazy! he pleaded silently. Then being the businessman he was, he tried bargaining with his Creator, I'll change, I promise. I'll use my energy and money to help the poor. I'll start a foundation for orphaned children or the homeless or anybody you say. I'll even scrub toilets and cook food and all that stuff that good people do. I'll do anything, just please don't let Caroline die. She's the most important thing in my life.

Suddenly David remembered the Sunday School lessons of his youth, the teachers' insistence that God was a jealous god who must be placed first, so he quickly revised his last statement. No! I didn't mean that, God. You're the most important thing, of course. Caroline is the most important person, I mean, human being—oh, God, I'm not getting this right. I know I'm not. Forgive me. Help Caroline. Do anything you want with me. I deserve anything you do to me. Just please don't take Caroline away from me. Tears filled David's eyes and began to run down his cheeks. Fiercely he wiped them away.

"Is there anything I can do for you, Mr. Randolph?"

"Yes, get this plane off the ground!" David snapped. "And get me a scotch. Make that a double."

"We've just been cleared for take-off, sir, so I can't serve you anything right now. Perhaps a newspaper would help?" She held out a London Times, and David snatched it from her. He stared at the lead headline as the stewardess hurried away to prepare for take-off. "Japanese Banks Fail" bold black type proclaimed. I'll read this article to get my mind off things, David decided. I'll read the whole paper. Eagerly he began to scan the lead article, but his panic escalated and hit him like an iron fist in the diaphragm. It's not working! What am I going to do? I know. I'll read it slowly, word by word. David began to form each word with his lips in a desperate effort to stop his mind from reeling totally out of control. When that didn't work either, he clamped down on his concentration and began to spell the words to himself, but even intense concentration on single letters would not release him from his terror. Finally he dropped the newspaper, slouched over in defeat and whispered, "Okay. I give up. I won't run anymore. I'll remember the pain, if that's what You want. I'll do anything, just don't take Caroline. Please, God!" Somewhere, far away from his mental location, he heard the roar of the jet engines as they lifted the plane off English soil to return to America. He was finally on his way back to

Caroline, in more ways than he knew. David had finally relinquished control and was ready to allow his memories to surface.

*　*　*

"Danielle, just calm down," Philip DuBois was pleading with his daughter, as David stood helplessly by hoping Philip could reason with her, hoping he had a believable explanation for whatever was going on in Zurich. "Baby, you've got to listen to me. This is not what you think. I know it's suspicious and frightening—"

"Is my mother alive?" Danielle screamed the question at her father. "Just answer that one question. Is my mother alive? Is she?"

"No." He took his daughter by the shoulders, leaned over and peered into her face. "No, your mother is not alive."

"I don't believe you." She wrenched free of him, walked away several steps and turned on him. "You're paying that mental institution to take care of a woman named Mrs. Pontellier. Pontellier was mother's maiden name. Don't you think I know that?"

"Of course you know that. You're not stupid, and neither am I. If I were hiding your mother away, would I use her maiden name? Of course not. The Mrs. Pontellier they told you about is my sister-in-law, Chloe Pontellier. She is the wife of your mother's brother, Jean Pierre. Or rather she was his wife; he died many years ago."

"Why haven't I ever heard of this aunt before now?"

"Danielle, listen to me. Your Uncle Jean Pierre died before you were born, and your Aunt Chloe became mentally ill after his death. Your mother and I tried to help her in every way we could, but finally we had to accept the fact that a compassionate institution was the best place for her. Chloe had totally lost touch with reality, and the doctors insisted she could not be helped, only tenderly cared for. We placed her in an institution in Zurich. We were in Zurich visiting her when your mother died."

"Killed herself," Danielle corrected. "Mother killed herself, Daddy."

"Yes, I know, baby," he murmured sadly, "believe me, I haven't forgotten one moment of that day. In fact, I have often wondered if she took those pills because of Chloe Pontellier. You see, we had just returned from a visit to the institution when your mother— when she—"

"Killed herself."

"Yes."

"Why didn't you and Mother tell me about Aunt Chloe?"

"That's just not the sort of thing you burden a child with, Danielle. Look, baby, you always knew that your mother was having some emotional difficulties. You knew she was under the care of a psychiatrist and had to take pills. You were frightened by all that. I was not about to tell you about your Aunt Chloe. You would have been petrified that something like that would happen to your mother."

"I see," Danielle said as she nodded her head. "You're right. That would have really frightened me."

David finally started breathing more normally. It's going to be okay, he thought. I don't know if it's the truth, but she's buying it.

Philip walked to Danielle and once again put his arms around her. "You do remember hearing your mother talk about her brother Jean Pierre and his wife Chloe, don't you?"

"Yes, but I thought they both died in a car accident before I was born."

"You thought that because that's what your mother and I told you, Danielle. You do see that we couldn't tell a little girl about mental institutions, don't you?"

"Yes, Daddy, it all makes sense now," she smiled sadly up at him, then embraced him briefly before asking, "but why didn't you tell me the truth after I was grown?"

"I could have, and maybe I should have, but I just couldn't see any sense in burdening you with it. Besides, I didn't want to think about it anymore than I had to. It's just too painfully connected to your mother's death. You see, baby, I've always blamed myself for what happened to your mother. I should have forced her to stay away from that sanitarium. There was nothing she could do for Chloe, and I should have forced her to stay away."

"Philip, you did the best you could at the time," David broke in, hoping to turn the conversation to a less dangerous topic. "You know what they say. 'Hindsight is 20/20.'"

"You're right, David," Philip readily agreed, "We can only act in the moment, and I did the best I could at that time. And speaking of acting in the moment, let's put this behind us and think about the happy fact that I'm going to be a grandfather in a few more months. Can we do that, baby?" he asked Danielle. "Can we drop the past and think about taking care of you and my grandchild?"

"But what about Aunt Chloe?"

"I've always taken care of her, Danielle; I always will. Trust me, baby. Trust me to handle this; you don't need to think about it again. Get on with your own life, and give your old man the happiness of seeing you happy. Okay?"

"Okay, Daddy. You're right, of course. It's sad, but if there really isn't anything I can do for Aunt Chloe, then I'll just have to file it away."

"That's what your mother would want you to do. She would want you to take care of yourself and your baby."

Danielle nodded, "I know. I'm sorry I got so mad at you. I should have trusted you, Daddy. I love you very much."

"And I love you more than anything." Philip's eyes filled with tears as he spoke. "There's nothing I wouldn't do for you."

"I know, Daddy. Goodness I'm tired."

"Of course you are," David came to her side and put his arm around her. "This has been an upsetting situation, but it's all settled now. Let's get you upstairs for a nap. Your father's right. You have to think of yourself and our baby. We have nothing but happy times ahead of us." Gently he escorted her toward the door, but as they exited the room, he looked back at Philip's face.

"I knew he was hiding something," David whispered; "I didn't know what, but I just didn't trust him. I should have confronted him privately." David continued to condemn himself silently as the jet raced across the Atlantic, but I took the coward's way out, buried my head in the sand and hoped that Danielle would let it go. I chose to believe what I wanted to believe, so I could do what I wanted to do. And I wanted to go to London to open the new office of Randolph Industries. Dad had finally decided to trust me with something really big, and I wanted to show him that I was tough enough to make it work. So I convinced myself it was safe to leave Danielle, that she believed her father and would spend her days shopping and socializing just as she always had.

Then Philip's frantic call came to me in London; Danielle was on her way to the sanitarium. So I hopped the first plane to Zurich. I caught up with her all right. At the sanitarium. David leaned forward and buried his face in his hands as he remembered the horrors of that scene.

"Danielle, don't do this," David pleaded with her in a corridor of the sanitarium. "Just let it be. Your father has explained everything. Why can't you just believe him?"

"Because he lied, David."

"How do you know that?"

"At first I believed him. I told myself that everything he said made sense, and I really wanted to believe him, David. Or at least part of me did. But part of me just couldn't let go of it, and I didn't know why. Then yesterday a memory suddenly flashed into my mind."

"What?" David demanded. "What memory? Honey, let's go somewhere and talk about this. You're too upset; you're not thinking straight. You've got to think about the baby. No memory is worth endangering our child."

"This one is, David, because I have to know the truth. No matter how ugly it is, I have to know. I will never have peace until I know."

David's mind churned frantically as he grasped at ways to deter Danielle. "At least, tell me about the memory, honey. Let's go back outside, and you tell me what you remembered."

"I'll tell you, David, but I'll tell you here and now, and then I'm going into that room and see the woman my father has kept here. I am going to see for myself because I have to."

David fought for time and information to use to stop her, "The memory, Danielle. Sit down and tell me."

She refused to move. "It's quite simple, David. When Daddy told us that Mother had gone to see Aunt Chloe on the day Mother took the pills and killed herself, something began to gnaw away in the back of my mind. Finally, yesterday I remembered that I spent that entire day with Mother. We left the hotel early that morning and spent the day in the mountains skiing together. You see, Mother had been very depressed, and I heard her psychiatrist say that if someone could just get Mother's mind off herself, she would be better. I thought I could do that, so I begged her to take me skiing. I thought that if she spent the day away from everyday things, up in the beauty of the mountains, she couldn't possibly think about herself. I thought she would enjoy herself and not be depressed."

"So you spent the day skiing? Couldn't she have gone to the sanitarium later?"

"No. It was past dinner time when we got back to the hotel. I remember Daddy was upset with us for staying gone so long, so he told us to take warm baths while he ordered dinner from room service. That's exactly what we did, and after we ate, we went to bed because we were so tired. Daddy went downstairs to play cards. About 1:00 in the morning I woke up from a nightmare and went into my mother's room and found her on the bed with the pills—" Danielle choked up, stopped for a moment, then regained control of herself. "David, she did not go to any sanitarium that day."

"Maybe it was the day before, maybe your father just got his days mixed up, maybe that's why she was depressed the day before you went skiing—"

"Maybe! Maybe! Maybe!" Danielle exploded. "I can't stand another 'maybe.' I want to know. And I can know by going into that room and seeing the woman in there, and I *have* to do it."

"Then I'm going in with you," David insisted. "If going in there is the only way to calm you down, let's do it and get it over with. Can we just walk in?"

"No, we push this button, and the nurse inside let's us in." She walked across the corridor to the door and pushed the button. David hurried to her side, and when the nurse opened the door, he followed her in.

At first David saw no one in the room except the nurse. He was stunned by the fact that the room was beautifully decorated, but that everything in it was white. "It's all white," he whispered.

"White is the only color Mrs. Pontellier is comfortable with," the nurse explained quietly. Then she pointed toward a window draped with sheer white curtains.

David saw a woman, dressed entirely in white, sitting there staring out the window, apparently oblivious to everything around her. Then he watched as Danielle moved across the room, knelt down before the woman and looked up into her face. A sob escaped Danielle's lips, and she buried her face in the woman's lap. The woman was startled and turned her head to look at the nurse. David strode across the room to reach the woman's side, peered down at her face and discovered an aged copy of Danielle looking up at him.

"Mother, mother," Danielle cried, her voice muffled by the folds of her mother's skirt.

"Honey, please—" David reached over to lift Danielle up and hold her.

"She doesn't know me, David! She doesn't even know me. Do something, David!"

David felt totally helpless. He turned to the nurse who rushed over and took Danielle in her arms and kindly stroked her hair. "She knows no one," the woman comforted Danielle in heavily accented English. "She has never known anyone since she came here. I know it is hard for you, but your aunt is not suffering."

"She not my aunt! She's my mother!"

Suddenly Danielle crumpled in the nurse's arms.

"I can serve you a drink now, Mr. Randolph," the flight attendant broke into his thoughts. "Do you still want a double scotch?"

"Never mind," he mumbled. "It doesn't matter anymore."

"Are you sure, sir?"

David nodded.

"We'll be serving dinner soon," the attendant said.

Once again David simply nodded.

After she walked away, David sat, his mind settled in a pool of despondency. His panic was gone because he was mentally surrounded by the past, things that were already settled, things that he had no control over. We lost the baby, he thought. After five months of expectation and hope, we lost our son. Oh God! I was so afraid for Danielle after she lost the baby. I even tried to pray the way Mother had taught me. Do you remember, God? I tried, but all I could hear was Danielle's hysterical cries. No matter what I've done since then, I've heard her cries "My baby is gone! He's dead! I killed him!" I could never make her see it any other way. And now, twenty years later, it's Caroline!

Dad was right about me; I just don't have the strength to take command of things and control them. He saw my weakness when I was a boy, and as hard as he tried to toughen me up, it just didn't work. I learned how to run the business, but I never learned how to take control of people. If only I had asserted myself years ago with Philip DuBois, I might have saved Danielle and my son, but no. I let him convince me that things were better than they were, that things were under control. I can't lie to myself any more. I knew Philip was lying about Danielle's mother the minute he made up that story about his sister-in-law. But did I step in and privately confront him and get the truth out of him? No! So I was totally unprepared to deal with Danielle there in Zurich. Why did I let her go into that room? Why didn't I stop her?

And why didn't I stay in Dallas and keep Caroline at home so she wouldn't be having this baby prematurely? Because I couldn't let go of the past or at least keep the lid on it. I couldn't even keep control of myself! So I did the same thing I've always done; I ran! Why are we even having a baby? I absolutely said no to having kids from the minute I proposed to Caroline. I shouldn't have to live through this nightmare again. All of this could have been avoided if I had just taken control of my own sexuality. Why did I put Caroline in charge of birth control? What was I thinking?

Well this baby is probably dead by now, but I don't have to lose Caroline. I won't make the same mistakes I made with Danielle. The minute I get to that hospital, I'm taking control of Caroline.

I'm getting her out of Charleston, and I'm taking care of her. She's going to be really torn up about losing this baby, and all this spiritual stuff Aunt Kathleen has been drumming into her head is probably going to make her feel really guilty. I'm taking her away from there, and I'm going to see to it that she returns to living the carefree, happy life she had before all this pregnancy stuff began.

Dad may have been right about me, but my life isn't over yet. And he's going to look down from heaven, or wherever he is, and see that I know how to act like a Randolph!

ELEVEN

A little less than an hour later, Caroline suddenly threw the covers back from the bed and painfully stood up. She was through waiting.

"Don't bother to say a word, Aunt Kathleen," she addressed her aunt firmly. "I have no intention of waiting another minute for a doctor or for anyone else to show up in this room and tell me how my baby is. I'm going to see for myself."

A slight smile played around the corners of Aunt Kathleen's mouth as she nodded affirmatively.

"Betsy, get my clothes," Caroline commanded.

"They ain't in very good shape, Miz Caroline."

"I don't care what shape they're in. Bring them over here." Betsy found Caroline's clothes and brought them to the side of the bed. They were stained, but Caroline jerked off the hospital gown she was wearing and began putting them on.

"You can't go out of this room looking like that," Betsy protested.

"My appearance is not going to keep me away from my baby, Betsy. If you're concerned about such things, get me a clean hospital gown over there, and I'll put it on top of my clothes, but nothing is going to keep me from seeing my baby."

Betsy looked at Aunt Kathleen for support, but she received none, "You'd better get the hospital gown, Betsy." Then she addressed Caroline. "Do you feel like walking, dear? Or should we get a wheelchair?"

"I'll walk," Caroline said.

"Then we'll walk with you."

Caroline winced as she took the first steps, but as she started down the hall with Betsy on one side of her and Aunt Kathleen on the other, she put away thoughts of her own pain and let her mind be filled with her anticipation of seeing her first-born child.

Aunt Kathleen spoke with quiet firmness as they proceeded. "Now, Caroline, this is not going to be a pleasant sight for you in many ways, and you need to prepare yourself. Your baby is going to be smaller and weaker than you expect. She is going to have an I.V. and probably some other tubes in her. I don't know exactly what you're going to see, dear, but I know that a premature baby requires a lot of assistance. So prepare yourself, if you possibly can."

"If I can just see that she's breathing, Aunt Kathleen, I'll be fine. I have to know that she's really alive, that no one's keeping some dreadful secret from me."

"Of course you do, dear. It's time for you to see her."

When they reached the ward where the newborns were kept, Caroline knocked on the glass door. A nurse came out and closed the door behind her.

"I'm Mrs. Randolph," Caroline said firmly. "My baby girl was delivered prematurely several hours ago. I want to see her."

"You need to go back to your room, Mrs. Randolph, and wait for the doctor to come to you."

"I have no intention of going back to my room or anywhere else. Furthermore, I am not waiting any longer for the doctor. I want to see my child, and I want to see her now. So let's get the procedure started. What do I need to do?"

"Well, you can't just come in like that."

"I am not going away, nurse."

The nurse sized her up a moment before saying, "Wait here. I'll get the doctor."

"Miz Caroline, there's a chair over here. Why don't you sit down while you wait for the doctor," Betsy suggested.

"I don't plan to wait for the doctor more than a few minutes, Betsy. I have no need to sit down."

"Now, Miz Caroline, you've got to be reasonable—" Betsy started, but Aunt Kathleen interrupted.

"Let Caroline make her own decisions, Betsy."

"No one needs to let me do anything, Aunt Kathleen," Caroline said. "I don't mean to be rude. I love you both, but something has changed in me. I don't plan to be stopped by anyone. I don't understand it, but I feel empowered somehow, and I am going to see my baby."

"You have become a mother, Caroline," Aunt Kathleen smiled as she spoke. "You have become a mother."

"Mrs. Randolph," a man called from the doorway, and Caroline turned toward him.

"Yes, I'm Mrs. Randolph. Are you the doctor taking care of my baby? I want to see her."

"Yes, I'm Dr. Jorgansen, and I have been in charge of your little girl since she was born. Really, Mrs. Randolph, it's too early to see the baby. We are still trying to stabilize her condition."

"Doctor, I'm sure that you want the best for my baby, but this is not going to be a debate. I'm going to see my baby, and I'm going to see her now. I assure you I will do nothing to get in the way of your caring for her, but I'm going to see her."

"Wait a minute," Dr. Jorgansen assumed his best bedside manner. "Now let's just calm down a bit. Of course, you're overwrought, and you're having a perfectly natural reaction considering—"

"You can drop the patronizing tone, Doctor. I am here to see my child. Take me to her."

Startled, Dr. Jorgansen froze for a moment as Caroline glared at him. He decided that there was no point in arguing.

"You'll have to put on a sterile gown," he said.

"Take me to the gown and then take me to my daughter," Caroline commanded.

"I'll have a nurse bring out the proper attire, and then she will bring you back to your daughter. I will meet you there. I hope you're prepared for what you are going to see, Mrs. Randolph. Perhaps we should talk about it for just a moment."

"That would be very reasonable," Aunt Kathleen broke in. "Caroline, take just a moment to listen to the doctor."

"Is she alive?" Caroline demanded. "Is she breathing?"

"Yes, Mrs. Randolph, your daughter is alive. She is breathing, but we have her on a respirator."

"Then, she's having great difficulty breathing?"

"She's having enough difficulty that we don't want to take any chances. So we're going to leave her on the respirator for the first twenty-four hours, and then we will wean her from it. If she does well, we will be able to remove it tomorrow. She also has an I.V. It's taped to her foot, and there is a tube down her throat."

Caroline visibly winced at the image his words were producing in her mind.

"Furthermore," the doctor continued, "You need to realize that your baby is very small. She weighs about three and a half pounds—a few ounces more, actually."

"I want to see her," Caroline insisted. "I have read that even with the most premature babies, it is important for the mother to be there."

"It is," the doctor agreed, "if the mother is emotionally stable enough to handle it. I think you can, Mrs. Randolph, but it won't be easy. I'll order a gown for you and have the nurse bring you in." He turned and walked back through the door. Caroline allowed herself to slump against the door for a moment as tears gathered in her eyes and her throat tightened at the thought of her baby suffering.

"You are strong," Aunt Kathleen assured her. "Caroline, you have never known how tough you are, but you come from tough stock. You are Carrie's great-granddaughter," Aunt Kathleen insisted, and the significance of her statement was not lost on Caroline as she remembered the heroic acts of her great-grandmother's life.

"I'll remember that, Aunt Kathleen." She lifted her chin a bit. "I won't forget." They fell silent a moment, then Caroline added, "This would be a good time for me to practice praying by just talking to God, wouldn't it?"

"The very best time, dear," Aunt Kathleen agreed.

The nurse appeared at the glass door with a sterile gown for Caroline to slip into. Caroline quickly put it on, and the nurse led her back through the doors. She was physically separated from Aunt Kathleen and Betsy, but as she began to pray silently, she felt that they and even greater forces of love were at her side.

"You'll need to wash your hands first," the nurse said and took Caroline to the sink. "Mrs. Randolph, you are going to be visiting your baby quite a few times over the next month or so. It's very important that you have a sterile gown on and that you have your hands clean."

"Of course," Caroline agreed as she carefully washed her hands under the faucet the nurse had turned on. When she had finished, the nurse beckoned her to follow her. They walked just a short distance before facing another set of glass doors.

"Your baby is in here, in the ward for premature babies. Did the doctor tell you what to expect when you saw your little girl?" she asked compassionately.

"He told me," Caroline said simply. "I am ready."

The nurse pushed open the door and guided Caroline over to an incubator that was close to a window. Caroline approached the clear box that held her daughter with both eagerness and apprehension. Holding her breath, she stared through the plastic at a very small, very pathetic-looking creature. She was overwhelmed with a desire to scoop her baby into her arms and run out of the hospital in a frantic attempt to rescue her. But she asserted her reason, clamped down on her emotions and reminded herself that every tube she saw going into the body of her beloved child was somehow nurturing her.

"Breathe, Mrs. Randolph," the nurse said quietly as she reached up and patted Caroline on the shoulder. Caroline looked at her quickly. "Take a deep breath," the nurse said. "Take several deep breaths. This is not easy. You're going to have to learn to be very strong, and part of that means taking care of yourself. Now take a deep breath." Caroline did as the nurse suggested and turned her eyes back to her baby.

"Can I touch her?" she asked.

"Yes, you can. In fact, the more touching you do, the better for her. She needs to know that you're here, that there are people around who care about her."

"Oh, I care!" Caroline exclaimed.

"I know you do. Here, let me show you how you can put your hand into the incubator and touch your baby."

Caroline moved closer to the incubator, and the nurse showed her where to stick her hand through. With no hesitation whatsoever, Caroline stuck her hand through the opening and put her fingers on her child's chest. She ran her fingers along the tiny chest and then, carefully avoiding the tubes around her daughter's face, she reached up to her child's head and stroked the top of her baby's head. She felt the softest hair she had ever felt in her life. And as she stared down at the child through the plastic of the incubator and past all of the tubes, she whispered fiercely, "I love you. I love you."

The doctor approached Caroline and said briskly, "As you can see, she has quite a battle ahead of her, Mrs. Randolph, but I think she has a good chance of making it."

"You mean there's a chance she won't make it?" Caroline demanded as she withdrew her hand from the incubator and faced the doctor.

"She wouldn't be in this unit, Mrs. Randolph, if she wasn't in critical condition."

"I see," Caroline said quietly. "I want everything done that can be done for this child. Do you understand? I want everything done."

"We do everything for every baby, Mrs. Randolph," the doctor insisted. "And, of course, we'll do everything for your baby."

"And I want to know anything and everything I can do," Caroline added.

"For the most part, right now it's a matter of keeping oxygen in her lungs, keeping her from being dehydrated, giving her all the nutrients she needs through the I.V., and waiting. A good bit of what we have to do now is wait."

"Exactly, what are we waiting for?" Caroline asked.

"We're waiting for her to survive the first two days. The first forty-eight hours are critical. And eventually, if she survives the first forty-eight hours, we'll wait to see if she gains weight. She cannot leave this ward until she weighs enough. But first, let's just get through the next forty-eight hours."

Caroline nodded, and the doctor walked away.

"He may seem brusque, Mrs. Randolph," the nurse said gently, "but you see, he has to keep a certain distance from the babies. He can't allow himself to become too attached."

"In case they die," Caroline added as she turned and stared down at her own child.

"Yes, I'm afraid that's the situation."

"My baby is not going to die!"

"We're going to do everything we can, Mrs. Randolph—"

"And it will be enough," Caroline finished the woman's sentence.

"I'll get you a chair, so you can sit next to your baby for a while."

"Thank you." Caroline turned her attention back to her little girl and once again felt an overwhelming urge to touch her. She reached her hand through the incubator opening and stroked her daughter's head. The nurse brought her a chair, and Caroline sat down. When the nurse had moved away to take care of other babies there, Caroline was as alone with her baby as it was possible to be in such a place. She listened to the sound of the respirator, both hating and loving it at the same time. She hated it because it sounded so unnatural, and the thought that her daughter needed it upset her terribly, but she also loved the sound because it meant that her daughter was getting the oxygen she needed. She stared at the tube down the baby's throat and shuddered.

Slowly, but surely, avoiding all the tubes, Caroline tried to touch every inch of her child. "At least she's warm," Caroline thought as she ran her finger over the baby's tiny arms and counted the baby's diminutive fingers. She placed her hand on the baby's tiny chest and took great joy in the thought that it was moving up and down as oxygen came both in and out of the child's lungs. Suddenly, more than anything she had ever wanted in her life, she wanted this little being to breathe and move her chest up and down without the aid of a machine. "Oh, God," she whispered fervently. "Please help her. Please. She's so helpless. I know they're doing everything they can, but in the end, You will have to do it. I know that. Please, please, help her." Caroline withdrew her hand from the incubator for a moment and clasped both of her hands together and stared down at the tiny being she loved so much, her baby who was connected to and seemingly overwhelmed by so much medical equipment. The stress of the day caught up with Caroline, and she began to cry quietly.

I don't want this for you, she thought over and over again as the tears continued to roll down her face. Suddenly, she felt a firm thump on her right shoulder, and she heard a voice whisper brusquely, "I'll see you outside in the hall."

Startled, Caroline looked up into the obviously annoyed face of a nun. "Who are you?" Caroline demanded coldly.

"I am Sister Angelica. I am the head nurse of this neonatal unit, and I want to talk to you outside."

Caroline sensed that there was a great reservoir of love beneath the woman's commanding exterior. She also realized that this woman would be the most informed person in the unit. She winced as she rose from the chair, but she wiped the tears off her face and followed the grim-faced nun outside the glass doors.

"There will be no tears around my babies," Sister Angelica informed her.

"Your babies?" Caroline was startled by the woman's possessiveness.

"My babies. As long as God leaves them here, they are mine, and they will be surrounded by joy."

"But—"

"No arguments, young lady. Those babies are fighting for their lives, and you won't be a hindrance to them. Now, sit down here." She pointed to a chair and Caroline obeyed. "I'm going to give you the facts of life—the real ones." Sister Angelica plopped down onto a chair next to her. "Don't think I don't understand why you're crying, Mrs. Randolph. Every time they bring one of those little souls in here, I want to burst into tears myself. But that won't do the children any good, so I hold my tears till an appropriate time, and that's what you're going to have to do."

"I'll do anything to help my child," Caroline insisted.

"You've got spunk, and I like people with spunk. Some of the women who come in here are basket-cases from the beginning, and they stay that way. You won't be a basket-case. I can see that already, but you're starting out all wrong. Now, here's what you must do. For your own sake, you need to shed those tears. You need to allow yourself to feel anything you feel—and you're going to feel some pretty rocky things in the next few days and weeks—but you can't express them in this ward. When you come in here to see your baby—and I want you to come often—you come in here with joy. You come in here with the love you feel hanging out all over you. I want to hear a soothing voice come out of your mouth. I want you to touch that baby as much as you possibly can and talk to her."

"Yes, yes," Caroline agreed. "That's what she needs. I know that's what she needs."

"Of course it's what she needs. These doctors are going to do the best they can with their tubes and machines and so forth, and those things will keep your baby going, but we have to give her a reason to try as hard as she can, and that reason comes from experiencing love. And you and your husband are the main sources of that love. Where is he, by the way?"

"Probably over the Atlantic somewhere," Caroline said bitterly. "He's trying to get back from London."

"And you don't think he should have been there in the first place?" Sister Angelica was quick to pick up on Caroline's tone.

"No, I don't think he should have been there," Caroline retorted. "I think he should have been with me."

"Maybe he should have, and maybe he shouldn't have. I don't know," Sister Angelica said. "The problem with premature births is that they're not predictable. But whatever has happened in the past, don't you bring that into this ward. If you and your husband have any disagreements, you can have them somewhere else, but when either one of you comes in here, you come in here with the right spirit. The life of your child depends on it."

"Yes, Sister. You can count on us. I promise you."

"Good. Now, let's talk about a few other things here. You have been through a shock to your body. While giving birth is a perfectly natural thing, it's also a very tiring thing. You need some rest, and of course, you need proper food. I know you're going to want to be down here constantly, but you also must take care of yourself."

"I'm not leaving my baby alone."

"Your baby is not going to be alone. The nurses and doctors will be taking care of her constantly. But you are correct. Your baby needs more than the doctors and nurses can give her. The baby needs you, her father, and if possible, other members of her family. My point is that even though you want to be in there, touching that baby twenty-four hours a day, that's not the best thing for the baby because it's not the best thing for you. How long will it be before your husband gets here?"

"I don't know for sure. Probably another six or eight hours. But my mother is also on her way from Dallas, and she should be here quickly, and my great Aunt Kathleen is out in the hall."

"Good. That's the kind of thing we need. We need other people from the family to touch and talk to your baby and give you a chance to get off of your feet and rest."

"I understand," Caroline said. "But now, I'm going back to my baby." She stood up, turned her back on the nun and walked back through the doors.

Sister Angelica smiled broadly and nodded her head vigorously. "She'll do just fine, Lord. She'll do just fine." She rose and hurried in the opposite direction out to the hall where Great Aunt Kathleen waited. When she saw the elderly lady sitting on the other side of the hall, she marched over to her, "Are you Mrs. Randolph's great aunt?"

Aunt Kathleen rose with dignity and responded, "I am, Sister. I am Kathleen Kendall."

"Good," Sister Angelica said. "I'm here to tell you that your great niece will do just fine. Her baby, however, is in great danger, and the next forty-eight hours are going to be very critical. We of the medical profession will do everything we can, of course, but that baby needs a lot of encouragement from members of the family. On the other hand, your great niece needs some rest and some food."

"I understand," Aunt Kathleen said. "I'm here to do anything that I can do to help. And her mother will be here soon."

"Yes, family is what we need," Sister Angelica agreed. "Let's give her a few more minutes with the baby, and then if you are up to it, I believe that you better go in and stay with the baby while Mrs. Randolph goes and eats and rests for at least an hour before she comes back—preferably two hours if you can get her to do it."

"Does somebody need to be with the baby all the time?" Betsy asked.

"No, not all the time. In fact, many times the family member who is there will be asked to step out into the hall while various medical procedures are being performed. But the baby will progress more quickly if she hears soothing supportive voices and is touched gently. The nurses, of course, can't do enough of that. That's the part the family members can play."

"We will do anything that is necessary," Aunt Kathleen insisted.

"Is Miz Caroline's baby going to live?" Betsy demanded.

"That baby doesn't belong to Miz Caroline," Sister Angelica retorted. "She belongs to God, and He'll decide whether or not she lives, but you can be sure we're going to do everything we can to persuade Him that this world will be a better place with that little girl in it. Now, Mrs. Kendall, if you will come this way, I'll give you a sterilized hospital gown, and you can wash your hands and go in and see the baby with your great niece. Then I want you to persuade her to go back to her room and have a good meal and some rest." Sister Angelica turned toward Betsy. "That will be your assignment.

"I don't need to be assigned to take care of Miz Caroline," Betsy informed the nun. "I always takes care of Miz Caroline when she's in Charleston."

"Shall we go in?" Aunt Kathleen asked as she moved past the nun, toward the door, hoping that her movement would stop any confrontation between the two strong-willed women she had left behind. Sister Angelica chose to follow her. As Great Aunt Kathleen entered the door, she glanced back over her shoulder, and when she saw that Betsy had both hands on her hips, she was relieved that Sister Angelica had followed. When she reached the incubator, she put her arms around Caroline and hugged her as she stared through the plastic at the small, fragile-looking child. Caroline was gently stroking the baby's head.

"I wish I could ask, 'Isn't she beautiful?'" she whispered to Aunt Kathleen.

"She's alive, dear, and she has every chance of becoming beautiful in the physical way that you mean. I know it's hard, but try to look past the physical and see that she is indeed beautiful. She has been sent to you by God, and she embodies a beautiful spirit already."

"I never dreamed it would be like this. I always dreamed that I would deliver her and they would put her in my arms."

"Don't think of what might have been, Caroline. This is what we have. This is what we'll work with with God's help. It's not the beginning you wanted, but it is a beginning."

"If only we can keep her alive," Caroline added gravely.

"It will be God who keeps her alive, Caroline. We'll do everything we can to assist, but in the end it will be God who keeps her alive."

"I'm praying for her, Aunt Kathleen. When I really needed to just talk to God, it was the most natural thing in the world." Caroline looked into her aunt's face for the first time since the woman had entered the room.

"Yes, dear. He made it that way, natural and easy. We're the ones who try to make it hard."

"Do you think He will listen to me?"

"Why wouldn't He, Caroline?"

"Because I've lied to David, and now my baby has been born prematurely and is suffering."

"Do you remember when Carrie had Robert's child and the baby's foot was malformed?" Aunt Kathleen asked. "Do you remember that part of the journal?"

"Yes, I do, but Carrie was a victim of her father's sins. I brought all this on myself," Caroline insisted.

"You didn't make your baby come into the world prematurely, Caroline. You took care of yourself; you know you did."

"But—"

"You're missing the point of Carrie's journal, Caroline—of her experience. Remember when her mother demanded whether or not she loved her newborn son less because of his deformity?"

"Yes, and Carrie was appalled at the question. She loved her son with all her heart. She didn't care about his imperfect foot."

"And her mother told her that God loves his children the same way. He loves us in spite of our imperfections, our mistakes." Aunt Kathleen watched Caroline's face closely. "Do you remember that part?"

"Yes, I do."

"And what does that say to you in your situation?" Aunt Kathleen quietly asked,

"I don't have to be perfect or even sinless to be loved by God."

"That's right. Keep that truth in the front of your mind. Now, we need to take care of you. And Betsy's waiting for you out in the hall. She's going back to the room with you, and you're going to have some food and some rest and perhaps take a shower."

"No, I can't leave."

"You can leave, Caroline, because I'm going to stay. I'll be here with your baby. Each one of us has our task, and we're going to each do what is necessary. Your task is to rest."

"But if I leave her, something could happen to her."

"If you stay, Caroline, something could happen to her. She is in God's hands. We're only here to encourage her, and I'm going to be here doing just what you're doing."

"The truth is, I don't know if I can leave her. I feel a wave of panic just thinking about it."

"You're going to have to do a lot of leaving her in the next few weeks, Caroline. The best way is to go quickly. Just get up and go."

Caroline looked into her baby's face, stroked her head one more time, then she clenched her jaw, removed her hand from the incubator, stood up and abruptly turned around.

"Go, Caroline," Aunt Kathleen ordered. "I'll be here."

Caroline nodded and left the room as quickly as she could. By the time she reached the outside hall, she was ready to burst into tears. Betsy put her arm around her and walked with her back down the hall, and when they reached Caroline's room, she broke down and sobbed into Betsy's strong shoulder.

"Go ahead and let it out, Miz Caroline." Betsy patted her on the back. "You's gonna have to hold it in when you's with the baby, so you best let it out now."

When Caroline emerged, freshly showered, from the bathroom half an hour later, the first sight she saw was her mother standing there.

"Mother!" she cried as she hurried across the room as quickly as she could.

"Oh, Caroline!" Marian exclaimed as she threw her arms around her. "I'm so glad to see that you're okay and to hear that the baby is safe."

"But she's *not* safe!" Caroline wailed. "Oh, Mother, she's nowhere near safe. She's hooked up to every kind of tube you can think of, and she's so tiny." Caroline began to cry again.

"But she's alive, Caroline," Marian insisted. "She's alive, and she simply needs time to develop further."

"But the doctor says the next forty-eight hours are critical. That means she could die in the next forty-eight hours."

"I know, Caroline, I know. Betsy has told us everything."

"Us?" Caroline asked.

"Yes, dear. Your father's here also. He's gone back down to the car to get my luggage so that you can have some of my clothes to wear."

"I don't care about clothes, Mother. My baby is down there at the edge of death. I've got to get back down there."

"Caroline, your baby is down there at the edge of life. I know that the next forty-eight hours are critical. I know that she is in great danger, but let's think about the positive things here. What's wrong with your baby is that she has not developed fully yet, but the doctor says, according to Betsy, that there's no disease, there's no dysfunction that has forced this premature birth. She was simply born too soon, and thanks to medical science and technology today, she can be protected as if she were still in the womb."

"I know. I know all of that, Mother. I've been told that over and over again, but everything in me just makes me feel desperate to get back to her side."

"That's perfectly normal, Caroline. After all, she was in your body a few hours ago."

"Your mother's right," a masculine voice spoke up.

"Daddy," Caroline cried as she looked across the room and saw her father standing there with a small bag. Once again she hurried into the arms of someone she loved dearly. "Oh, Daddy, I'm so glad you're here."

"Where else would I be? I'm here, and I'm not leaving as long as you need me."

"I need you, but most of all, I need to get back to my baby." She let go of her father and leaned over to pick up the suitcase.

"I'll get that, honey," he said, picked it up and walked briskly to the bed and opened it.

"Caroline, take anything out of there you need," Marian said, "and get dressed, and we'll go back and see the baby together."

"But she ain't even eaten anything," Betsy fussed.

"I can't eat," Caroline brushed aside the thought. "It's ridiculous to expect me to eat at a time like this."

"Let's just get you dressed," Marian said. "Then we'll go down there together and, eventually, we'll get you some food. Here, what about this denim dress? It won't be a perfect fit, but it will do.

Take anything else you see that you need."

Caroline snatched the dress and some other items from the suitcase and hurried back to the bathroom.

"Where's Aunt Kathleen?" Marian asked Betsy.

"She's down with the baby," Betsy answered. "And I's worried about her."

"Yes," Marian agreed. "We have more than one person to take care of here. We need to get Aunt Kathleen home, so she can rest."

"What we need to do is divide up duties," Walt suggested. "As soon as we have seen the baby, I'll take Betsy and Aunt Kathleen back to the house, and then I'll come back here, Marian."

"Sounds good," Marian agreed quickly.

"There ain't no need for you to take us anywhere, Mr. Walt. Mr. Kendall came this morning and brought us to the hospital after Miz Caroline left in the ambulance, and he left his car and driver here for us, so we already got a ride home."

"Good," Walt agreed, "that takes care of that. Let's get Caroline back down to the baby. We'll see the baby. We'll get Aunt Kathleen out of there, and, Betsy, you get her home."

Caroline emerged from the bathroom as he was speaking. "Yes, Aunt Kathleen must be exhausted. This kind of strain can't be good for her."

"This kind of strain isn't good for anybody," Marian said as she went to put her arm around Caroline's shoulders, "but if we all pull together and share the burden, we'll all come out fine. Now, let's see that beautiful baby of yours."

A tortured look flashed across Caroline's face, and she shook her head. "She's not beautiful, Mother. She's got tubes going in her everywhere. She's just a pathetic little thing fighting for—"

"Caroline, let's go," her mother interrupted. "All we care about is that she stays stable."

"I just wish David were here," Caroline said as they walked across the room.

"He will be, dear," Marian encouraged her "just as soon as he can get here."

"Have you heard anything from him?" Caroline asked Marian

as they started down the hall.

"All I know is that he got on the Concord from London to New York."

"Good," Caroline said. "That'll cut the transatlantic flight in half. How did you get here so quickly? It takes forever to get from Dallas to Charleston."

"We hopped David's corporate jet, and of course, we were able to bypass the Atlanta Airport by doing that and come straight here. The jet has gone on to New York to meet David. I'm sure as soon as he touches down in New York, you'll hear from him."

"Does he know the baby is born? Does he know anything?"

"I just don't know, honey. All I know is that he managed to get on that Concord." Marian looked at her watch. "I'm kind of confused about time, frankly, but I would think it's about time for him to reach New York. So I'm sure you'll be hearing from him soon."

"How will he ever find me? He'll probably call the room, and I won't be there."

"You let me take care of that," Walt spoke up. "I'll take care of communications, Caroline. If David calls this hospital, I'll see to it that he finds you."

"Here," Caroline said as they turned the corner. "Here's where we go in. We'll have to wash up and put a hospital gown on and all that kind of thing, or they won't let us in."

"They may not let all of us in at once anyway, Caroline," Marian suggested. "I'm sure the facility is crowded."

Marian's judgment was correct; after a few minutes of preparation she and Caroline stood before the baby's incubator, and Great Aunt Kathleen was back out in the hall with Betsy and Walt.

"Oh, Caroline," Marian exclaimed quietly, "she's so precious. In spite of all the tubes, there she is—born and determined to live."

"I just want to hold her," Caroline whispered fervently. "I just want to hold her in my arms."

"Of course you do. Of course you do," Marian held Caroline close. "That's the most natural feeling in the world, and I'm so sorry that you can't have what you want. I do understand what you're feeling. It's a deep, deep longing, Caroline, that's perfectly natural, but it can't be now, and you know that. But she's here. She's born, and she's safe. And while it's hard to see past all the tubes and the respirator, you can see her now. Look, see her tiny hand? Look at her little fingers—those perfect little fingernails."

Caroline inserted her hand into the incubator and stroked the baby's diminutive hand, and with her little finger, touched each of the fingernails on the baby's right hand.

"Put your finger in the palm of her hand," Marian suggested. When Caroline did so, the baby instinctively grasped what she felt in her palm. "See," Marian encouraged her, "she knows you're here. She knows someone is here who cares about her."

"Does she really know, Mother?"

"Somewhere in that little baby's brain, she knows," Marian insisted. "I don't know what doctors or scientists would say about it, but I'm convinced she knows. That's why they want someone from the family here. She needs to be touched."

"I'm here, and I'm not going to leave her," Caroline insisted. "And then when David comes, he can stay with her."

"That's right, dear, but you're going to have to eat, and you're going to have to sleep."

"Everybody keeps saying that, but I can't worry about food. I don't even have an appetite."

"We're not worried about your appetite, Caroline. We want you to have the strength to stay here as much as you can. We understand that this baby is your focus, your only focus, just as she will be David's focus when he arrives. We just want to make it possible for you to stay with her. Now, as much as I hate to leave her, I'm going to go out so that your father can come in, and I'm going to get Aunt Kathleen to go home."

"Yes, please take care of Aunt Kathleen. I owe her so much."

"Oh, my dear," Marian insisted. "This has been one of the great moments of her life. She wouldn't have wanted to have missed it."

"Still, she needs to go home, and tell her I love her, will you? And thank her, too."

"I'll take care of it all. Bye for now; your father will be in soon."

In the next few hours, a lot of things happened that Caroline was only vaguely aware of. She knew that her Aunt Kathleen had gone home with Betsy to rest. She knew that at one point her mother had forced her out into the waiting room to eat some soup that her father had brought up from the cafeteria. But through all of those hours, she was most aware of two things, being as close to her baby as she could get and longing for David's arrival.

When David did arrive, he came striding down the hall and into the neonatal waiting room in his characteristic fashion. He was there to take charge of things. The moment he saw Walt and Marion, he demanded, "Where's Caroline? She's not in her room."

"David," Marian exclaimed in relief. "I'm so glad to see you."

David ignored her. "Where's Caroline?"

"She's in with the baby, David. And she's waiting for you."

"We haven't been able to get her to leave the baby," Walt interjected. "She seems to feel that the baby's only safe if she's there or if you're there."

"I'll handle Caroline," David said brusquely. "Now tell me about the condition of the child."

"David, I don't much like your tone," Marian said.

"He's just stressed," Walt insisted.

"All right," Marian agreed. "We're all stressed, but, David, you can't take that tone with Caroline. Believe me. She'll fall apart."

"All right, all right," David softened his voice. "I assume Caroline is in good shape."

"She's in relatively good shape," Marian answered, "considering that she gave birth this morning and has been sitting next to that incubator most of the day."

"Don't worry. I'll get her out of there."

"I mean it, David," Marian warned. "You better back down. You better go slowly. Caroline is immovable."

"Caroline has always been stubborn and hasn't had enough sense to know what's good for her," David said sharply.

"Caroline is not just being stubborn," Marian's own temper rose. "She's acting like any mother would who has been through a traumatic birth and is worried about the life of her baby."

"Tell me about the baby," David insisted. "What's the prognosis on the child?"

"The child, your daughter, was born too soon as you well know. Her lungs are underdeveloped, and that's the major threat to her life. She's on a respirator; they have her hooked up to an I.V., and she has a tube in her stomach. You need to be prepared for what she's going to look like. She's very small, very frail-looking."

"This isn't the first dying baby I've seen," David snapped. "You forget. I lost another child."

"Your baby is not dying," Marian insisted. "She is living, and it's just a matter of time before she will be living with more vigor. David, you're not going to do Caroline any good if you go in there with the attitude that your baby is dying."

"Marian, I've been down this road before. I'm not getting my hopes up, and I don't want Caroline to get hers up. Caroline's baby is probably going to die."

"Caroline's baby!" Marian exclaimed. "David, this is not Caroline's baby, this is your baby. This baby belongs to you and Caroline."

"This baby was entirely Caroline's idea, as you know, Marian. I never chose to take this risk. Losing one child in my life was plenty for me."

"David, that was a long time ago. What, twenty years ago? Everything in the medical field has changed in the last twenty years. I don't know the details of the loss of your first wife and child, but I do know that it's twenty plus years later, and the medical field is totally different now. They can do remarkable things with premature babies. You must not go in there and see Caroline with the attitude that your baby is dying. She will pick up on that, and she will not be able to handle it."

"I'm not going to give Caroline false hopes, Marian. It just makes it that much harder when you lose."

"David, I forbid you—"

"Let me handle this, Marian," Walt broke in firmly. Marian turned and walked over to the windows and stared out at the parking lot as she prayed that her husband could talk some sense into her son-in-law.

Walt took several steps toward David and placed a reassuring hand on his shoulder. He spoke in a calm, reasoning way, "David, we just need to keep her steady. We've done everything we can do for her, and now we just need to keep her steady."

At Walt's words David's exhausted, anxiety-filled mind began whirling back in time. He no longer saw Walt standing in front of him, quietly reasoning him into accepting a path of action he felt was wrong. He saw Philip DuBois. It was the voice of Philip he heard, and for a minute David believed he was trying to save Danielle.

"What do you say, son?" Walt asked. "Can we agree just to keep her steady?"

David's mind remained stuck in the past, and as anger at his father-in-law's manipulation of him rose to fury, a stronger voice from the past suddenly roared into David's mind. "Take control!" David heard his father yell. "Be a man, be a Randolph! Take control!" Those imagined, but potent words that came hurtling into his mind from his youth were the words David was most conditioned to respond to. His attention snapped back to the present as he took control of himself and the situation.

"Get out of my way!" he ordered and turned and strode out of the room.

"Walt! What have you done?" Marian cried as she turned. "What is he going to say to Caroline?"

TWELVE

"David!" Caroline cried out the moment she saw him enter the door of the neonatal unit. "Oh, David!" She jumped up as quickly as she could from the chair, paused for just a moment as she winced with pain, and then hurried to his side. The moment Caroline called out, Sister Angelica jerked her head up, ready to object to the overly loud noise in her unit, but when she saw the man entering the door and Caroline rushing into his arms, she decided that it was best to let it go. Silently she observed what took place.

"David, I thought you would never get here," Caroline said more quietly once she had actually reached him and thrown herself into his arms. He held her tightly but said nothing at first.

Finally, in a choked voice, he asked, "Are you all right, Caroline?"

"Oh, yes, David. Yes, I'm fine. A little sore and very tired, but I'm fine—really I am."

"What does the doctor say about your condition?"

"The doctor says I'm okay—really. It was an easy birth because the baby is so small."

"It may have been an easy birth, Caroline, but I understand

that you've been down here all day."

"Of course I have. I want to be near my baby, and she needs me. It's very important that she knows we're here for her. Everybody on staff agrees with that."

"Caroline, I don't think it's wise for you to get too attached—"

"Oh, David, wait till you see her!" Caroline exclaimed, obviously not hearing what he had begun to say. "Come over here and take a look. Oh, first, before you do, remember that there are an awful lot of tubes and things—well, you just have to learn to look past those, David, and it really upset me at first to see them, but now when I come in, I don't see the tubes and things anymore. I just see our baby. She's so beautiful, David! She's very tiny, but she's perfectly formed, and it's just so wonderful that she's here, and I can finally touch her."

"Caroline, you really need to be cautious about your feelings—"

"Oh, come look at her, David. Try not to see all the plastic, try not to see the incubator walls and all the tubes. Just look at *her*." Caroline was slowly pulling him across the room.

David's face turned white, and he was obviously reluctant to be drawn any further into the neonatal unit, but his father's words once again leapt from his memory and spurred him on. "Take control! Be a man!" He was determined not to be afraid, so he looked in the direction that Caroline was pulling him and saw a window with the light of a sunset flowing through it. The light was bouncing off of a plastic rectangle which he knew contained the baby. Everything in him wanted to take Caroline firmly by the arm, jerk her out of there, force her out of the hospital and never allow her to return. But he pushed those feelings down deep inside of himself, tightened his jaw and prepared himself to see the baby he had never wanted in the first place.

When they reached the incubator, Caroline said, "Just look at her, David. Here she is—alive and breathing in this world." David looked down at the incubator but would not allow his eyes to focus on the baby. "Look," Caroline continued, "you can put your hand through here," she demonstrated as she spoke, "and you can touch her. Look at her beautiful, beautiful hands. They're so tiny but so perfect. And look, see? It's wonderful. You can put your finger here on her chest and feel her breathing. And, oh David, look at her little ears. Aren't they the sweetest things you've ever seen?" Caroline moved her hand up to the baby's head. "I can't believe she actually has hair. It's the softest thing I've ever touched."

David had closed his eyes and was seeing nothing that Caroline was showing him. He was struggling deep inside of himself just to remain conscious and to deal with the flashback scenes from his past that were seeking to overwhelm him. Suddenly Caroline realized that her husband had said nothing. She looked up at his face and saw that it had turned ashen. "David!" she cried in alarm, and as she did, Sister Angelica decided it was time to move into the situation.

"Mr. Randolph," she said as she moved forward quickly. "Would you like to sit down?" She pushed a chair under him and jerked him down firmly just before he fell into a faint.

"David!" Caroline cried again. "Are you all right?"

"Put your head down on your knees," Sister Angelica ordered.

"I'm fine," David mumbled. "Just leave me alone."

"I'm not going to leave you alone, Mr. Randolph," Sister Angelica informed him "because I'm not going to have you fainting in this unit."

"I'm not going to faint," he insisted.

"You certainly aren't," Sister Angelica confirmed, "because you're going to put your head down." She took him by the back of the neck and pushed him forward. Normally he would have been strong enough to resist her push, but in his weakened condition, he was easily controlled by the nurse. "Now, you just sit there for a minute," she commanded, "and you'll feel better." She looked at Caroline's alarmed face. "He's going to be all right, Mrs. Randolph. This is just quite a shock for him."

"He's come all the way from London," Caroline suddenly focused on what David had been through.

"I'm sure that's part of it," Sister Angelica agreed. "This is a lot to take in and especially after such a long flight. He must have been really anxious the entire time."

"Oh, David," Caroline said as she reached over and stroked the hair on his head. "I'm so sorry. I'd forgotten what you've been through today, the hours and hours of waiting and worrying."

"That's right," Sister Angelica confirmed what Caroline was saying. "Sometimes it's harder to wait and worry than it is to actually do something." She patted David on the shoulder. "Sometimes we medical people get so accustomed to dealing with the babies and the mothers, we forget about you fathers sitting on the sidelines and the anxiety that you're feeling."

"I'm perfectly fine," David retorted as he began to raise his head. "I don't need to be hovered over." Sister Angelica leaned over and stared at his face to check his color.

"Yes, I think you're much better," she agreed. She patted him on the shoulder once again. "Now why don't you just sit here for a moment, and I'll get another chair for your wife. You take your time and get to know your daughter just a little bit. And then, I think, it would be a good idea if both of you go have some dinner and have a little time away from this place." She looked at Caroline and nodded firmly. Caroline understood the message the nun was sending her.

"Yes, that's a good plan," Caroline agreed as she once again stroked David's head. Sister Angelica brought a chair up for her, and Caroline sank into it gratefully. For a moment, she just held David's hand. "I'm so glad you're here, David. I'm just so glad you're here, and we're all together at last. It's been the longest day of my life."

"Yes," David said coldly. "It has been a very long day."

Caroline felt totally inadequate in this situation and indecisive about what to say next; David seemed so distant. Finally, she felt some strength returning to David's grip, and she realized that he was more in control of himself. Very quietly she asked, "Would you like to look at the baby now?"

"Yes, Caroline," David's tone was mechanical and cold. "I'll look at her, but then I want us both to leave."

"But don't you want to be with her, just be with her for a few minutes? Spend some time with her?"

"No, not now," David said more strongly. "I think it's too early, Caroline. It's far too early for us to get attached to this baby."

"But, David, we *are* attached to this baby. This is our child!"

"I understand the biological facts of that, Caroline, but I'm talking about the emotional situation. We need to maintain some distance until we see what's going to happen. Believe me, I've been down this road and the pain of losing a child is overwhelming."

"But we're not going to lose this child," Caroline's voice rose as she began to feel panicky.

"We don't know that yet, Caroline. We don't know what is going to happen."

Caroline stared at him for a moment, amazed at his ability to detach himself from someone who seemed so precious to her. "This is my child. I can't detach myself from my child, David. This is your child. This is our child, and we can't just distance ourselves and wait and see what happens. What happens depends on us to a great extent. You can leave if you want to, but I'm not leaving my baby." As Caroline's voice rose closer to a hysterical tone, David remembered Marian's warnings.

"I'm not asking you to leave her, Caroline," he quickly tried to soothe her. "Of course, we're not going to leave her. We're not going to abandon her, but we're going to find some happy medium. We'll be involved here in a way that's helpful to the baby, but we'll try to protect ourselves emotionally, too."

"I don't care about my emotional protection, David. I care about my baby." Caroline turned away from him, put her hand into the incubator and caressed the baby's head. "How can you ignore the fact that she's here, that she's alive, that she's real?" As Caroline's voice rose to an even higher pitch, Sister Angelica took a step in their direction.

"I'm not ignoring the fact that she's here, Caroline. Believe me, I'm not ignoring it. I'm just trying to deal with it in a way that is slightly different from yours. That's all."

"She needs us!" Caroline cried. "She needs us, David. Don't you understand that?" The tears coursed down Caroline's cheeks as she turned her head and stared defiantly at her husband.

Sister Angelica intervened in the situation, her first thought to calm Caroline down. "That's right, Mrs. Randolph. The baby does need you. The baby needs both of you." She gave David a warning look. "But what the baby doesn't need is for you to be upset. And you're too exhausted to keep this up."

Caroline was so choked up she couldn't respond. The tears continued to flow down her cheeks as she stroked every inch of her baby that was not connected to a plastic tube. Sister Angelica put her hand on Caroline's head and gently rubbed it.

"Now, Mrs. Randolph, you just sit there quietly for a minute and be with your baby. We're going to work everything out," she soothed. "We're all in this together; we're all on the same side, aren't we, Mr. Randolph?"

She looked back at David, demanding with her eyes that he say something supportive. "Of course," he agreed. "I'm just worried about you, Caroline."

"And you're exhausted yourself, Mr. Randolph," Sister Angelica coached him along.

"Right. Absolutely. I've traveled from one side of the Atlantic to another, holding my breath the whole way."

"You're just too exhausted to feel anything," the nun continued to give him the right words, "and you hardly know what you're saying." He resented her taking control, but he went along for Caroline's sake.

"That's right," he agreed.

"He hasn't even looked at her," Caroline condemned him.

Sister Angelica looked at David, and motioning with her head, she urged him to move forward.

"But I want to now, Caroline," David lied. Everything inside of him was saying "no," but he was determined to get past this moment. He stood up and leaned over Caroline's shoulder and stared down into the incubator. There he saw exactly what he expected to see, what he had trained his mind to see hours before, as he sat on a plane crossing the Atlantic Ocean. He saw a maze of tubes, and somewhere deep in that maze, he saw a tiny bit of flesh. He struggled to think of something to say, and finally blurted out,

"She looks like quite a fighter."

"Oh, she is, David. She is!" Caroline turned to him eagerly. "She's going to make it. She has what it takes. All we need to do is support her."

David didn't believe one word of what Caroline was saying, but he saw how close she was to the edge, and he chose to heed Marian's warning. "I'm sure you're right, Caroline. She is quite a fighter. That's obvious, and I'm sure she's going to be fine. It's just going to take a lot of time."

Sister Angelica listened intently, and with David's last word, she realized that he had said as much as he would be able to come up with. "Yes," she broke in. "That's the ticket. We just need some time here and a lot of good care, and we have an excellent staff here, Mr. Randolph. Your baby's going to get great care, and I'm sure that you and your wife and other members of the family are going to be in here encouraging her every inch of the way."

"Of course, we are," David made himself agree because he was determined to get Caroline out of there.

Caroline looked back at him and smiled weakly; then she turned back to look down at the baby. When she turned her back, Sister Angelica made a motion with her hand to suggest to David that he should try to touch the baby. David turned white again, but determined to take control of the situation, he lied, "I'd like to touch the baby, Caroline. Just for a moment, if you don't mind."

"Of course, David." Caroline was instantly pleased and removed her hand from the incubator. "Just put your hand through here." She took her husband's right hand and put it through the opening of the incubator. "Now, just take your forefinger and run it along her head. Feel how soft her hair is, David." David did as he was told, all the while telling himself that this was not his child and that he need not become attached. One part of him heard Caroline instructing him to touch the baby's beautiful ears and to feel her breathing by putting his finger on her chest, so he mechanically did as he was told. Another part of his mind was far away in some safe place that he had long ago found to retreat to.

"See, David," Caroline's spirits had risen even higher, "she's going to make it. She's going to be fine."

David could think of nothing to say, so he fell back on his original comment. "Yes, she's quite a fighter, Caroline." He removed his hand from the incubator and looked over at his wife. "And so are you," he added although he wasn't sure he was making sense.

"You're both going to be just fine," Sister Angelica insisted. "But now I want you both to have some time together and have a good meal. Mr. Randolph, if you've been on a plane all day, I'm sure you need some food, and Mrs. Randolph hasn't eaten much. You two go have some supper together."

Caroline looked hesitant, but Sister Angelica hurried on, "Your mother can come in and stay with the baby, Mrs. Randolph, or your father."

"Yes," Caroline finally agreed. "They're out in the waiting room."

"Perfect," Sister Angelica responded enthusiastically. "You see, that's what families are for. When these kinds of difficult situations come up, everybody shares the load, and then no one is totally wiped out by it. And Mrs. Randolph, you're the one most likely to be wiped out, so we need to get you some rest and some food, and Mr. Randolph has had a hard day, too, so let's get your mother in here."

"Well, yes, I guess that's a good idea," Caroline agreed. "I am suddenly very tired."

"Well, of course you are. Of course you are," Sister Angelica agreed as she started gently helping Caroline from the chair and encouraging her toward the door. "After all, you gave birth to this baby this morning." She didn't have to push David. He was walking ahead of her and extending his hand to reach out to the door handle, long before he reached the door. Caroline stopped at the door and looked back at the incubator. "Don't worry, Mrs. Randolph. I'll stay right with the baby until your mother comes," Sister Angelica soothed. "You go with your husband now."

"Okay," Caroline finally agreed, and David quickly ushered her out the door.

When they entered the waiting room, they found Walt pacing the floor and Marian staring out the window.

"Mother," Caroline said quietly. Marian whirled around, and Walt stopped his pacing. Both of them were taken aback at Caroline's obviously weakened condition and the strain on David's face. "Mother, would you go stay with the baby, please, while David and I get something to eat?"

"Yes," Marian quickly agreed. "Of course, dear. Of course, that's a wonderful idea." She looked at David, whose face hardened into a mask and told her nothing, then back at her daughter and realized that Caroline had been crying. "I'll be able to stay with the baby as long as necessary. You and David take plenty of time. Go down to the cafeteria and get something good to eat. No. On second thought, why don't you and David go back to your room where you can have some peace and quiet, and Walt will go down and get you some food."

"Yes, I can do that," Walt agreed. "And some quiet would really be good for you, Caroline. You could lie down."

"That's the best plan," David agreed. "Caroline, we're going to go back to your room and let you lie down, and we'll send Walt down for food."

"And you could rest, too, David," Caroline added.

"Yes, yes, that's right. I could rest too. We both need to rest, Caroline."

"Well, that's all settled," Walt said, far too exuberantly. "Marian, you go stay with the baby, and Caroline and David, you go back to the room, and I'll go to the cafeteria. Now what do you two want to eat?"

Caroline shook her head vaguely, so David answered, "Just bring whatever looks good to you, Walt."

Caroline looked at her mother and said anxiously, "The baby, Mother." Marian nodded and waved and left the waiting room.

"I'm off to the cafeteria," Walt said. "I'll meet you in your room as soon as I can."

"Let's go, Caroline." David put his arm around his wife's shoulders. "It's time for you to get off your feet."

When Walt brought the food back to Caroline's room, he was grateful to discover that David had encouraged her to get into bed. She was propped up and ready to eat. As he opened the containers of food, he announced, "I'm going back to the cafeteria to eat, myself, so you two can be alone."

"Is Mother still with the baby?" Caroline asked quickly.

"Yes, honey. She's with the baby, and she's going to stay there until someone comes and takes her place. Don't worry now. You eat and you rest." He left them alone.

"Your father's right, Caroline," David insisted as he put the food in front of Caroline. "I want to see you eat every bit of this."

"And you eat, too, David. It's going to be a long night."

"Okay," he agreed and sat down with his own food. They ate in silence, both grateful for a few moments to think of nothing but the food they were putting into their mouths. As soon as Caroline was finished eating, she started to get out of the bed, but David stopped her.

"Where are you going, Caroline?"

"Back down to the neonatal unit to be with the baby. Where else would I be going?"

"Caroline, it's dark outside. You can't go through the night sitting down there by that incubator. It will kill you. It's too much."

"I'm not leaving my baby, David," Caroline said with resolve. "There's nothing you can say that's going to change my mind."

"Look, Caroline, I know how you feel—"

Suddenly Caroline's temper flared. "You don't know how I feel! You don't have the slightest idea what I'm feeling. You haven't been involved in this pregnancy from the beginning. You've been gone. You've put your business before me—before us. You've abandoned me through this whole time."

"Caroline, let's not dredge up all of that—not now. The baby is here. I'm here. Just tell me what you want me to do now. What will make it possible for you to rest?"

"I guess I just need to know you love our little girl. I know Mother could stay with her, but somehow I need our baby to have me or you with her right now. That doesn't make any sense to you, does it?"

David was sickened at the thought of going back to the neonatal unit, but he calculated quickly and realized that Caroline would never rest unless he did. "It doesn't need to make sense to me; it needs to give you the peace of mind you need to rest. Will you stay in bed and try to sleep, if I go down there and stay with the baby?"

"Yes, I will."

"Do you promise, Caroline, you will actually rest—I mean allow yourself to go to sleep—if I stay down there with the baby?"

Caroline hesitated, not at all sure she wanted to make such a vow. "I'll try, David. I'll definitely stay in bed. I can't promise you I'll sleep."

"Then I'm on my way," he came to the bed, leaned over and gathered her into his arms. "Listen to me, honey. If there was anything I learned in that endless flight over the Atlantic, it was how much I love you. I can't stand to see you so worn out. Please let me take over now. I love you, Caroline; let me take care of you."

"Oh, David, I love you too," she sighed in his arms. "And now we're really a family."

"And I plan to take care of my family, honey. You can count on me. Now you rest."

"I will," Caroline agreed as David kissed her and turned out the light next to the bed.

"Sleep," David encouraged. "Just for an hour—sleep. I'll take care of the baby."

"Okay," Caroline said, as she watched him go. She was amazed at how the exhaustion seemed to rise up from the bed and pull her down into it. In moments, in spite of herself, she was asleep. David had not left immediately; instead, he stood outside in the hall, and when he briefly looked in five minutes later, he saw that Caroline was asleep. Good, he thought as he forced himself to go back to the neonatal unit to relieve Marian of her duty.

"Is Caroline asleep?" Marian asked when she saw him approaching the incubator.

"Yes, she drifted off very quickly when I promised to stay with the baby."

"Are you sure you're up to this?"

"I've eaten and gotten my second wind. I'll be okay for a couple of hours. Besides, it seems awfully important to Caroline."

"It is important to her. I know it's hard to understand her right now, David. To you she must seem quite fanatic. She's just so scared. Her baby has lived for seven months because it was physically attached to her; it's almost impossible for Caroline to believe it can live unattached to her."

"You're right, I'm sure. I guess we just have to get through a day or so before Caroline comes to her senses. In the meantime I'll do what she wants, no matter how irrational it seems."

"I know you must be exhausted. I'll just go down to the cafeteria and join Walt. We need to go to Bradford House and check on Aunt Kathleen and call the family in Dallas, too. If you're sure you'll be okay for a couple of hours—"

"I'm fine, Marian. Go on." David urged her.

As soon as he was certain that she was gone, he too left the unit. He went across the hall to the waiting room and was grateful to find it empty. He threw himself down on a long couch, stretched out, and thought, I've got to keep Caroline from being hurt. I know how to protect myself; I just won't allow myself to get emotionally involved with the baby. But it's not going to be easy to get Caroline to keep some emotional distance. What I need to do is get her away from this hospital as quickly as possible. Then, when the worst happens, as no doubt it will, she won't be here to see it. She's going to have a difficult enough time when we lose the baby, but at least, maybe I can keep her from actually seeing the baby die. As for now, I'm just going to get some sleep. Caroline will probably sleep most of the night, and Marian won't be back for at least two hours. I'll set the alarm on my watch and get back in there before she returns.

An hour later Caroline awakened and immediately thought of her baby. Adrenaline surged through her as she looked at the clock,

"I've been asleep over an hour; I've got to check on the baby." She got out of bed as quickly as possible, wincing as she moved, and started for the neonatal unit. After she had donned the required sterile gown, she hurried to join David by the baby's incubator. She pushed open the glass doors and immediately looked over at the incubator. David was not there.

Caroline left and went across the hall to the waiting room. There she found David asleep. "What are you doing in here?" she demanded. "You promised me!"

"Caroline, be reasonable, you're exhausted, I'm exhausted—"

"I don't care!" Caroline began to cry. "The truth is you don't love our daughter. You don't even really love me. I never want to see you again!" She turned to storm out of the room as Marian and Walt walked through the door.

"Caroline!" Marian called after her, but Caroline kept going. "What have you done, David?" Marian demanded.

"Something reasonable. I took a nap."

"And Caroline found you in here? Great! She'll never trust you again. She may not trust any of us."

David clamped down on his temper, determined to reason with them. "Marian, sit down. We need to talk about this."

"What is there to talk about? You told me that Caroline was asleep and that you were going to stay with the baby. I would never have left if—"

"I know, I know," David broke in, "but the baby doesn't need me in there. There's plenty of professional help to take care of her."

"But Caroline needs to know you're in there," Marian insisted.

"What Caroline doesn't know won't hurt her, Marian," David said brusquely. "She just needs to go to sleep and stay asleep. In fact, we need to give her a sedative to make her sleep. Whatever is going to happen to that baby is going to happen. Nothing we're going to do is going to make any difference."

"David," Walt intervened. "We could debate that from now to eternity. All I know is what the nurse has told us about the importance of interacting with the baby at this stage; we need to do what they say we need to do."

"We also need to do what Caroline thinks we need to do," Marian interjected. "In a way, Caroline is the one most at risk here."

"But Caroline is being totally obsessive about this," David insisted as he rubbed his forehead and massaged his temples. "Marian, even you have to admit that she's past reason. It's absurd to hang over that incubator. I think we need to get her a psychiatrist."

"A psychiatrist!" Marian exploded. "That's the answer to everything, isn't it? David, Caroline *feels*. There's nothing wrong with Caroline. She just allows herself to feel, and this is a time in her life when her feelings are rightfully very strong. Maybe you don't feel anything, but she does. Caroline loves. Whatever the risk, she loves. She can't withhold her feelings the way you do. I don't understand you. Are you so unfeeling that you don't care what your own wife is agonizing through?"

"I'm just trying to interject some reason into this situation," David insisted. "I have flown here from London and have found all of you—even you, Walt—acting like a bunch of hysterics. A baby has been born too soon. Maybe she'll make it, maybe she won't, but the rest of us aren't going to make it if we don't gain some kind of detachment from this situation. This excessive emotionalism is not good for anybody. The reasonable thing to do is for all of us to get some rest. Now, I propose that we get the doctor to give Caroline a sedative, something that will knock her out for the whole night and give her a good rest. Then the three of us ought to go somewhere and get a good night's sleep. We just need to leave this baby in the hands of the professionals."

"And how is Caroline going to feel when she wakes up from this sedative that you force on her and discovers that all of us have abandoned her and her baby?" Marian demanded. "You can stand here and theorize about this until you turn blue. I'm going to be with Caroline."

"That's what I mean by excessive emotionalism," David said to Walt after Marian had left. "Surely you understand that we have a very restricted predicament to deal with here. Caroline needs rest; we all do, and that baby won't be helped by having anyone hanging over the incubator."

"You may be right about the baby's needs, David. I don't know, but I do know that Caroline thinks that the baby needs us and that the baby won't make it if we're not there. And at the moment, frankly, I'm more concerned about Caroline than I am about the baby. I can understand that you don't feel very close to this baby—that you haven't done what they call 'bonding.' I'm just another man like you. I don't claim to understand all this, but I am the father of three children, and I've watched Marian go through pregnancy, give birth, and be inseparable from her baby three times. This is a very emotional time for new mothers. We men don't feel it as strongly as our wives do. Maybe we should; maybe we shouldn't. I don't know, and right now I don't care. At the moment all I care about is that Caroline feels as good about this as she can."

"That's all I want, too, and she's not going to feel good if she's sitting there when the baby dies."

"Maybe you have your defenses up a little too high because of your first marriage. Maybe you're overly concerned that the baby's going to die, or maybe you're right. Maybe the baby's not going to make it. The question still comes back to Caroline. *She's not dying.* You're not going to lose Caroline unless you abandon her. And if you don't play an active role by sitting by that incubator, Caroline is going to feel abandoned. If you want Caroline, you better give her what she thinks she needs if you possibly can."

"I can give Caroline anything she needs," David insisted, "and I don't need you telling me what that is."

"Can you stay in that neonatal unit and sit next to that incubator?"

"Of course I can, but that would be a ridiculous way for me to spend the night."

"Maybe so, but it's what Caroline needs."

"I don't agree. What Caroline needs is for someone to take a strong hand with her and force her to rest."

"You're not going to force a sedative on her as long as I'm here, David."

"I'm her husband, Walt. I'll decide."

"I don't care if you are her husband. I'm her father, and we're going to handle this another way."

"You're actually going to give in to these female hysterics and spend the night here?"

"If Marian's staying, I'm staying, too, David."

"You're crazy! You're all crazy," David hurled the comment over his shoulder as he stalked toward the door. "I'm going to the nearest hotel and get some sleep, like any sane person would."

After having picked up his bag in Caroline's room, David walked to the nearby Armstrong Hotel and checked into a room. "How am I supposed to take care of my wife with her father in the way?" David fumed aloud after he had closed the door to his room. "He's no different from Philip DuBois. Well, I'm different. I'm not a kid anymore. I won't be told what to do or what to think." He threw his bag down, took off his trench coat, walked straight to the bed and pulled the bedspread back. "I lost Danielle because I didn't think for myself." David reached for the corner of the crisp, white sheet and snapped it back. "I lost Danielle because—" He stopped his tirade and stared down at the white bed. Slowly he sat down on the edge of the bed and took the top sheet in his hand.

It wasn't really that simple, he admitted to himself. The truth is, I was glad to let someone else take over. I didn't want the responsibility. I was over my head, and I knew it. It was so easy to just let Philip get Danielle a psychiatrist and turn my attention back to work. He got her the best help money could buy, and we saw to it that she was never left unattended until she seemed stable again. We were all so careful, but not cautious enough. And so that phone call came, the call that changed my life. David slumped forward and gripped the sheet in both hands. "As long as I live, I will never forget that day," David murmured as tears flooded his eyes, and all the ghastly hours of his failure sprang to his mind.

"Mr. Randolph, I'm sorry, sir," David's secretary ran into the boardroom and interrupted the meeting. "There's an urgent call, sir, from Mr. Dubois' housekeeper, someone named Molly."

David didn't need to hear any more. He sprinted out of the room into the outer office and snatched up the phone. "Oh, come quick, sir!" he heard the housekeeper plead. "It's Miss Danielle. I found her in her father's bathroom. Oh, Mr. Randolph, she's unconscious, and there's pills all over the floor."

"Call an ambulance, Molly!" David ordered. "I'm coming, but call an ambulance now!" He flung the phone on the desk and yelled at his secretary as he bolted toward the door, "Get an ambulance to 3000 Westview."

David was oblivious to the traffic as he tore through the streets to his father-in-law's house. One self-condemning question raged repeatedly through his brain, "Why didn't I think of this possibility?"

He heard the ambulance coming as he took the steps three at a time up to the second floor of the DuBois house. He crashed down the upstairs hall, through his father-in-law's bedroom and into the bathroom. In a split second his eyes recorded the scene—Danielle, totally limp, lying on the tile floor—and he knew she was irretrievably gone. Nevertheless, he scooped her cool body up and shook it. Her arms and legs flew around him like a ragdoll's as he cried, "No, Danielle! No!" Finally, he quit shaking her, and hugging her tightly to him, he sat on the edge of the tub and wept into her hair.

An ambulance attendant walked to his side and silently felt of Danielle's neck, looking for a pulse. Several other quick checks convinced him she had been dead a while, so he quietly withdrew from the bathroom and left David alone with his beloved.

In the end they had to force her out of his arms, but he followed close behind them as they laid her on a stretcher. When they covered her with a white sheet and drew it up over her face, David snatched it back so she could breathe. Part of his mind just refused to believe she was gone.

After he had followed the stretcher down the stairs, Molly came to his side, caught hold of his arm, and spoke the words he had already condemned himself with, "I knew Mr. DuBois was out of town; I should have remembered Miss Danielle had a key to the house and that her father kept those sleeping pills in the bathroom. I should have remembered."

"I left Danielle when she needed me," David sat in the hotel room in Charleston and whispered to the white sheet in his hands. "I wasn't there for her and look what happened," he glanced down at the sheet crumpled in his grip, and when he did, he saw his wedding ring. "Caroline! Oh no! What's wrong with me? I've done it again!"

He dropped the sheet as he jumped up, strode across the room, and out the door.

When Caroline awakened at dawn, she was startled to see her mother standing by the window. "Mother! Is the baby—"

"The baby is fine," Marian whispered as she put her fingers to her lips. "Your father is with her; I just came to check on you."

"What time is it? I've got to go to her."

"She's fast asleep, Caroline. She looks very peaceful, and the nurse says she is stronger."

"Thank God."

"And look who's here." Marian pointed to David who was sound asleep on the sofa in the room.

"He came back. Why?"

"To take care of you, I'm sure."

"Why?"

"He loves you."

"David doesn't know the meaning of love!" Caroline whispered fiercely. "Just let him sleep." She slipped out of bed and began hurriedly donning her clothes. "I don't even want to talk to him."

"Caroline, put yourself in his shoes as much as you possibly can. He was so exhausted yesterday, so—"

"I can't believe you're defending him, Mother," Caroline started for the door.

"Caroline, you must forgive him," Marian pleaded as she followed her out.

"I can't. I won't. Tell him to go back to London. I'm going back to my baby now."

When Caroline arrived at the neonatal unit, she found her father standing in the hall, but before she could express her alarm, he said, "There's nothing to worry about. The doctor's doing a routine check. She had a good night, honey."

"Thank God! And thank you for staying with her, Daddy."

"Where else would I be when you need me, honey?"

"Oh, London or Tokyo," Caroline answered acidly.

"David isn't either place, honey," her father responded. "He's here in Charleston, and he came as soon as possible."

"He's asleep down in my room, actually."

"Is he?" Walt decided not to mention that he thought David was in a hotel. "Doesn't that say something good to you?"

"I don't care what he does anymore," Caroline began, but she saw Dr. Jorgensen exiting the neonatal unit and hurried to his side.

"Doctor, how is my baby doing?"

"She's definitely holding her own. In fact, I'm somewhat encouraged. She has stabilized nicely, but let's don't get too over-confident. We have at least another tricky twenty-four hours ahead of us."

"But she is stronger, isn't she?"

"She's stable, Mrs. Randolph, and that's the best we can hope for at this point."

"It's helping her to know we're here," Caroline insisted. "I know it is."

"Well, it's not hurting her," the doctor agreed, "and if it's helping you—"

"It is!"

"Fine, fine," Dr. Jorgensen murmured as he turned to leave.

"I have to go see her," Caroline announced to her parents as she started through the glass door.

Aunt Kathleen arrived an hour later to visit Caroline in the unit. The baby was sleeping quietly, so Caroline was just sitting next to the incubator trying to stay calm in spite of the many questions that were plaguing her. When she saw her great aunt approach, she was overwhelmed with gratitude. "You are just the person I need to see," she exclaimed as she rose from her chair to hug her great aunt.

"And you are just the person I need to see," Aunt Kathleen whispered in Caroline's ear. "I was sitting outside in my garden praying for you and our new little one, and suddenly I just needed to be right here, and I knew it."

"Thank you, thank you for coming! I need so desperately to talk to you."

"I'm here, Caroline," Aunt Kathleen assured her as Caroline pulled up a chair for her. "Let's just sit quietly with your little girl and with God, and let's talk about anything you need to discuss." Aunt Kathleen sat down and leaned over to look at the baby. "She looks very peaceful, Caroline; God has her in His hands."

"She just looks helpless to me," Caroline sighed. "Aunt Kathleen, why did she have to be born so early? I know she's struggling, even suffering, and it's my fault. Why didn't God just punish me? Why is he letting her suffer?"

"Now Caroline, listen to me. We'll probably never know why she was born prematurely, but her early birth is not God's punishment for anyone. It's just a medical fact."

"He could have stopped it."

"But He didn't choose to. I don't know why, but I know that He has a plan and that He can and will do something good with this situation, if you work with Him."

"But even if she lives, she's not going to have a father in her life. Why is God allowing that? Don't tell me that's not a punishment. She's totally innocent, but she's being victimized by my choices. Why does God allow such things to happen?"

"You know the answer to that question; we talked about it very recently. 'Choice' means having the freedom to choose. God wanted to give us legitimate choice, and we wouldn't have legitimate choice if He stepped in and overrode our choices. Sometimes we do make wrong choices, and we suffer the consequences. Worse still, innocent people suffer from our wrong choices, often people we love dearly." Aunt Kathleen paused and seemed to reach deep inside herself for special strength. "Caroline, do you remember the story of Allison?"

"Oh!" Caroline drew in her breath sharply. "Oh, I see! Allison died because the pilot was drinking."

"Yes, she did. He made the wrong choice, and Allison suffered, and so did I. Eventually, after much anguish and questioning, I learned to forgive that pilot and to allow God to do what He wanted to with that experience in my life. It wasn't easy, and it took time. Most importantly it required me to make some positive choices, namely to let go of my anger and bitterness."

"What you're saying reminds me so much of Carrie's life, of all the things I read in her journal, Aunt Kathleen. She suffered because of her father's choices, and her baby suffered."

"What we're discussing here actually applies to every life, doesn't it? Because we're all in the business of making choices and because we're not perfect, we do make wrong choices. But let's narrow the discussion down to you because that's what you need to deal with."

"I don't want my baby to suffer all her life because her father abandoned her because I lied to him; I am the one who broke faith with David; she shouldn't pay the price for my bad choice."

"Caroline, the good news is that your baby knows nothing at present. There is still time to rectify this situation. Much depends on what you do in the next few days."

"If you're going to tell me to try to make peace with David, I have to tell you in all honesty that I never want to speak to him again. He lied to me; he told me he would stay with our baby, and he abandoned her."

"And how does that make you feel?" Aunt Kathleen asked.

"Hurt."

"Can you see a way that you can use your current hurt feelings to understand David's hurt?"

"I've never thought of that."

"It is a good time to try to understand him."

"I guess I do understand, actually. How can I not understand? I'm feeling what he's been feeling ever since I told him I was pregnant, but I still don't feel like forgiving him. I'm sorry, Aunt Kathleen! I'm just not as spiritual as you are, as Carrie was—wait a minute."

"What is it, dear?"

"Carrie couldn't forgive her father. I read about it in her journal. She and John Kendall both had trouble forgiving him."

"So what did they do?"

"They *chose* to forgive him. That's it, that's what they did over and over again. They chose until they truly felt it."

Aunt Kathleen nodded, and the two women sat in silence two or three minutes as each thought her own thoughts. Then, quite gently, Aunt Kathleen asked, "Do you remember the part of my garden that died, Caroline?"

"Yes, yes, I do." Caroline reflected for a moment. "You can leave it the way it is—dead and barren—or you can replant it. That's what you said about it. I remember. You can leave it the way it is or you can replant it."

"That's right, and if I choose to replant it, I can redesign it at the same time. It can be better than ever, but not until I choose to clear the old out and start over."

Caroline looked down at her baby, thought a long moment, then said quietly, "This is the perfect time for me to start over, for her sake."

"And for yours, Caroline. Carrying around anger and hurt is so debilitating. You might as well throw a burlap sack of heavy rocks over your shoulder and leave it there."

"That would be incredibly stupid of me."

"It's always stupid to give your power away, to waste your strength on something worthless, and believe me, Caroline, anger and hurt feelings are worthless because they never do anyone any good."

"I can choose, Aunt Kathleen, but I can't make David choose, so how much good can I do? How far can I get in redesigning our lives?"

"It's true, Caroline, that you can only change yourself, but you are not alone in your attempt. God is here, and He's actively involved, and He loves all of you so much. God didn't put your baby's life at risk by making her be born prematurely, but He did allow it to happen. Now, if you allow Him to, He will use this situation to bring healing into your relationship with David."

"How can He if David won't cooperate?"

"He is God, Caroline, and even David Randolph cannot resist the power of God. I think David is hiding something, and I can't figure out what it is, but he can't hide anything from God. He may or he may not choose to cooperate with Him, but he can't hide from Him."

"So what should I do?" Caroline asked.

"Your part. You need to forgive David's hurtful actions and actively express your desire for a better union."

"But Aunt Kathleen! I have repeatedly asked David to work on our relationship, and he has consistently refused to and made me feel worthless."

"Caroline, because I love you, I must be severe with you on this point. If you are allowing David to make you feel worthless, it is because you are choosing to make David the source of your worth when you *know* he is not. Who is the source of your worth, Caroline?"

"God is! Why can't I remember that? God is."

"Correct, and you know it. So if you choose to allow anyone to make you feel worthless, I can only conclude that you are enjoying your hurt feelings."

Caroline sighed heavily. "You're right, Aunt Kathleen. It's not a very appealing picture of me, but it's a true one. I know it is."

"Remember the true source of your worth, Caroline. Then forgive David and try again to open a meaningful dialogue with him. Regardless of his reaction, put yourself and your relationship with David into God's hands. Then try your best to live and respond as God wants you to."

"But how do I know what God wants?"

"It isn't complicated, Caroline. He wants you to love. Did He not come to earth and live with us thirty-three years to demonstrate how we should live?"

"Yes, he did." Caroline's eyes filled with tears, but she was smiling through them. "He did."

"And can you forgive David and love him?"

"Yes, yes, I can. I'll talk to David again."

"Then things will get better, Caroline. I am sure of it."

THIRTEEN

David re-entered the neonatal unit as surreptitiously as possible. All morning he had taken long shifts when he was supposedly watching over the baby so Caroline would rest. In actuality he had been coming in to relieve Caroline, then waiting fifteen minutes to be sure she wouldn't return and as soon as he had deemed it safe, he had left to conduct business over the phone. He had been rigidly cautious to return fifteen minutes before he expected her back. Every time he returned, he fumed silently to himself, this will do no good for anyone, but I don't really have a choice. I came mighty close to losing her after she caught me napping in the waiting room last night. Thank God for Aunt Kathleen; whatever she said to Caroline this morning really worked. Something about forgiveness and starting over. And something about replanting a dead part of the garden. At least that's what Caroline told me about their talk. I don't understand most of it, but I did manage to listen to her patiently, and if it works for Caroline; that's all I care about. I can't get her away from here if I can't regain her trust, so once again I'll stay in this suffocating place and stare death in the face until the baby dies or Caroline gives up hanging over the incubator.

He stopped by the side of the incubator and thought for a moment about pulling a chair up to sit next to it as Caroline always did. I better be sure she finds me here next to the baby, he decided as he pulled up a chair. He looked down at the chair and lost his temper. "This is perfectly ridiculous," he muttered. "The baby doesn't really know I'm here. She doesn't really know anything." He touched the exterior plastic of the incubator and sighed angrily. "I've never felt so helpless in my life. No, that's not quite true. This is the second time in my life I've felt completely helpless."

David walked away from the incubator and stared out the window. The blazing early afternoon sun reflected off the wide expanse of white brick on the building across the quadrangle, and David allowed his mind to wander back in time.

He walked by Danielle's side as the nurse rolled her in a wheel-chair down the long, gleaming, white hallway of the hospital. Danielle's head was down as she stared at her lap and repeatedly intertwined her fingers and then separated them. As the nurse paused at a desk close to the exit, David squatted down by the wheelchair so he could look straight into Danielle's face.

"I'm taking you home, honey," he encouraged her. "Everything will be fine once we get home. We'll just rest up, and then we'll get on with our lives."

Danielle didn't look at him or respond, so he continued, "Are you listening, Danielle? I need you to talk to me. I don't know what you're thinking if you don't say anything." He waited, but Danielle remained silent. He tried a different approach, "Are you worried about your mother, honey? You know she's being well cared for, and she doesn't understand anything. She's happy, honey, and we can't do any more for her. You do know that, don't you? I mean, if there was anything we could do—Danielle, please talk to me."

"I want my baby," she mumbled without raising her head or looking at David.

"I know, honey. So do I. It's all you've said for two days. Please talk to me. I'll lose my mind if I can't help you! I love you! I love you, and I can't stand to be separated from you. Talk to me!"

"I killed him."

"What? What did you say?"

"I killed my baby."

"Danielle, no! That's not true!"

Dr. Mann, the physician who had cared for Danielle, approached the couple and signaled to David to step away from the wheelchair. "Don't press her now, David. Just get her home and get a good psychiatrist for her. This is going to take time. Monitor her closely for the next few months. Take control and keep control awhile."

David dragged his mind back to the present, back to the neonatal unit. "I didn't take control of Danielle," he whispered, "so I lost her." He turned away from the window of the unit and walked back toward his daughter's incubator.

"It isn't easy, is it?" a male voice spoke quietly from a corner and startled David. When he turned to find the source of it, he saw a man about sixty, sitting in a rocking chair, holding a very tiny infant. David quickly sized up the man, as he was accustomed to doing in his business activities, and he was startled by what he found. Although the man's hair was gray, he was trim and athletic-looking. His tanned face said quite clearly that he was a sportsman, but even under the sterile hospital gown he wore, David could see the man's gray suit, crisp, white shirt and conservative silk tie. He was obviously a business man. He looked at David with keen, ice-blue eyes that communicated that he would see through any mask David tried to wear. "It isn't easy," he said again, "Is it?"

"No," David muttered. He turned back to the window

"Would I be right in presuming the baby is your daughter?" the man asked.

"Yes," David responded curtly.

"I hear she's not doing too well," the man said calmly.

"I hear the same thing," David said without turning around.

"But they've sent you down here to make a difference, haven't they?" the man asked.

"Yes," was all David said, but his tone communicated clearly that he felt it was useless to try.

"This little girl's doing very well," the man said, referring to the baby he held. "She's had a rough two months of it, but she's definitely going to make it. I was actually able to give her a bottle today."

"This little girl?" David questioned as he turned briefly to look at the man, but carefully averted his eyes from the baby the man was holding. "Is she your granddaughter or something?"

"Oh, no. Not this one. It's been a long time, actually, since my grandson was here. I'm afraid he didn't make it."

"I'm sorry," David muttered. He wanted to turn back and stare out the window, but the man had aroused his curiosity. "What is the relationship of the child to you?"

"Oh, this little girl is not related to me at all. She's just one of the babies I come and see and hold a little bit everyday; you know, when I can get away from my business—usually about lunch time. Today I'm a little late." David stared at the man in disbelief. "This one was a crack baby," the man continued. "She was really a pathetic little thing in the beginning, delivered very prematurely like your daughter over there. But, oh boy, did she have a heap of extra trouble! These crack babies, you know, they go through hell on earth the first few weeks of their lives. They have to fight a lot more than being premature."

"Yeah, I suppose so," David said. He wasn't at all sure he wanted to hear anymore.

"Now your little girl, on the other hand, is actually blessed in a way. Of course, she's got a fight ahead of her, but at least she wasn't born addicted to something as destructive as crack. And if you can get her through the next few days, certainly the next week, anyway, she'll have a very good chance of living a normal life. This little baby," he paused and looked down at the infant he held, "we won't know for a long time how she's going to turn out."

"Why not?" David asked in spite of himself.

"Well, you see, the crack babies, or those that are born addicted to any substance, they were formed while the mother was taking drugs, and we just don't know how well they're formed."

"She looks the same on the outside," David offered.

"Yeah, she does," the man agreed as he stood up and walked toward David with the baby. Without saying another word, he pushed the baby toward David's chest. David froze with a horrified look on his face. "She won't break if you hold her," the man said quietly, "but maybe the real question is, will you break?"

David flushed with anger, but put his arms out, and the man placed the baby in them. He stood in front of David and looked first at him and then down at the baby.

David struggled to think of something appropriate to say, finally gave up and repeated, "She looks the same as the others on the outside."

"But there's no telling what has happened to her brain, you see. We won't know that for a long time. Your baby ought to be just fine if she can beat this lung thing."

David felt like he would faint if he didn't get rid of the baby. "Well, I hope she'll be all right," he said hastily, as he thrust the baby back at the man. The man took her, threw a cloth across his shoulder, placed the tiny baby on top of it, and began to massage her back. "I guess you have other children," he suggested to David.

"No," David said curtly. "No other children." He didn't want to get into his own history.

"Well, then you need to learn a few things like what I'm doing right now. After a baby's had a bottle, you can't just put it back down; you've got to do this kind of thing—putting it on your shoulder, rubbing its back, patting it a little bit until it burps, you know."

David said nothing but turned back to the window and stared down at the street. "Come on, sweetheart," the man whispered to the baby girl. "I know this was your first bottle, so we've got to learn this burping stuff. I've been through it before, but you haven't. Come on, now, let's have a big burp. I've got to go back to work and make some money, but I'll be back to see you for a late supper. You and I have a date."

In spite of himself, David turned again to stare at the man. "You're coming back to this place?" he demanded.

"Sure. I told you, I come over here all the time."

"Why?"

"Because these babies need somebody. A lot of them are abandoned, you know. It's something I can do."

"Surely there's something more significant you can do with your time," David said. "I mean, you look like some kind of business man or something. Are you retired?"

"No, I'm not retired. I run a hotel chain, but there's nothing more significant I do in any part of my life than this hour I spend over in this unit."

"You run a hotel chain?" David couldn't believe what he had heard.

"Yeah, you've heard of Armstrong Hotels, haven't you?"

"Sure. I stay in them all the time."

"Well, I'm Clifton Armstrong. I own the joints."

"You own Armstrong Hotels? Those are the most luxurious hotels in the world."

"Yeah, I know. I make them that way so I can sucker guys like you out of a lot of money. Then I can come over here and do something worthwhile with that money and a little bit of my time."

"What do you mean you sucker guys like me? You don't know anything about me," David's temper was beginning to rise.

"Sure I do. You're David Randolph, aren't you?" David nodded. "Well, I know all about Randolph Industries. In fact, I'm one of your stockholders. And I know that you're from Dallas, Texas, and that your child was born while your wife was visiting relatives here. I also know you haven't spent much time in this place, and I know you need to."

"That's none of your business," David retorted.

"Well, it kind of is, and it kind of isn't. So, I'm going to make it my business one-hundred per cent. You see, I don't really care how angry you get with me, David. I'm going to tell you something that I learned too late. My first experience in a ward like this with babies in trouble was when my daughter, a crack addict, who had run away from the perfect life that all my money had provided for her, ended up here giving birth to my grandson. He was also a crack addict, thanks to his mother. Only he was born that way; he didn't choose it. And he didn't make it; he died and so did my daughter. But I spent a lot of time in this place, trying to help that little boy make it, and when I lost both of them, I felt helpless and furious. I had to do something to fight back. I couldn't help my daughter or my grandson, so I decided I would help other babies and their mothers if I could."

"Why didn't you just give some money to the place?" David demanded.

"I could have done that. That would have been the usual approach. In fact, that would have been my usual approach, just to write out a big check. But you see, that's the mistake I made during the entire life of my daughter. I just wrote out big checks. I never gave her any of me, and then it was too late."

David shuffled his feet and looked down at the floor. "Do you have any other children?" he quietly asked Armstrong.

"No, I had just one daughter, but in a way, now I have a lot of children. You see, a lot of these babies do pull through. Some of them are not totally developed, not ever what you would call normal, but some of them are. And I can do for them what I would not do for my daughter. I can do more than write out checks. Oh, I see to their needs. I write the checks that are needed to provide for them materially, but I've got to come up here and hold them. I want to show them a little love, whether they're going to hang around in this world or die, whether they're ever going to be what the world considers normal or not. I've got to do that, you see. I can't distance myself just by writing out checks. That would be too easy."

"I respect you for what you're doing," David said. "It must be painful for you."

"It's always hard to revisit tragedy, David. I think you're finding that out. I understand that you lost your first wife and child. I know I'm not supposed to know something like that, but you know, these things get around."

"Yeah, I know," David said. "It's true. I lost my first wife and child. It was over twenty years ago, though."

"It's still hard to revisit tragedy. We always feel that if we'd done things differently, there wouldn't have been a tragedy. It's hard to confront the guilt we feel."

"I don't feel guilty! Why should I? I didn't kill my first wife," David retorted. "Or my child. If anybody was responsible for that, it was God, not me."

"Typical response," Clifton Armstrong said. "I remember it well. I carried that baggage around for a long time. You're lying to yourself, Randolph. You do feel some kind of responsibility for their deaths. And you're afraid you've done it again."

David said nothing. A nurse came in to take the baby from Clifton Armstrong and put her back in her incubator.

"Well, I guess I better be getting back to the hotel business. Listen, Randolph, I've made a lot of mistakes in this family thing, and I'm no expert now, but I do know one thing. That baby of yours has got a better chance of living if she feels you want her to live, and the only way she has of knowing your feelings right now is for you to touch her, to talk to her. I know she seems like a foreign being there with all those tubes in her. I know you don't feel any real attachment to her, but you are attached to her. You're her father, and you're going to have to play a part in helping her live just as you played a part in giving her life. Listen, man, it's true that it's going to hurt if she dies. It's not going to hurt less because you never touched her, because you didn't spend time with her. In fact, it may hurt more because then you may wonder if you could have made a difference, but you didn't have the guts to try." Armstrong turned and strode out of the room.

As David turned back to the window, he clenched his jaw and shut his eyes tightly, then the tears began to come down his cheeks. Furious with himself, he muttered an oath, brushed the tears away hastily, and turned to see if there was anyone else in the room who might have seen him. The room was empty except for the incubators, one of which contained his own daughter. He took a deep breath and walked back to her side and stared down at the helpless infant surviving with the aide of a respirator and other tubes. "But she is surviving, and Armstrong's right," he muttered. "I know

I'm going to hate myself if I don't make some attempt."

David sat down in the chair at the side of the incubator, clamped down on his nerves and pushed his hand through the opening. For a moment, he held his hand above the tiny body, and then he willed himself to touch his daughter. He stroked her tiny chest and touched the hair on her head, and finally, he ran one finger down her tiny arm until he reached her diminutive hand. Instinctively, she opened her hand and clasped his finger. He knew that this was supposed to be some great moment of bonding, but he couldn't allow himself to do that. With a forced voice, he finally managed to whisper, "It's going to be all right." He couldn't think of anything to call her, any way to address her. So he just sat there letting the baby hold onto his finger with surprising strength as he repeated, "It's going to be all right." But he didn't mean it. He didn't believe it. The only thing he really thought would be all right would be the fact that he could always look back and know that he had tried. Even more important, Caroline would know he had done his best.

He sat there for a long time, letting the baby clasp his finger, but he intentionally moved his mind to business matters, for in that arena, he could find some comfort. There he felt he had some control over his life. Carefully, he thought through the problems in the Japanese economy and how they could impact Randolph Industries. Methodically, he made a list in his mind of various involvements in the Pacific countries that Randolph Industries had and created a strategy for what Randolph Industry's response would be if those economies should drop to dangerous levels of instability.

He was so absorbed in his thoughts he didn't notice when Caroline entered the room and stood at the door watching him. To her perception he was leaning forward toward the baby concentrating on communicating with her. Tears of gratitude welled up in her eyes as she quietly approached him. "Oh, David," she whispered, "she's holding on to you."

Startled, David wrenched himself free of his business thoughts and smiled up at her. A nurse approached the two of them and commented, "Mr. Randolph, I'm afraid you're going to have a terrible cramp in your arm, if you don't move, sir." For the first time David realized that his arm was painfully cramped.

"It's hard to let go of her, isn't it?" Caroline beamed down at the baby.

"Sure is," David agreed.

"But you've had your arm in the same position for about an hour, Mr. Randolph," the nurse insisted. "You better move it."

"A whole hour!" Caroline was thrilled. "Oh, David! You do love her, don't you?"

"Of course," he murmured as he removed his hand from the incubator. He looked at his watch and was startled to find that he had been in the room for almost two hours.

"I'll be here, Mr. Randolph, if you'd like to stretch your legs," the nurse offered.

"Yes," David agreed hastily as he stood up. He was stiff all over. "Yes, I think I do need to stretch."

"Why don't the two of you go have lunch?" the nurse suggested. When Caroline looked doubtful, she encouraged, "Now don't worry. I'll be right here, I promise."

"Let's go eat, Caroline," he pressed her to leave.

"Okay," she agreed, then immediately announced, "Oh, David, I'm so glad you have finally bonded with the baby."

He smiled at her and said nothing. He was just grateful that he had spent two hours with the baby, that he had touched her, and even more grateful that he had managed not to think about her through most of that time. *I have finally found a way to cope with this situation,* he silently congratulated himself; *I can just go through the movements. I can do everything Caroline thinks I should be doing, but I don't have to think about it.* Then he remembered Clifton Armstrong. *I don't know what to think about that man. Either he's crazy or he's some kind of saint. What kind of business man would spend his time that way? I don't get it. He's practically a legend in the hotel business, and he spends his lunch hour in the neonatal unit of this hospital, and he's not even related to any of those babies. He's definitely crazy,* David concluded as he walked down the hall by Caroline's side, but he didn't believe his own judgment of Armstrong, not really.

FOURTEEN

Around sunset David was standing in the neonatal unit about ten feet away from the incubator that held his daughter. He was staring out the window, blankly gazing at the tops of the flat-roofed hospital extensions that spread out beneath him, and then lifting his eyes further out and staring at the parking lots. It had been a bright sunny day, the kind of day when David ached to be very active. He had been working on various business projects via his cellular phone and e-mail, but three times he had returned to the unit to relieve Caroline by watching over their daughter. Most of the time he didn't stay more than a few minutes; instead he slipped out to work. He had just returned to the unit after an hour's work so he would be in place before Caroline returned. Also, he was expecting Aunt Kathleen to come stay with the baby so he could get Caroline to have supper with him.

It was rush hour time, and David looked at the long streams of cars out on the freeway and wished that he was bottled up in that traffic rather than being a captive in this neonatal unit. He took a quick look at his watch. He'd only been there for five minutes, so he knew he had a wait ahead of him before Aunt Kathleen and

Caroline would come.

He looked through a glass partition into another part of the unit and saw Clifton Armstrong walk in. He watched, still amazed by this man's determination to be a part of the recovery of crack babies. Armstrong walked over and picked up a baby and settled into a rocking chair to hold the child and give it a bottle. For some reason he didn't understand, David felt angry the moment he saw Armstrong's behavior, so he turned around and stared out the window again.

He tried to concentrate on the sunset, but in his mind's eye he kept seeing Armstrong holding the baby and rocking. How could I admire him and hate him at the same time, David asked himself. Well it's easy to see why I admire him. He manages to be extremely successful as a businessman, but still gives so much of himself away to these babies who shouldn't mean anything to him. I'm not sure why he makes me so angry. David thought a little longer before confessing to himself, I guess the truth is I do know why he makes me angry. He makes me feel inadequate. After all, those babies are not even his children, but this little baby, David turned and looked at the incubator, is my daughter, but I can't make myself attach to her in any way. Armstrong's definitely got something that I don't have, and seeing him makes me feel absolutely worthless.

David rubbed his forehead and walked over to the incubator. He sat down next to it like he was supposed to and tried to make himself put his hand through the opening to stroke the baby's body, or at least pat her, but he couldn't do it. He could almost never do it unless Caroline was present, and he had to. He just sat there and stared down at the tiny life form that was supposed to be related to him in some way. She looks a little better, he thought, but I guess it's really just that they've taken that respirator off of her. Fewer tubes and no mask over her face, still she looks about half-dead. That thought sent a surge of anxiety through him, and a sweat broke out on his face. He stood up hurriedly and went back to the window. After pulling an immaculately laundered, monogrammed, linen handkerchief out of his pocket, he wiped his face. He made a ritual of doing this, then carefully folded the handkerchief back up, all in an attempt to forget what he had just felt.

He looked at his watch again. Another five minutes had passed. I really should go sit by the incubator before Caroline comes back, he thought, but he didn't move. I wish Armstrong would leave. The guy makes me feel guilty. He folded his arms across his chest as if that would somehow protect him from everything around him and stared out at the cars again.

I'll buy Caroline a new car when this is all over, he thought. Yeah, that's what I'll do. I'll get her a new car. Let's see. What kind shall I get this time? He looked at the long stream of cars out in the distance trying to spot something special for Caroline. No, those are all so ordinary, he thought. I've got to come up with something really special for her this time.

David heard a strange noise, and suddenly a nurse came rushing through the door. He turned to look at her, wondering which of the incubators she would go to. She was obviously distressed, and he watched in horror as she ran to his daughter's incubator. Another nurse followed quick on her heels, and the first nurse barked an order, "Get the doctor!"

The second nurse ran out of the room. David stood, paralyzed, realizing that something had gone wrong and that the nurse's face showed extreme stress. She had reached her hands into the incubator and was doing something to the baby.

"What's wrong?" he asked.

"I'll have to ask you to leave now, Mr. Randolph," she said tersely.

"What's wrong with the baby?" David demanded as he took a few steps toward the incubator, cautious not to get too close. He looked down into the incubator and saw that the baby was squirming out of control. "What's wrong with her?" he demanded.

"Her heartbeat is very erratic. I think she's having problems breathing again. I've called for the doctor. I'll have to ask you to leave, Mr. Randolph." David looked at his baby again and saw that her color was changing to a gray tone.

No one needed to order him out. He ran across the room and bolted out the door. He hurried down the hall to the elevator and stabbed his finger at the button. When the elevator didn't open immediately, he took the staircase next to it and started down. He had gotten down one whole flight of stairs before he realized that someone was following him.

"Wait a minute, David," a male voice called. It was Armstrong's voice. David ignored him and charged down another flight of stairs. "David, just wait. It may not be as bad as you think."

David kept descending the staircase as fast as he could. His heart beat wildly; he was sweating all over, and he felt so dizzy he was afraid he would end up tumbling head first down to the bottom. He gripped the handrail but continued to charge downward.

"David, wait!" Armstrong insisted. "Let's talk about this."

Even though he realized Armstrong was close behind him, it sounded like Armstrong's voice was coming from the end of a deep tunnel. All David could think of was that he had to get outside. He had to get out of this horrible building. He had to get out to the parking lot to get to fresh air before he passed out. Finally, he ran out of steps. He burst through the door in front of him and found himself in the main lobby. He was totally disoriented. He stared wildly around until he found an outside glass door and went charging toward it. He shoved the door open and staggered another twenty feet before he had to stop and hold on to a pillar. He stood there taking deep breaths of the fresh air trying to keep from passing out. He was hardly aware of the strong arms that took hold of him from behind.

"As soon as you can, let's go over there and sit down," Armstrong said. David couldn't answer. He couldn't think. He felt like he was slipping into unconsciousness, and he was petrified he was going to fall. I have to stay on my feet, he thought, I have to stay on my feet. The words kept running through his head as he gasped for more air. "David, you're hyperventilating," Armstrong said. "Breathe normally. Don't worry. I won't let you fall. Just breathe normally."

"Do you need some help?" David heard a woman's voice and in his peripheral vision he saw a white uniform. It panicked him further.

"No," he said and lunged forward and ran across the walkway out into the parking lot. He got thirty feet into the parking lot before he started to fall. Just as he was sure his face was going to hit the asphalt, strong arms took him and pulled him down onto a curb.

"Get your head down between your knees," Armstrong ordered, and he obeyed. "Now, don't gasp for air, David. Take normal breaths. Slow it down. You're going to be all right." He felt Armstrong reaching for his wrist and knew that he was taking his pulse. "Just keep your head down and breathe slowly."

David fought the frantic desire to take in great gulps of air. He knew what hyperventilation was. He had been a runner in college and had been forced to work his way through hyperventilation at quite a few track meets.

"Nice and easy," Armstrong said. He was rubbing David's shoulder to help him calm down. "Nice and easy. Just in and out, slowly, slowly. That's good. You're going to be fine." The numbness around David's mouth began to recede, and he could feel his hands and feet again. Past experience told him he was getting better.

"Just keep it up," Armstrong said. "You're getting better." David nodded. He sat there and concentrated on breathing normally for almost five minutes before he was finally able to raise his head. He still felt terribly wobbly and unsure of himself and didn't dare try to stand.

"Let's just sit here a while," Armstrong said as he took his hand off of David's shoulder and turned loose of his wrist. David nodded again, not sure that he was ready to try to talk.

"Boy, the traffic around here gets worse all the time," Armstrong said, obviously trying to give David something to think about other than his own breathing. "Must be those condominiums they built down the road. I can't blame people for wanting to move to Charleston, but to tell you the truth, I hate to see it get bigger."

David concentrated on the man's words, knowing that that was the best thing he could do for himself at the moment. "Of course, I guess it balances out," Armstrong continued. "A lot of people are building condos, but a lot of young people are going back to the inner city and restoring some of the beautiful old homes. It's kind of exciting to walk around down there and see the place coming back to life. One house will be an absolute wreck waiting for somebody to come and take care of it, and right next door there will be a house that's obviously been reclaimed by somebody. You're feeling better, aren't you?"

"Yes," David finally trusted himself to speak. "I think I can stand up."

"Better give it a few more minutes," Armstrong advised. "Be sure you're good and strong before you go back in."

David whipped his head to the left and stared at Armstrong for a second before blurting out, "I'm not going back in there. I'm never going back in there."

Armstrong took his eyes off of David's face, stared out into the parking lot, then said quite calmly, "You've got to go back, David. You're needed in there."

"I won't go back," David insisted. Armstrong said nothing. Then David stared down at the asphalt between his feet and admitted, "I can't."

"Why not?" Armstrong asked as he continued to stare out into the parking lot.

"The baby is going to die," David said tersely.

"You don't know that," Armstrong finally turned and looked him in the face. "You don't know that, David."

"I do know it. The baby is going to die."

"I don't think so, but even if your baby dies, you can handle it. You can—"

"No, I can't handle it," David raised his voice and stood up suddenly.

Armstrong rose from the curb and calmly took David's arm. "Why not?"

"I can't."

"Why not?"

"I just can't."

"Why not, David? Why can't you handle it?" Armstrong knew he was pushing David hard, and David looked dazed, but his breathing was still normal. "Why can't you handle it, David?"

"I just can't."

"Why not, David?" Armstrong punctuated each word.

David suddenly turned on him. "Because Danielle is going to kill herself!"

"Danielle?"

"She's going to kill herself, and it's my fault."

Armstrong looked at the confusion in David's eyes for a moment, then asked calmly, "Why is it your fault?"

"I could stop her."

"How?"

"By remembering she has a key to her father's house."

Armstrong was confused about David's words, but he knew that David was speaking some truth from deep within him, some truth that had to be released. "She has a key to her father's house?" he asked to prod David to go on. "Why is that so important?"

"There are sleeping pills there."

"And you think she will get to the sleeping pills and try to kill herself?"

"Yes."

"How do you know, David?"

"She's already tried once, but I found her in time and called an ambulance. Don't you see? She's going to try again, and this time she'll kill herself. I can't stop her!"

Armstrong frantically tried to hang information together, then asked, "Because the baby is dead?"

"Yes, because the baby is dead and because—because—"

"Why, David?" Armstrong pressed.

"Because I'm not strong enough to stop her. I can't control her. I can't think far enough ahead of her, and she's going to think of using the sleeping pills before I get control of her. I'm a weak, worthless man." David's breath was now coming in quick gasps.

"Okay," Armstrong said quietly. "Okay, David. Take a slow breath now. Let's just sit back down here on the curb. It's okay. You don't have to go back in. Let's just sit down. I'll sit down next to you. We'll just sit here and relax." Slowly he talked David into returning to his seat on the curb. "Take another normal breath. That's it. Just look out there past the cars at that sunset. Watch the sun go down slowly. Take normal breaths, David. That's it."

Armstrong waited until David's breathing sounded normal again. "You feeling better?"

"Yes."

"Good. Now, I need to ask you one question. Who is Danielle?"

Startled by the question, David turned and looked at Armstrong. "Danielle?"

"Yes, you just told me about Danielle trying to kill herself."

"I did?"

"You did. Who is she?"

"My first wife," David murmured.

"Did she kill herself, David?"

"Yes." Harshness crept into David's voice.

"Did she kill herself because her baby died?"

"Yes," David was beginning to sound angry.

"Is that Danielle's baby in the hospital now?"

"No," David answered forcibly then stared back at the sunset a moment before saying more quietly, "No, no, it's Caroline's."

Armstrong leaned a little closer to him. "Would Caroline kill herself?"

"No. Never. She's just not like that." David fell silent, and Armstrong said no more. Finally David turned and asked, "What happened to me?"

"You got the past and the present confused, I think. I would bet that you've been confusing the two for a long time, that you've been coloring the present with the trauma of your past. Is that possible?"

"Yes, I guess so, if people do things like that. And they do, don't they?"

Armstrong nodded.

"You see, I never planned to remarry after Danielle killed herself, but then I met Caroline, and I fell so deeply in love with her. I just couldn't help myself, but I made her promise me she would never have a child."

"You must have been awfully worried ever since you found out she was pregnant."

"Yes, worried and running away," David answered sarcastically. "You see, I'm a coward, a worthless coward. I've been running, but the running didn't do me any good because no matter how far I ran, every time I stopped to think I thought about Danielle, and every time I went to sleep, I dreamed about Danielle. I wasn't even strong enough to control my own thoughts."

"So you think you're worthless because you can't control your thoughts, and you think you're worthless because you couldn't control Danielle, because you couldn't keep her from killing herself."

"That's about it." There was a long silence between the men. Then Armstrong spoke.

"I must be worthless too, David."

"Why?"

"I didn't control my daughter. I let her go on using crack."

"No, that's different, Armstrong."

"How come, David?"

"Because she made her own choices. She was your daughter, but she was grown, wasn't she?"

"Yeah, she was grown."

"You probably didn't even know she was doing drugs, did you?"

"Sure I did. I put her in rehab three times. Did you get Danielle any help?"

"Of course, but it didn't do any good."

"Because she was grown and made her own choices?" Armstrong asked quietly.

David stared deep into the man's steady eyes, and he began to understand that they had both walked the same path, but he respected this man. He admired him. He envied him his strength, the peace he had made with the world, but they had both made the same mistakes. They had both fallen down.

"We can't control everything, David, and we can't make control the basis of our worth."

"But you must have eventually gotten control of yourself

because now you're able to spend so much time up here at the hospital. You do all these wonderful things. You go up there, and you take care of those crack babies even though your grandchild died and your daughter died."

"I do all those things, David, but they don't make me a bit worthier."

"Sure they do."

"No, they don't. They don't make me worthy, David, and what I did wrong in the past didn't make me worthless. It took me a long time to understand that. You see, after my daughter and her baby died, I hated myself. I kept telling myself there must have been something I could have done that would have turned her around and saved her life and saved my grandchild. I felt totally worthless. I had power, I had money, I was intelligent, but my daughter was dead and so was my grandchild. I felt like the scrapings off the bottom of the barrel. Then I got the idea that if I came up here and helped somebody else, I would start earning my worth. I'd start feeling better, but it never worked. No matter how many days I came, no matter how many hours I spent, how many people I tried to help, how many babies I held in my arms, I never felt anything but worthless."

"What did work?" David demanded quietly. "I know you feel good about yourself now. It shows all over you."

"Yes, I do, David. I feel good about myself because I know where my worth comes from."

"Well what happened? How did you get to where you are?"

"Well, I kept coming up here, and of course that meant that I kept seeing all these addicted teenagers and young people. I saw them at their very worst, when they had to tie them down, when they were raving and convulsing and vomiting all over the place. I mean, David, I saw them at their worst, and I saw how they had passed on their addiction to the babies they gave birth to. I watched those babies struggle to live and then struggle to become unaddicted. It was awful. It still is, but one night I was trying to help a young woman about my daughter's age. She was going through the worst part of detoxification. She had already given birth to her baby, and the baby was fighting for its life, but this poor teenager—about eighteen—was in the deepest hole any human being can get into, and I felt compelled to stay and help her even though she was vomiting all over me and hallucinating and clutching at me. Finally, I was so tired I took a break and staggered out into the hall and leaned against a wall.

"An orderly walked by and saw me, and he stopped and said, 'Mr. Armstrong, why don't you go home and get on with your own life? She ain't worth your time. If you get her past this detox, she'll just go back out on the streets and find that stuff again and ruin her life all over again. Give it up. She ain't worth worrying about. She's just like all the rest. This is the third time she's been in here. She's the scum of the earth. What is a fine man like you doing down here worrying about the scum of the earth? She ain't worth it.'"

"What happened?" David asked.

"I was so angry I thought the top of my head would blow off. I took that man by the arms, and I threw him against the wall, and I gave him a lecture. I can't even begin to tell you what words I actually used, but I know what the theme was because I heard myself saying it over and over again. 'She is worth it.' I was practically screaming at that man, 'she is worth it. She is worth it.'"

David was mesmerized by Armstrong's voice and totally unable to tear his eyes from Armstrong's face. He knew that for the rest of his life he would never be able to explain this moment, but somehow this was a turning point in his life, and he knew it. He knew that Armstrong was going to utter the words he needed to hear, and he wanted desperately to hear them. "What happened?" he asked.

"After I quit yelling at the man, he just looked at me and said, 'Well, if she's so worthy, Mr. Armstrong, why ain't you?' I couldn't say anything to him. I just stared at him. 'Why ain't you, Mr. Armstrong?' he asked again. 'That addict in there vomiting all over the floor. She came from the same place you did. She came from God. He made her. He made you. He made me. He made us all, Mr. Armstrong. He thought we were worth making. We all mess up our lives in different ways, but He still thinks we're worthy because He knows He made us that way, and no matter what we do, we can't unmake our worth.'"

Armstrong stopped talking, and David continued to stare into his eyes. He had heard what the man said, and the whole basis for his life was shifting.

Finally David asked, "Are you saying that nothing that we ever do that is right makes us worth anything?"

Armstrong nodded his agreement.

"And nothing we ever do that is wrong makes us worthless?"

Again, Armstrong nodded.

"Because it's not about what we *do*," David concluded.

"Right," Armstrong agreed. "It's not about what we do. It's about what God did when He made us. We can mess up, or we can succeed in this world, but we can't change the fact that we are made worthy."

"Danielle and our baby are dead, but Caroline's still alive, and maybe the baby is too."

"Right," Armstrong agreed. "Maybe you messed up in the past. That didn't make you worthless then, David, because you couldn't control everything. Maybe you'll mess up now. That won't make you worthless either."

"What do I do, Armstrong?"

"Accept the fact that your worth is intact, David. You can't do that suddenly, in a moment's time, but start embracing that fact. It is a fact. Your worth is established. It was established the minute God thought of you. Also, accept the fact that the past is the past. It's over. We can learn from it, but we have to live now and do the best we can now. We have to act in love now, knowing that sometimes we're going to stumble, sometimes we're going to fly like an eagle, but either way, we are worthy, and our present life can be happy if we are loving."

David's eyes filled with tears. They brimmed over his lashes and spilled down his cheeks, but for the first time in his life he was not ashamed to cry in front of another man. "Thank you, Armstrong," he said. "Thank you." Then he stood up and pulled a handkerchief out of his pocket and wiped his eyes. Armstrong stood up beside him and waited. "Caroline's probably in the neonatal unit by now," David said. "She must be scared to death. She needs me. I want to go help her."

"Do you think your baby is dead or alive, David?"

"I don't know. I know I have to leave her in the doctors' hands and in God's hands, but I can help Caroline."

"Yes, you can help Caroline, and she does need you. But what if your baby is dead, David? How are you going to feel about that?"

"Grieved. There'll be another hole in me, and I'll probably blame myself. You know, think of a thousand things I could have done, should have done." David paused and tears sprang to his eyes as he remembered his father's insistence, over the years of his youth, that he wasn't strong enough. David brushed the tears away and swallowed hard before continuing with obvious effort. "But then, I hope I'll focus on what you said, that I can't make or break my basic worth through my own actions. And I hope I'll let go of the past, quit letting it define me now. I hope I'll quit running, know I'm an okay person, and just love Caroline the best I can." He turned and smiled weakly at Armstrong. "That's a lot of hoping, isn't it?" David swallowed hard, "I better get started."

"You're up to the task, David. You're a strong man, an essentially good one. You adore Caroline, and even though you haven't let yourself know it, you love your baby." Armstrong clapped him on the back, and together they started back toward the hospital entrance at a fast pace.

"David!" Caroline threw herself into his arms the minute he exited the elevator. "Are you all right? Aunt Kathleen and I were coming to look for you."

"The baby, Caroline, the baby started—and I couldn't—I feel like I failed—"

"The baby is fine, David." Caroline drew away from him so she could look up into his face. She was shocked to find that tears were brimming over his eyes and flowing down his cheeks. "David, she's fine, really." She waited, but he was so choked up he couldn't talk. "Honey, what's wrong?"

"Thank God, thank God," he finally whispered, then after a pause, while he grappled with his emotions and struggled to gain control of himself, he added, "I have to talk to you, Caroline."

"Sure," she agreed, "but really, honey, everything's fine, isn't it, Aunt Kathleen?"

"No, it's not. We're not fine," David insisted.

"Yes we are," she argued gently, "we're finally both wanting and supporting the baby. Our future is—"

"Caroline, I've been lying to you." She stopped her attempts to soothe him, stepped back, and became ominously still and quiet.

"Aunt Kathleen said you were holding something back, but—"

"She is right, and I have to tell you."

"I don't want to know!" Caroline insisted. "The baby's going to be fine, and we can just go on from now."

"No, we can't. We can't be close, like you've been wanting us to be, unless I tell you the truth. The lies will always separate us."

"He's right, Caroline," Aunt Kathleen stepped toward her, reached up, and gently touched her cheek. "Don't run from what your heart needs most. Choose courage. Your baby is safe. I'll stay with her. Go with David and let him talk to you. Choose courage. Let David become the soul mate you have so desired."

"Like Carrie," Caroline murmured, "courageous like Carrie."

"Yes, dear, exactly." When Caroline nodded, Aunt Kathleen took Caroline's hand and put it in David's. "Go be with your husband, Caroline, and listen to him."

David put his arm around Caroline's shoulders and guided her toward the elevator. "There's a quiet courtyard off the chapel downstairs. I walked by it yesterday when I came inside from a different direction." Caroline just nodded her approval, and they continued down to the first floor in silence. When they exited the elevator, she glanced up at David's face and knew from the deep lines she saw there that he felt as tense as she did.

"That bench looks kind of hard." David pointed to a wooden garden bench in the courtyard. "Will you be okay if we sit there?"

"Fine," Caroline responded tersely as she sat down. She looked around her as David seated himself, and she discovered that part of the courtyard landscape included a climbing pink rose trained to grow up a wrought iron trellis. Concentrating on the porcelain pink blossoms soothed her nerves a bit, "Look, David," she pointed to the flowers, "a touch of Aunt Kathleen's garden."

"And a very appropriate one, too," David added softly. "Aunt Kathleen said last spring that I wanted you to be a pink rosebud that never opened to full flower. She said I was a coward, and she was right. Caroline, I've wronged you in so many ways I don't even know where to begin."

"This mess is my fault, David. If I hadn't lied to you about taking my birth control pills—"

David reached out and gently placed his forefinger over her lips. "No, Caroline, it began long before that. I lied to you about Danielle."

"Danielle?"

"Caroline, Danielle didn't die in childbirth. She killed herself."

Caroline stared at him a moment, then asked quietly, "Why?"

"She miscarried and lost our son when she was about six months pregnant."

"But, David, lots of women miscarry, but they don't kill themselves."

"Honey, just let me start from the beginning. When I married Danielle, I knew she was emotionally volatile, but I was no more than a kid myself, so I told myself she was just high-strung. I told myself I could make her so happy she would level off. The truth was she was actually mentally disturbed, and no one told me."

"You mean her family hid the truth from you?"

"She only had her father, and yes, he didn't tell me about the trauma Danielle had endured."

"What trauma?"

"She found her mother apparently dead from an intentional overdose."

"Apparently dead? What do you mean 'apparently'?"

"Danielle believed she was dead, but she wasn't. She was so brain damaged that Danielle's father put her in a sanatorium and told Danielle she was dead. He even had a funeral."

"How horrible!"

"It was even more horrible when Danielle discovered that her father was paying the bills for a woman in a sanatorium. She went to Switzerland to the sanatorium and found her mother. The shock of discovery was what made her miscarry."

"I can't believe this! David, why didn't you tell me?"

"Oh, Caroline, it's all so complicated. I just wanted to forget it; it was so painful I couldn't even think about it." David stopped talking and stared blankly ahead. Caroline said nothing as she struggled to assimilate what he had told her and to evaluate their lives together in light of it. "That's not really the truth either," David suddenly blurted out. "At least not all of it. The truth is I hated myself because I had been so weak I couldn't control my own wife. I couldn't take care of her; I couldn't save her."

"But, David, no one could have saved her."

"I should have been able to."

"Why? Why should you have been able to? Did you know about all this trouble in her past?"

"No. I didn't know any of it."

"Then, how can you hold yourself accountable? If you didn't know, you didn't know."

"A man should be able to take control."

"Of things he doesn't know about? That's preposterous. Where is all this obsession with control coming from?"

David stared at the brick floor of the courtyard, but in his mind's eye he was on a blazing hot tennis court. "From my father," he murmured.

"Your father? You've never told me much of anything about him." Caroline paused. "Except what he owned."

"He was my idea of a real man. Strong, very strong. He knew what he wanted and how to get it."

"He sounds like James Bradford to me," Caroline commented, but David said nothing. "Did he love you?"

"Sure, I was his son, his heir to Randolph Industries, his—"

"Did you feel his love, David?" Caroline demanded.

"No, I felt his disapproval." David hung his head to avoid looking at her

"Because you weren't as strong as he was?" Caroline asked, and David nodded. She was silent for a moment before commenting, "Well, I would define strength the way John Kendall did."

"John Kendall? Who's John Kendall?" David asked as he looked back up at Caroline.

"The man who married Carrie when she was pregnant with Robert's child. You remember? She couldn't stay married to Robert because he was her half-brother, so John Kendall stepped into the situation and married her to protect her from being ostracized by Charleston society."

"Yes, I remember the story. How did he define strength?"

"He said that strength is the courage to love in spite of all obstacles. That's a real man to me, David. That's the man I want as a husband, as a father to my child."

"I do love you, Caroline. I never knew how much until I spent those endless hours in that plane crossing the Atlantic trying to get to you."

"And our little girl?"

"I don't really know her yet; I haven't let myself." David stood up and crossed the courtyard to the rosebush. He broke off a fully-opened pink rose and returned to Caroline. He knelt on one knee in front of her so he could look her directly in the eyes. "Here's that fully opened rose you've become in spite of me." He handed her the rose. "As for our daughter, she's part of you. How can I not love her?"

"She's going to live," Caroline insisted with quiet assurance.

"Yes, she is," David agreed. "I really think she is, honey."

Caroline smiled happily up at him. "So she needs a name, David, doesn't she?"

He laughed quietly before asking, "Doesn't she already have one?"

Caroline's smile became more mischievous, "Does she? What is it?"

David stood, gently pulled her to her feet, stroked her smiling cheek and answered, "Kathleen, of course."

Enjoy another captivating story from
Kay Moser

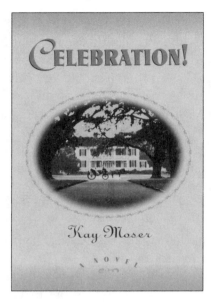

Chapter 1

The man lunged at Rachel and pinned her arms to her sides the instant she stepped outside the back door. Her heart beat wildly as she gasped for air and fought to make her numb mind work.

Turning, she struggled to wrench herself loose from his arms. Then suddenly she realized that he wasn't restraining her at all. He was leaning on her. She jerked her head back and stared up into his face, and there she found the drunken, dazed eyes of her husband, Collins.

"You scared me to death!" she screamed as she pushed him away from her. The enormous adrenalin flow continued to surge through her body as her fear turned to fury.

"Where have you been?" she shouted. "I've been up all night. Where have you been?" He swayed toward her, obviously on the verge of passing out there in the doorway.

Rachel grabbed him, held him up as best she could, and helped him drag himself into the den and on to the couch. There he collapsed, just barely able to sit up, and stared at her with glazed eyes. As she opened her mouth to blast him out, his eyes showed a glimmer of perception, and he slurred some words.

"Shocking, isn't it, Darling?" He laughed sarcastically. "Absolutely disgusting for anyone to lose control like this! Not at all the thing to do.

Not at all like you." He leaned toward her, leering as he laughed. "You never lose control, do you, my darling Rachel?" He wagged his finger at her as if he were correcting a child. "Never, never, never!" Then his voice turned icy cold, taunting, "You always land on your feet, don't you, my Darling?"

Before she could respond, his eyelids sank, and he would have fallen forward to the floor if she had not caught him and pushed him over on his side. "Oh no!" she wailed. "He's unconscious! What am I going to do?" She glanced at his feet which were still on the floor. "Leave them there!" she ordered herself. "Let him wake up with a half-broken back. Serves him right!" She turned away and walked back to the door, picked up her scattered briefcase and keys and started out. She got to the point of locking the door behind her before she stopped herself and went back.

As quickly as possible she dragged his leaden legs up on the couch, pulled off his shoes, and went to the bedroom for a blanket. "Why am I doing this?" she demanded of herself. "Heaven knows where he's been, who he's been with." Then she stared down into his face, and there she found her answer, there under the two-day beard and the swollen features. He's still Collins, she thought. In spite of every awful thing he's done, he's still Collins. My Collins. And I guess I still love him. She sighed and paused long enough to tell herself, "You belong in a loony bin, Rachel D'Evereau Greyson. You're nuts!" Then she picked up her things for the third time and left.

As she slid into the driver's seat of her car, she remembered Collins' crumpled figure on the couch and tried to calculate how long he was likely to sleep. I better call that smart-mouthed secretary of his, Shawna whats-her-name, after my first class, she decided. Then I'll come home at noon and check on him. If I'm going to be an idiot, I might as well be a total one! She inserted the key and turned it, but the car made only a clicking noise, followed by total silence. She tried again and again. Nothing but the click. Frustration and anger burned through her as she recognized the undeniable sign of a dead battery.

"Not now!" she cried, "not today!" She felt like beating her head against the steering wheel but settled for slamming her fists against it instead. Then she glared at her watch. Thirty minutes until my first class. No time to get the car fixed. I'll have to call a neighbor.

Grabbing her things, she jumped out of the car and started toward the house. Then she saw Colllins' car parked in front of the house, one front wheel over the curb on the grass. "He was driving!" she gasped. "He didn't even call a taxi this time. When I get him sobered up—no, I can't think about that. I've got to get to the university. I'll take Collins' car! Heaven knows he's not going to need it." She headed for his car, started it, and drove quickly down the street.

When she did, the breeze through the open windows sent a stack of envelopes floating around the front seat. Several ended in her lap.

Angrily she slammed on the brakes and gathered up the envelopes to secure them. As she hurriedly stacked them, she noticed that the top one was an electric bill. I pay the bills, the thought raced through her mind. What's he doing with an electric bill? She glanced at the name and address and froze, paralyzed by what she read. As she shuffled through the envelopes, she moaned over and over, "no, no, no, no." Something in her was dying. Mrs. Shawna Greyson. The envelopes were mostly addressed to Mrs. Shawna Greyson at an address Rachel recognized as an exclusive condominium complex close to Collins' office. A few envelopes were addressed to Mr. Collins Greyson at the same address.

A fury like she had never known seared through her veins. She whipped the car around and roared back down the street. When she reached the front door of her house, she jabbed the key into the lock and banged open the door. Even from the entry she could see Collins snoring on the couch. Slowly she walked to his side and stared down at him. I want to kill him! she thought. I want to kill him, but not while he's asleep!

Turning abruptly, she stomped to the kitchen where she filled the mop bucket with cold water. When she returned to the couch, she threw half the cold water in Collins' face.

"Wake up!" she screamed. "Wake up, you lousy liar!"

Collins bolted to a sitting position, his head swaying, and tried to focus on her. "What the—"

"You're having an affair with Shawna, aren't you?" she yelled at him. "You're living with her at the North View Condominiums, aren't you?"

"No—" Collins stammered.

"Don't you lie to me! I found your utility bills in your car!"

Collins stared at her in confusion, obviously trying to force his hungover mind to work.

"Say something!" Rachel screamed. He was silent. "Say somethng!" she yelled again as she threw the rest of the cold water in his face.

"Okay, okay! It's true!" Collins shouted back at her as he wiped water out of his eyes. "But you have to let me explain," he began as he tried to rise from the couch.

"Don't bother! How many times do you think I'll stand for this?" Rachel shouted as she shoved him back on the couch. He was so weak and befuddled he fell backwards and sat there staring up at her.

Much to his surprise, Rachel jerked up the telephone book, fumbled through it, and grabbed the phone. "This is Rachel D'Evereau Greyson," she spoke sharply into the receiver. "I want a cab to meet me in twenty minutes at the North View Condominiums, No. 12. Do you have that? Twenty minutes."

"What are you going to—" Collins began.

"Get up!" Rachel interrupted.

"Now, Rachel, we need to talk—" Collins tried again.

"I've done all the talking I'm going to do. Get up!" Still he didn't move, so she reached down and slapped him across the face with a strength born of pure wrath.

Collins struggled to his feet and tried again to talk to her.

"Move!" she yelled as she shoved him toward the door.

"Rachel, for heaven's sake—" he pleaded outside the front door.

"Move!" she yelled repeatedly as she shoved him down the sidewalk. She kept pushing him, and he kept stumbling forward until he reached the passenger side of his car. She opened the door and ordered, "Get in!" Motionless, he stared at her in confusion. "Get in!" she ordered and pushed him down onto the seat. "Put your feet in," she commanded. He was too hung over to argue, so he pulled his feet in, and Rachel slammed the door.

When she slid behind the steering wheel and started the car, he asked nervously, "What are you going to do?"

"You'll see," she warned as she turned the car around and started down the street.

"Rachel, what are you going to do?" Collins demanded, as his nervousness turned to panic.

Rachel stared straight ahead in stoney silence until she had maneuvered the car onto the freeway and was driving at high speed. Then she glanced over at him and spat out, "I'm going to deliver you to your wife!"

The taxi driver arrived at the condominiums just as she pulled into the parking lot. When she reached Collins' condominium, she slammed on the brakes, jumped out and yelled at the taxi driver, "I'll be right with you!"

Then she jerked open the passenger door of Collins' car and commanded, "Get out!"

"Rachel, please, let me—"

"Get out, Collins!"

Reluctantly he stood up, but he was so unstable he had to steady himself for a moment by clinging to the car.

When she saw that he had his balance, she ordered, "Walk!" and pointed to the front door. He began to shuffle along, but he was too slow for her taste, so she grabbed his arm and dragged him to the door. Once there, she rang the doorbell.

Several minutes later the door was opened, and there stood Shawna. Her expression turned to terror.

"Don't worry, Shawna," Rachel spoke with detached coolness, "I'm not here to claw your eyes out. I wouldn't risk breaking a fingernail on the likes of you! You want to be Mrs. Collins Greyson? Fine! Here's your husband!" She shoved Collins at Shawna, turned her back, and walked away.

When she reached the taxi cab, the driver was standing by the passenger door. "What's going on?" he demanded.

"Nothing," Rachel responded nonchalantly as he opened the door for her. "Just delivering some drunk home."

The driver closed the door, hurried around to the other side and started the cab. "Where to, Lady?"

Rachel gave him her address, and he drove her out of the condominium complex. She didn't look back. Collins had done enough this time.

She was finished.

On the way home she thought over the names of lawyers she knew and settled on one to handle the divorce for her.

When she entered her house, the phone was ringing. It was the secretary of the Education Department at the university; she had forgotten all about her classes. Mentioning only the trouble with her car, she reassured the secretary she would be in as soon as possible. When she hung up, she called the local garage to come start her car. Then she called and made an appointment with the lawyer she had chosen.

Finally there was nothing to do but wait for the auto mechanic. Standing next to the phone, she surveyed the den where an hour before she had still been able to find love in her heart for Collins. It looked perfectly normal to her except for the large water spots on the couch. But they were drying fast.

She absolutely refused to be upset or to break down in any way. She was determined to go to the university, to make her professional life go on. I must make this work, she insisted, it's all I have left now. Collins can never mean anything to me again. Never! Oh why do I feel so numb about that when I should be so determined? She demanded and then answered her own question.

It takes a long time for loss to sink in, to be felt. I should know that from living through Justin's death. Rachel shuddered. My little brother and Viet Nam. Tragedy guaranteed. Justin dead, mother breaking down. Seven years ago I stood by that gaping hole in the red clay of Louisiana and watched it swallow up Justin's coffin. The soldiers folded the flag that covered the coffin and gave it to me. I will never forget the feeling of that cloth in my hands as I heard the first clods of clay hit the top of the coffin. And there was Daddy, watching silently, broken-hearted but proud. Very proud. I stepped toward him, "This belongs to you." I shoved that taut bundle of flag into his diaphragm. "Take it! You killed him for it. You sacrificed him to uphold your D'Evereau pride!"

Stop it! Rachel reined in her thoughts. What are you doing? Trying to kill yourself? It was a long time ago. Leave it there. Forget them. You don't need them! This is now, and you have to do something about Collins. You can't go on in this marriage.

Two days later she saw the divorce lawyer and instructed him to keep it simple. "I want nothing that belongs to Collins," she explained. "I simply want you to see to it that he gets nothing of mine."

"Are you sure, Rachel? Your husband is a very wealthy man," the lawyer argued.

"Only I know what my husband is worth," she responded coldly, "and I tell you he has nothing I want."

Available from Seton St. Clare Books or at your favorite bookstore.

Another fascinating novel from
Seton St. Clare Books

ℛENDEZVOUS WITH THE ℛOCK

Edith Buck

A NOVEL

Misty Morrow is a young journalist determined to make a name for herself as an investigative reporter. Her fiance is an aspiring politician who insists that Misty marry him immediately and give her talents to helping him win his first political race. His excessive pressure has made Misty doubt his love for her and wonder if he wants her only for her talents and connections.

When Misty learns about two opportunities for head-line catching stories in the Rocky Mountains, she packs her bags and heads for Colorado in spite of her fiance's objections. Once she arrives, she secretly joins the staff of a camp for terminally ill children so she can obtain a close-up view of what is really going on in the privately funded camp.

At the same time she is investigating the disappearance of a famous painter who was last seen in the Rockies near the camp. He is reclusive by habit, but no one has been able to make contact with him for months. Furthermore, it has become obvious that someone is trying to sabotage his career by damaging the commissioned paintings he is sending to museums.

Misty is really on a journey of self-exploration as she attempts to define herself personally and professionally.

While in the Rockies she is befriended by members of a cult, and soon she is torn between the demanding "love" of the cult members and the love of family and friends she has left behind. She also meets a man she loves more than her fiance, but life with him would require her to give up some of her independence.

A tragic accident finally forces Misty to make difficult choices in both her professional and personal lives.

Rendezvous with the Rock is a fast-paced, contemporary novel of romance, intrigue, and adventure.

Seton St. Clare Books
P.O. Box 8543, Waco, TX 76714-8543

Please send me the following books:

QUANTITY	TITLE	AUTHOR	PRICE	AMOUNT
_____	**CELEBRATION!** ISBN 1-890236-22-5	by Kay Moser	$11.99	_____
_____	**COUNTERFEIT LEGACY** ISBN 1-890236-38-1	by Kay Moser	$11.99	_____
_____	**DAVID'S GIFT** ISBN 1-890236-16-0	by Kay Moser	$11.99	_____
_____	**RENDEZVOUS WITH THE ROCK** ISBN 1-890236-23-3	by Edith Buck	$ 9.99	_____

Mailing & handling: $2.00 for one book;
             $3.00 for two or more books   _____

(Texas residents please add 8% sales tax)   _____

                                      TOTAL   _____

(Please print clearly)

NAME _____

ADDRESS _____

CITY _____ STATE _____ ZIP_____

E-MAIL_____

We would love to hear from you!
e-mail: setonbooks@aol.com